Light Up the Cave

Books by Denise Levertov

Poetry

The Double Image
Here and Now
Overland to the Islands
With Eyes at the Back of Our Heads
The Jacob's Ladder
O Taste and See
The Sorrow Dance
Relearning the Alphabet
To Stay Alive
Footprints
The Freeing of the Dust
Life in the Forest
Collected Earlier Poems 1940–1960

Prose

The Poet in the World
Light Up the Cave

Translations

Guillevic/Selected Poems

Denise Levertov

Light Up the Cave

A New Directions Book

ACKNOWLEDGMENTS

Grateful acknowledgment is made to publications in which some of the
material in this book first appeared: *American Poetry Review*, *Chicago Review*, *Dreamworks*, *Follies*, *Gangrel*, *In These Times*, *The Literary Review*,
The Malahat Review, *Poetry Wales*, *Ramparts*, *Real Paper*, *Resist Newsletter*,
Virginia Quarterly Review, *Worldview*, and *Herbert Read: A Memorial Symposium* (Methuen, London, 1967).

Grateful acknowledgment is also made to the authors and publishers of works
quoted in these pages: "The Awakening," from *For Love: Poems 1950–1960*
by Robert Creeley; Copyright © 1962 by Robert Creeley (New York: Charles
Scribner's Sons, 1962), reprinted with the permission of Charles Scribner's
Sons. Excerpt from *Portraits from Life* by Ford Madox Ford (Copyright
1936, 1937 by Ford Madox Ford); reprinted by permission. "Howl" from *Howl
& Other Poems* by Allen Ginsberg (Copyright © 1956, 1959 by Allen Ginsberg);
reprinted by permission of City Lights Books. "New Beginning" from *Collected
Poems* of Paul Goodman, edited by Taylor Stoehr (Copyright © 1972, 1973 by
the Estate of Paul Goodman); reprinted by permission of Random House.
Poems and prose by Kim Chi Ha from *Cry of the People and Other Poems* of
Kim Chi Ha (Autumn Press, Japan; Copyright © 1974 by Kim Chi Ha) and *The
Middle Hour: Selected Poems of Kim Chi Ha*, translated by David R. McCann
(Human Rights Publishing Company; Copyright © 1980). Excerpts from *Things
I Didn't Know I Loved: Selected Poems of Nazim Hikmet*, translated by Randy
Blasing and Mutlu Konuk (Copyright © 1975 by Randy Blasing and Mutlu
Konuk); reprinted by permission of Persea Books. By Denise Levertov: "The
Park," "A Ring of Changes," and "The Dead" from *Collected Earlier Poems
1940–1960* (Copyright © 1959 by Denise Levertov); excerpt of "Fragrance of
Life, Odor of Death," from *The Freeing of the Dust* (Copyright © 1973 by
Denise Levertov); excerpt of "A Son," from *Life in the Forest* (Copyright © 1978
by Denise Levertov); excerpt of "Four Embroideries III: Red Snow," and "The
Broken Sandal" from *Relearning the Alphabet* (Copyright © 1967 by Black
Sparrow Press, 1970 by Denise Levertov Goodman; "The Broken Sandal" was
first published in *Poetry*); "Life at War," and "Living" from *The Sorrow Dance*
(Copyright © 1966 by Denise Levertov Goodman)—all reprinted by permission
of New Directions. "Images" and "Postcards" by Bert Meyers, first published in
Windowsills by The Common Table in 1979 (Common Table Books are
available from: Hugh Miller, Bookseller, 216 Crown Street, New Haven, CT
06510); "To My Enemies" from *The Wild Olive Tree* by Bert Meyers, published
by West Coast Poetry Review & Press. "Grain" by Barbara Moraff first
appeared in vol. II, nos. 3 & 4 of *Potpourri*, Summer 1966; reprinted by

Manufactured in the United States of America
First published clothbound and a New Directions Paperbook 525 in 1981
Published in Canada by George J. McLeod, Ltd., Toronto

Library of Congress Cataloging in Publication Data
Levertov, Denise, 1923–
    Light up the cave.
    (A New Directions Book)
    I. Title.
PS3562.E8876L54   819'.5408   81-11295
ISBN 0-8112-0813-3   AACR2
ISBN 0-8112-0814-1 (pbk.)

New Directions books are published for James Laughlin
by New Directions Publishing Corporation
80 Eighth Avenue, New York 10011

Contents

Author's Note

Most of this book was written since *The Poet in the World,* my other prose book. Of the earlier pieces, the memoir of my experiences as a civilian nurse in London during World War II ("Three Years") is by far the oldest: chronologically it is a companion piece to the poems of *The Double Image.*[1] "My Prelude," which describes an episode of my adolescence, was not written until the early 1960s.

Although diversity of topic and genre is a temptation to browse, as I know very well from my own browsing experience, I have had in mind also those ideal readers who demand that a book have some internal shape and logic, and for them—and for my own satisfaction—have attempted to place these pieces in a logical progression, both within each section and, by the implicit links between the last item in each section and the first item of the next, throughout the sequence of sections.

[1]First published in 1946. Included in *Collected Earlier Poems* (New York, New Directions, 1979).

I THREE STORIES

Growing Up, or When Anna Screamed

All day we had been caught up into a special happiness, as the song of birds might get caught up into a sonata someone was practicing in a room with open windows, or as the raindrops shaken off the leaves flew with our laughter into sunlight when we came from beneath the trees after a passing shower. To wander all day—hiking, we called it, though we were never resolute and athletic, nor burdened with more than a packed lunch and a book—in the fields and trafficless lanes of Essex was a private satisfaction to me and my sister, experienced jointly and with conscious intensity. We cast ourselves adrift on the ocean currents of footpaths, rights-of-way maintained since long before Enclosure.

The nine years between us never seemed so negligible as on those days when I was let off lessons, our mother would make us a surprise picnic, and we'd hurry out to take whatever bus came along that was going some miles into the country. The adventure began at the bus stop, for the busses had many destinations; then it began again, like dreams do sometimes—everything tuned a pitch higher—when we alighted at our random point of departure, anywhere beyond the last outcrop of newbuilt houses, for the hike itself.

On this day there were four of us. We had never brought anyone else with us before—never considered it. No one we knew—children I sometimes played with, or people her age whom my sister knew from the Drama Society or from church—could have picked up our style, the tacit understandings we had. Even our quarrels were a part of it, in a way; for swift reconciliation was to be counted on, and almost made the pain of a falling-out worthwhile, just for the exhilaration of relief that followed. Gerhardt and his cousin Anna were different from other people we knew,

Written 1979.

3

and could come with us without spoiling anything. We took that for granted. All that year they were constantly at our house, or it seemed so. Days when they didn't come were duller. Both were around my sister's age—Gerhardt about twenty, Anna seventeen or eighteen—and it was Olga they came to see; but though I was only ten they didn't snub me or try to exclude me. I suppose that formed the basis for our feeling able to invite them on a hike; but maybe, too, it was because we believed that back in Germany, before they became refugees, they'd been part of a world in which students wandered the countryside with poems in their rucksacks, and conversed, merry or melancholy, with the brook that ran alongside the road, as depicted in an illustration to the German songbook I was so fond of. I knew about *Wanderjahre,* and if we didn't have wander-years these expeditions were at any rate our wander-days; we trusted the cousins to get the feel of that without having it explained to them. *We,* I say—but of course I don't really know what Olga thought. I don't even know what may have been going on between her and Gerhardt. Probably not very much—some sentiment, some tension. I thought I was Olga's confidante in all things; she taught me to believe that, and some days it was probably true. It was years before it occurred to me it couldn't have been true all the time. I wonder why she wanted me to think it was.

Anyway, we were right to trust Anna and Gerhardt that day. We moved in a collective dream. Villages, groves of trees, isolated farmhouses concerning whose inhabitants we spun webs of fictive drama, were revealed to all of us in their charm and peculiarities. Together we mocked a pompous eighteenth-century epitaph carved in marble and set in the wall of a modest church centuries older than its monuments; deplored the locked door of another church and went to find the verger and demand entry. As "clergy daughters" Olga and I believed we had the right to insist on access to the houses of God, as well as to expect cups of afternoon tea from Vicars' wives—although we didn't go so far as to try anyone's hospitality this time, when there were four of us. We got lost together in some osier-beds, swampy

4

underfoot, dryly, thickly rustling bamboo-like leaves about our faces, an East Anglian jungle. No one complained when it rained a bit from time to time; the cousins were not provincial and could accept English weather with suavity. We all saw with admiration the way shadows of clouds smoothed their hands over the mild slopes which—defending my county, for I was Essex-born—I claimed were hills.

We ate our picnic of bread-and-butter and mutton, mustard-and-cress in a punnet, oranges, and Rowntree's Motoring Chocolate, under the elephantine protection of a beech, where stories were told. Gerhardt told about skiing in Bavaria. I thought him handsome. "My blue eyes," he would say, "are Aryan—but my nose, it is my nose gives me away." He had no trouble speaking English.

Anna never said much. She had short curly hair and frowned a lot. Come to think of it, she didn't really contribute much to our social life, the days they spent at our house, except by just *being* there, another presence to fill out all I vaguely imagined about the life of students, artists, Europe—a life more like what I supposed mine would surely be than anyone else, outside of books, represented. Gerhardt alone wouldn't have been enough, not quite enough, to do that; it took the two of them.

Gerhardt's hosts, his "sponsors," a few streets away from where we lived, were German Jews themselves, though long settled in England, and they liked to see him so debonair, so blue-eyed and leisurely, swinging his tennis racket as he strolled over to our house; the English family who had taken Anna in spoke no German and expected her to do a lot of housework in the afternoons, after she got back from her accountancy course. But under the beech tree even silent, overburdened Anna told something to entertain us—about her dog when she was a child, it was. And Olga: some outrageous tale of her adventures, so full of details anyone would believe it. She must have believed it herself. I was not inventive and told some silly story about a dragon. But everyone laughed indulgently, even hilariously; we were dreaming the same dream, the harmony was unbroken.

Much of the talk was about music, for Gerhardt played

violin a little, and Olga was a fine pianist. When she played the Waldstein sonata I would think myself in a forest at night during a storm, at first—then in a landscape of emotion, clear or turbid, abstract, ineffable, my not yet visible destiny. Gerhardt's Berlin sophistication, which my mother complained of, was exchanged for earnest enthusiasm when he spoke of music. We despised Wagner, we worshipped Bach. Though I'd never heard much Wagner, I was happy to despise him if Gerhardt did. Johann Sebastian Bach was a holy name. There was no pretense in our love of his works. Sometimes Gerhardt would whistle bits of a fugue; Olga and Anna would come in with their voices right on the beat—Olga's coloratura sweet and piercing as a blackbird's, though not strong, and Anna's thick, throaty mezzo, a woman's voice already. I wished I could sing.

For many hours it seemed that we danced the day, danced it into being, created afternoon out of a chocolate bar, a rainstorm, and the emerging sungleams, and so would dance through life, even though Gerhardt and Anna were exiles and their parents still in Germany, where the Nazi oppression kept getting worse. (Gerhardt's mother still thought it might all blow over.) We would dance through the world in the knowledge of comradeship. It was my first experience of such communion outside the little circle of the family itself, except for Christmas eves perhaps, when many invited strangers, people without homes of their own, exiles or isolate scholars, were transformed by the glow of real candles that dangerously lit our tree, and by the singing of old songs—English, German, Welsh, and Russian—into delightful intimates, though they might never revisit us.

Late in the afternoon we came to a place that hushed us in wonder, a scene magically appropriate to such a day.

Following a cart-track, we emerged from a copse into a long, narrow, enclosed field, with thickets on both sides of it and conifers at the further end. We came out of the dark of the trees together and stopped in a row transfixed, delighted. It was a field of short, nibbled grass, studded with molehills, tussocks of longer grass, clumps of thistle—and it was full of

6

rabbits. The sun was low in the sky, and the light, while we
had been passing through the copse, had grown tenderly
golden. Every molehill and tussock and thistle, and every
rabbit, had a long shadow.

The rabbits stopped browsing and sat up poised in alarm
at our intrusion. They were dispersed about the field in
many little groups of ten or twelve. A long moment of
immobility, held like a dance pose by the whole corps de
ballet—then they ran for the woods on the left. None of
them ran to the right or towards the dark woods at the far
end of the field. But what was more remarkable was that
each separate cluster of rabbits seemed to have a chief or
guardian, who remained upright and alert, not moving from
his post out in the field, watching us but seemingly watching
his little troupe also, until they reached the safety of the
thicket; and only then tearing off after them at top speed.
For a few moments the field was full of movement—of
fleeing rabbits, bobbing whitish scuts, resembling a flight of
birds, but all happening down on ground level. Then the last
of the leader rabbits had dashed for cover, and we drew
breath and laughed gaspingly to each other, and marvelled.

It was such a quiet, secret kind of place. One felt no one
had passed that way for a long time. The sun was still quite
bright, though slanting.

We noticed that immediately to our left, backed by that
part of the woods into which the tribe had vanished, was an
old barn. Vaguely curious, we moved towards its open
doors. It was not much more than a large shed. Some old
cartwheels, a haywain, some pitchforks and a tarpaulin
were stored in it. Nothing of much interest. But there was a
ladder leading to the loft, which we climbed to look at the
field from the height of the haydoor.

Up in the loft was a contained, warm ambience. Light
was pouring through the square opening in a thick, almost
palpable shaft, honey-gold and dense with motes. The place
was filled with old but sweetsmelling hay—a huge mound, a
mountain, of it. Instinctively we dove into its tickly softness,
in an instant we were bouncing and sliding in it. The three

big ones gambolled just as I did. That was the character of my happiness—that I was part of their grownup conversations some of the time and they were part of my childhood play some of the time, and no one mentioned either part with surprise. If I myself suspected it was unusual, I kept it to myself.

We breathed hard, we slid down hayslopes, climbed by beamhold up again to a vantage point and flung ourselves back, over and over, into the warm, amber haywaves. Our laughter, our exclamations, weren't loud; maybe a blind person hearing us would have thought a fight was going on, for the sounds we made, intent on the action of our bodies, resembled the grunts and sharp broken syllables of a struggle. It was the very peak of the day's joy, following on the mystery of the rabbits that had itself seemed a culminating marvel. Life was giving us a mode of utterance, a way to gesture delight with our whole untried bodies.

But all at once, from silent Anna, Anna the frowning one, homesick for the Germany that had ejected her, unplayful Anna who today had played and joked, who had sung folksongs louder than anyone, and was the only one who knew all their words, from silent Anna came a chilling scream. We stopped in our tracks as if playing "Statues." Horrified. And she opened her mouth and screamed again: she was staring at something. We looked—we saw it. It was a shining, grinningly curved scythe blade thrusting up through the soft warm gold.

There was nothing to say. No need to tell each other any one of us might have been killed, mutilated. That we had escaped the event seemed less forcible a recognition than that the deadly crescent had so mockingly been there with us the whole time.

Quietly we went down the ladder. Gerhardt took the scythe and brought it down with him: he leaned it carefully against the wooden wall, behind the old cart's graceful upturned shafts. We picked up our small packs, light and almost empty except for a book or a scarf or some treasure trove of moss or curious pebbles: the day's food was eaten, the thermos flasks drained. Walking through the field to where the track's ruts passed into a gated plantation of larches, we saw the sun had gone down, and though the clear sky was still pale, the last daylight was dull and abruptly cold. No shadows patterned the grass. We could see little heaps of rabbit-droppings here and there, otherwise one might have thought we had imagined those lively presences and their swift, highly-organized retreat.

I knew from many other country days the sadness of lacklustre twilight; fatigue would set in about this time, and Olga and I would trudge along in silence, aware of being far from home and not knowing just how we would manage to get back—maybe picking up a bus or a train somewhere, if we had enough money left, maybe begging a ride from a passing motorist if we came out onto a travelled road before it got too dark. We had always promised to be home before it was really night, and we never kept our promise; so our parents were always anxious and angry when we at last appeared at the kitchen door, though no one, themselves included, knew exactly what they feared, and by the next time we wanted to go hiking we were always given permission. It was grownup Olga who had to face the music when we came in late, but she never seemed to worry much. It was I who took on the anxiety, the anticipation of trouble; it seemed only fair: one of us to worry, the other to be scolded. Olga would ask me fretfully after a while why I was silent, and I would reply glumly that no one had to talk all the time, and we would bicker for half an hour before the real night, flashing with country stars, succeeded gloomy twilight and lifted our spirits again, keeping them high right up to the time we were almost home, among traffic and lamp-posts, and actually turning the corner into our street, when a moment of panic might make us run the last few yards.

Tonight, because Gerhardt was with us, we were free of the hour's usual trouble; there would probably be no scold-

9

ing. He and Anna would have supper at our house, and help tell the day's tale—the bits we would want to tell. And Anna would stay the night and go back to her sponsor's house in the morning. But though we had no need, this time, to worry about being late, we were very quiet—not silent, for silence would have doubled the blow our joy had suffered; just quietly talking about mundane matters—Olga's broken shoelace, and whether we could fill our water flasks somewhere when we got onto the road again, and about larches not being evergreens though they were conifers. It was dark in the wood, and we had to take care not to get whipped in the face by twigs. Dry twigs snapped underfoot, where they'd fallen in the little-used track with its old dried-up cart furrows. We walked along purposefully now, bent on return, and not looking anywhere but on the ground. We were still together, but if we were dreaming, it was not the same shared dream.

That was the only time Gerhardt and Anna came with us, and no one else ever did. A few months later Gerhardt got a special work permit and went into business. I heard that when the war came he wasn't even interned. His father died, but not in a concentration camp, and his mother got out in time. Anna's parents left Germany too and she went to join them in Prague. She and they were still there when the Nazis went into Czechoslovakia, so it turned out to have been a bad choice; but at the time she said good-bye to us she was lightheaded with happiness at leaving London.

Olga began to be away from home a lot, but we had some more hikes when she came back for a month or two now and again. The Spanish Civil War was on and she and I and my father and mother used to listen to the news reports on the BBC every day. Olga and I used to talk about the war fervently, and pretend, as we slogged up the edge of a ploughed field, that the heavy Essex clay was the soil of the Pyrenees and we were secretly crossing the border to join the International Brigade. Olga actually did go to Spain for ten days; but by then she had fallen in love with a married man as old as my mother and was fighting with my parents all the time, and didn't confide in me any more. She had no time to.

When she left home for good soon after, I took my parents' side in their bitter feud, because they were so angry and unhappy it frightened me.

The fields were white with frozen snow, but the wind had swept the snow off the surface of the lakes and revealed the black, polished ice. The English girl had never imagined ice would be anything but whitely transparent. The lakes were artificial, rectangular, the result of extensive and methodical cutting of peat in past centuries, she had been told. Intersecting them, and running alongside of the canals too, were narrow roads built up on causeways and bordered by rows of pollarded trees. At night, when the temperature dropped from cold to colder, the black ice groaned. It was cracking; but not melting, only growing more implacable.

The English *au pair* girl knew she was a poet. She was also beginning to know she was pregnant. Was it possible? Of course it was possible. She was ignorant and naive, and accustomed to behave with dreamy rashness; still, she was not without knowledge of possibility. It was not ignorance that made her wonder, but the unfamiliarity of disaster. She was nearsighted but had so far concealed the fact and not worn glasses. When she did steal a look through a pair that happened to fit her, the world looked sharp, shrewd, unpleasing. Was that reality? None of the risks she had taken up to now had had disastrous consequences. When she was seven she had secretly taken letters off her mother's desk, letters in various scripts too hard to read, and hidden them, to see what would happen. Surely she'd hear her mother say, "Drat, what have I done with so-and-so's letter"; and then after they had been secretly replaced, she'd hear, "Well I never, here it was right under my nose!" But nothing happened. So another day she took others, and burnt them in the drawing-room fireplace, where the coal fire was lit every day after breakfast and kept going till late at night. It was easy to do, charred flakes flew up the chimney in the

Written 1980.

draft or paper ash blended soft and grey with coal ash. She was prepared to feel remorse—but again nothing happened. She grew up, went to work, often fell in love, was loved a little and was cast aside. But being cast aside was a sorrow, not a disaster. That difference seemed clear. She cried a lot, laughed with her friends, and wrote poems as she always had. During the war, which now at last was over, she never went to an air-raid shelter, though one time a bomb blast lifted her clean off her feet, carried her several yards, and set her down on the ramp leading into one. Several times men she didn't know at all led her off to strange dwellings; she went along so as not to hurt anyone's feelings, or be thought timid, or simply for the idea of adventure; but no one had ever hurt her, raped her, made her sick—she wasn't afraid, because she scarcely believed such things occurred, but even if they did there was a ring of protective magic around her: it was not to her they would happen. Maybe her poems, her sense of destiny, protected her. Yet now disaster had entered her life. Would it be this way from now on, and what did one do next? It was no use telling her boyfriend, back home in England, because he had fallen in love with a young and very gentle friend of hers who loved him. Besides, she had not yet seen a doctor to make sure. But she was sure anyway. Though she never remembered when her periods were due, she did know she'd been here two months now without one—though if she hadn't started to feel nauseous in the mornings she might not have noticed. That's the way she was—vague.

The prospect of asking for the name of a doctor (it would have to be one who spoke English), and then having to go into town and speak to him, filled her with an embarrassment more oppressive than her fear. Until she could think up an excuse for needing an appointment, she just waited, paralyzed by surprise. English conversation with her employers, English lessons of a more formal kind with the children of the household, and light housework—those were her duties. They didn't take up much of the time. Fortunately, Mr. and Mrs. van Dam already spoke fairly well and

13

had acquired many English books. The *au pair* girl read for many hours each day. Often she was alone in the house, or alone with the young village girl who came in daily to do the heavier housework. With her she shyly tried to speak Dutch, but the little girl giggled in response. The English books ranged from classics to thrillers, and the *au pair* girl read steadily, rejecting nothing unless it was too familiar, and only fearing the day might come when she would have read them all. She wrote poems—poems that evaded any direct expression of her predicament—and copied phrases and ideas into her notebook; but what would she do if the books gave out? She hated the cold; and her rationed clothing, scarcer than ever now the war was over, wasn't heavy enough for her to stay long outdoors. The children were high-school students, too old to play with and not old enough to talk to; and Mrs. van Dam went in to the city almost every day to help her husband in his office. "I am in a state of suspended animation," the *au pair* girl said to herself. And it was true. She was frightened, now that *real life*, that is to say *disaster*, had announced itself; but her fear was quiet. It was as if a challenge had been received but the challenger was still travelling to where the duel was to take place, and the seconds had not even been decided on nor the weapons chosen. She had no idea how to set about obtaining an abortion.

There was only one element of her fear that threatened not to be quiet, and that was the possibility of her parents finding out. Abortion was illegal and dangerous but she felt passive about it, as if it were a dark staircase she might climb with a stranger. "Having a baby"—*that* was unimaginable; but as long as it could be kept a secret, here in "the Lowlands low," perhaps it could be undergone?—although, no, there must be a way to avoid it, there must. She might be dreaming, and would wake up. But having her parents find out any of this, anything about all the life she had hidden from them as easily, up to now, as she had burned the letters in the grate, that almost made her panic. To cause grief, to cause anger, to witness it—the idea terrified her. But she

14

didn't know *how* to panic. Did one scream? She could imagine jumping off a bridge in such a way that it would seem to everyone she had fallen. Everyone would be very sad, but not absolutely grief-stricken, not angry. But that didn't seem very real. Besides, how absurd, all the canals and rivers were frozen, and as for the shallow lakes, that black ice was solid, right through to the peaty bottom. She knew some kind of action must take place long before the thaw.

Into the doldrums arrived visitors. Decision could the more easily be put off. It was an English writer and his wife, whom she knew slightly. Indeed this was the man who had recommended her for the three or four month job here, polishing the family's English, improving their pronunciation. Her employers were well-to-do socialists, friends of the writer even before the war, and now eager to renew the friendship and tell their stories of the Occupation and the Resistance. The *au pair* girl and her boyfriend had attended left-wing meetings in London, but listening to the suddenly lively conversations that broke out now that the visitors had arrived, she felt at a loss. Names and events flew back and forth that meant nothing to her. Even more than before, she felt unsure where to put herself in the evenings after dinner. In the back sitting room where the three children, a boy and two girls, did their homework she was unwanted. They were supposed to speak only English with her, but they'd had their English lesson for the day and their mealtime conversations, and now was their time to chatter and gossip in Dutch, too fast for her to understand. They gave her cold looks and ignored her. In the front room the adults made her courteously welcome but soon forgot her. She knew the writer thought well of her poems and poorly of her boyfriend, and had suggested this job to her to get her away from him. She resented that, though she could see it was a piece of luck as it turned out. Although—would Colin have fallen out of love with her, and into love with Jessie, if she hadn't gone away? Wouldn't Colin have helped her if she'd still been with him when she found she was pregnant?

Perhaps they would have married, and had the child, and her parents would have accepted the situation? That scenario too seemed scarcely believable—not a disaster, exactly, but still not conceivable for a person with a magic ring around them. But the ring was broken anyway. She sat quietly, listened, laughed, or made a remark from time to time, but felt invisible and unheard.

After two days of this came the weekend, when an overnight sightseeing trip was planned. Always kindly, her employers told her she was to come along. The children, who had been brought up to be reliable and self-reliant, would stay home, delighted to have the house to themselves. They took for granted, in this family, a freedom that was surprising to the English girl. Her own freedom had been stolen, not given. Probably some of their high-school friends would come over to skate on the lakes. Skating on the canals was routine, people went to work or to school along them; but on the lakes among which the house stood there was scope for figure skating and for ice boats. The *au pair* girl was teased a little because she had not learned to skate. How she longed to! But the bitter cold deterred her. Pushing a chair in front of her, the horrible feeling of skidding, the pain of falling, feeling as if her coccyx were smashed; and her nose dripping the whole time. . . . How did people learn? Besides, the knowledge of her problem was constant in her mind, and created a gulf between her and the young people much greater than that which the few years of age-difference would have made by itself. She was thankful not to be left awkwardly in charge of the household.

The expedition lifted her spirits even though she felt superfluous. When she had arrived in Holland she had been taken straight from the boat to the little town and the still smaller, scattered, village. Now for the first time she saw the cities, the urban canals, the crow-stepped gables familiar from seventeenth-century paintings, and the great museums. She forgot her problems and the feeling of being neither child nor adult, not fish, flesh, fowl, nor good red herring, just an *au pair* girl. She became the poet again, losing herself in Rembrandt's profound velvet and his long-gazing faces that were luminous with grief survived. The lakes had not been dug out in Rembrandt's time, but his eye had rested on landscapes she saw on her unwilling, red-nosed daily trudges. And with Van Gogh her mind threw itself into the imagined sun, shook with earth's convulsions, whirled among the leaves.

The quick trains took them in a breath from city to city—the Hague, Amsterdam, Haarlem. The true ginevra, purest essence of juniper, was praised and quaffed in ancient bars where old men looked askance at the foreigners. She was borne along upon the tail of the van Dam's hospitable whirlwind.

Late in the evening, after a long dinner in a restaurant, they arrived at the house where they were all to spend the night: the home of a socialist newspaper editor and his Jewish wife, people who had worked in the Resistance, been hidden, known great hardships. Their son, a boy of fourteen, had T.B. and lay on a couch in an enclosed porch off the living room, muffled in blankets, where he could breathe fresh air at all times as if there were a Magic Mountain here in the damp Netherlands. The editor and his wife gave the five people a warm general welcome, with laughter and hot drinks. Then the *au pair* girl was taken upstairs and shown where to sleep. It was a couch in the small room where the editor's wife kept her sewing machine and made and mended the family's clothes. This woman was dark haired and rosy faced, with strong features and bright friendly eyes. The *au pair* girl seemed to feel more at ease with her than she had with anyone else in the last two months. After her hostess had helped her make up the bed and had gone downstairs to attend to her other guests, the girl wished she were going to stay longer in this house, for perhaps this woman would help her. She was very tired and fell asleep in a few moments.

In the morning she woke cramped and unrefreshed from the narrow bumpy couch. In the bathroom mirror her face showed pale and puffy. Subdued nausea was a nagging

17

reminder of this reality she had not practised for. Discouraged, she splashed cold water skimpily on her face though she knew there was a grey tidemark around her neck and her whole body felt unclean. No one would notice, she supposed.

Back in her room she folded the bedclothes neatly and stuffed her pajamas into her handbag. She was half-dressed, standing in her slip about to pull her lisle stockings on, when the door burst open and the host, the newspaper editor, rushed in, a small, dark, wiry man in his forties, with whom she had not exchanged a word the night before. Pushing the door shut behind him and in the same movement bounding across the room to where she stood, he seized her in a close embrace and kissed her passionately on the mouth. "Where have you been?—Why have you only come to my life now? —How long I have waited for you!—Where were you all these years?" he was exclaiming. She couldn't have said if he were murmuring or shouting. An absolute astonishment froze her—and before she had responded in any way, any way at all, there was a footstep on the stairs, he leapt back across the room, whipped the door open, and was gone.

Had these few seconds really happened? Disbelief came not only from the suddenness of the event, but from her sense of how unattractive she had become: secretly pregnant, unloved, unwashed. She had even forgotten her brush and comb. And he had hardly met her the night before; she had gone up to bed within an hour of their arrival at the house. Yet now she stood trembling, her shoulders and one breast could still feel his tight embrace; he had grabbed her so hastily it had pinned one arm to her side. But now her familiar acceptance of what befell, as if she were dreaming, returned to her. It was as if she were reentering her circle of immunity and vagueness, but with the tokens people in fairy tales bring back in proof of strange journeys. His breath was fresh, the cloth of his shirt was rough: she was left with that knowledge. It must have been true. But this reality, though incomprehensible, (or perhaps for that very reason?) was not terrifying like being pregnant—the hurried embrace of a man to whom she had not uttered a single word, his exclamations of love, only mystified without frightening her.

At breakfast—one of those strange Dutch breakfasts, bread and cheese, bread with chocolate hundreds-and-thousands—she dared not look at him. What was he going to do? When would he speak to her again? She didn't even consider whether she liked him or not—her soul was a feather, floating along a dark stream, seized in eddies, released into shooting currents, held pulsing for moments against mossy rocks.

Breakfast was over; the sick boy, who lay on his sofa with many books and games scattered around him, and looked up at each of them smiling confidently with his witty Jewish look, had been teased and cheered; laughter was bubbling, the house still fragrant with coffee. For a moment the English girl felt irrationally happy, and as if this house was where she belonged. But now they were consulting timetables and putting on coats and boots. The editor and his wife muffled up too, and prepared to see them off. It was a short walk to the train station. And now he will speak to me, the *au pair* girl thought. But the editor walked with the English writer, the editor's wife with her old friends Mr. and Mrs. van Dam, and the *au pair* girl and the English writer's wife were left to make conversation—awkwardly enough, for the *au pair* girl felt that she bored this brilliant cosmopolitan lady.

At the station the editor's warmhearted wife kissed the *au pair* girl good-bye, and she remembered with regret that the night before she had thought perhaps this woman would be the source of help, of a solution. . . . Clearly, that was not to be. Somehow in the flurry of boarding the train she was not sure if she even shook hands with the editor himself. Yet she still seemed to feel him hugging her half-naked body.

There was more travelling and sightseeing all day, and in the evening the long trip back to the house among the lakes of black ice. The *au pair* girl wondered very much that anyone had wanted to hug and kiss her now that disaster was making her so ugly. When would he write to her, and

19

what would he say? Could it be that he had felt she was a poet, that she had a destiny?

The English couple left, the days resumed their previous monotony, and now she knew she must overcome her extreme shyness and tell the van Dam's she wanted to see a doctor. It would be a lot harder to find one if she tried to do so on her own; and if she didn't do it, she would be cooperating with disaster. She had just enough common sense to know that, and enough instinct of self-preservation to recoil from such cooperation. With a dry mouth, her heart pounding, trying to sound casual but too flustered to remember her prepared excuses about a sore throat or stomach ache, she enquired at last. She could see that her employers guessed her reason at once (for all she knew, they'd suspected before . . .) but they didn't at once say so; instead, pleasant and calm, they sent her off on her bike to the nearby town to see their own physician, who confirmed what she knew already. Disaster was happening, but so quietly. Without fuss the doctor and her employers discreetly provided information about a trained nurse in Rotterdam. The *au pair* girl could not help contrasting the— what was it?—the hygienic sensibleness of these sophisticated strangers, among whom good fortune had landed her, with the dramatic, tragic, naive intensity of her elderly parents—whom, nevertheless, she loved, and who loved her.

Without reproach or excitement an abortion was arranged, when they had ascertained that that was the alternative she preferred. They offered her the option of staying on in Holland, having the baby, placing it with a Dutch family; but that she rejected without hesitation: it seemed only to compound all that terrified her. The abortion was accomplished with some secrecy, but efficiently; although, her pregnancy being almost too far advanced, the event was not without fear and gruesomeness. From dream to nightmare was only a step.

In the aftermath she thought she wanted to die. For a few days she lay in bed and refused to eat. Her employers scolded her for making a nuisance of herself, shooing her outdoors to work up an appetite. And even while she sought to give dignity to her experience by picturing it as a tragedy and magnifying her love for her false lover, she was taken unawares by a flood of joy. A sense of absolute identification with her earliest memories, of seeing things when she was two or three years old with the self-same eyes she looked out of now, a feeling of the continuity of that past with the long future she was walking towards even as she trudged along beside the black lake this very day, exhilarated her. She felt like a boat, its sails filled with wind, a swift current under it and the shrouds singing.

The stress of those weeks of intensified perplexity, of choice (even if it had only been choice by elimination of the impossible), of the violent intrusion of consequences into the drift of her days—all of that had taken up so much room in her that she had almost forgotten about waiting for the letter from the newspaper editor. She had not asked her friends—they were friends, now, not just her employers, though her relation to them remained one of gratitude rather than intimacy; perhaps, indeed, her *benefactors* was a more precise term for them—she had not asked them anything about the editor, what sort of person he was. To enquire about him would have been to risk telling about the isolated moment of his embrace and declaration. She would sooner remain mystified than betray him. And then, there was his wife, whose kind face and motherly kiss she remembered too. If she was also, by remaining silent, protecting herself from ridicule and disbelief, she was unconscious of it then— though the idea did occur to her a long time afterwards.

Spring came: the black ice became wind-ruffled black water. On the canals, iced-in boats began to work free. The water slapped against them and fragments of broken ice jingled against each other. When the snow melted off the fields, the Dutch earth was revealed as very dark—rich-looking. Among the mats of flattened, yellow grass which snow had smothered appeared conspicuous blades of new green cautiously testing the air. The *au pair* girl hugged her

21

employers good-bye and went away to Paris. There, in the unfolding of a fuller, leafier, abundant springtime, she came to feel that reality, with its disasters, was not so alien to her nor she to it. It was as if she were wearing eyeglasses and finding that the images they revealed were not crude but brilliant in their clarity, and this brilliance had its own glamor, a precision compelling as the fuzzier, softer forms perceived by naked, myopic eyes. *Now* if she had burned some letters they would surely have been missed and a hue and cry got up for them. She made decisions and expected consequences, and the consequences began to occur. But not every consequence was a disaster, and no disaster was final, it seemed. Reality included catastrophes but was not solely composed of them; it held relief, joy, and ordinary happiness too. Still, there was much that remained confusing to her. What weight did an event have? How was one to measure its specific gravity? In the span of a few months, events of obvious importance in her life-story had occurred. But these events blended into one another as she thought about them, and no single one of them was so dramatic, so clear-cut and memorable, as the brief moments when the editor had rushed into the room and embraced her, uttering those wild endearments. Yet she could puzzle out no interaction between that occurrence and anything else. It was as if a thread of violet had suddenly appeared in a fabric woven all of green and red. Had the editor been astonished to experience no result from his declaration? Had it been up to her, not to him? Could he have expected her to write, to turn up on his doorstep some spring day? But she never did hear a word from him, or learn anything about him, or solve in her mind the mystery of what his embrace signified; though she did find out that the young boy with T.B. had recovered.

Layer on layer of them: tightwrapped dense onion flesh of
feelings. Or no, not that, for each successive layer of onion is
nearer the center; even if the center is a space, still the last
layer is an innermost layer—and who could say which of
these was innermost? The feelings were experienced in
sequence, in time; but which of them was the deepest, the
truest, she couldn't tell.

The starting point of the sequence was that, in sleep, she
felt vague desire, and began, still asleep, to move her hips in
the rhythm of arousal, and began to wake and be aware,
and to remember that she was alone. But then her heart
jumped and she uttered a little shriek, for all at once she felt
the weight of his body beside her, and the warmth of it. At
that he stirred and murmured something, an endearment,
unintelligible, out of his warm sleep. He must have crept in
very quietly, climbed into bed without waking her, feeling
lonely, feeling affectionate. And she was sleepily glad. It
was after all a comforting sweetness, a tenderness, his being
there; even though she had no expectation that he would
turn to make love to her. But anyway, her desire had been
deep in dream, or not even dream, some depth of sleep into
which it had vanished. Now simply she felt the drowsy
comfort of his company.

But next came the thought: And if—now that our decision
is made—he *did* return to me? If he made love to me, if our
bodies met and caught fire from each other? After all the
long struggle towards decision, the slow realization that the
irritations and incompatibilities that had pushed them apart
would still be there even if Eros returned to them—would I
want that? Could I bear it? Would it be fair at all, make
sense at all? And she recalled the sense of relief that their
decision—made at last, only a few days before, less than a

Written 1974.

week—had given her, and seemingly given him too. Then she felt exasperated, almost indignant, that he had already backtracked from that relief, changing the rules of what was not a game.

And now came what was not perhaps the deepest layer of feeling, but was, in the sequence, the most dramatic, more startling even than the moment when she had uttered that little shriek at finding him there, weight, mass, body-warmth: a sudden doubt came to her as she lay on her side, back towards him, and made her reach out with arm and foot, behind herself, to touch him—

and no one was there. She was alone. Her first waking, in sleepy lust, her second waking, with a start, to find him; her acceptance of his being there, her increasing rejection of it, all had been dreamt.

And now she was—no doubt of it—stark awake. What she had to deal with now was this: in all the times of their being apart, even with all the uncertainty and anxiety of struggle and indecision, all the sense of bafflement and anguish, she had not been prone to *this* pain, of reaching out in the dark to a body that was not there. Sometimes when they were still together she would wake to the anxious awareness that he was gone from the bed, had gotten up unable to sleep. Many times she had gone down to join him in the kitchen for a glass of hot milk, or just to see if he was all right, not in some unbearable crisis of depression. But in the many months they had spent, in recent years, far apart, she had often actually enjoyed sleeping alone, the freedom, the luxury of extra space; enjoyed switching the light on to see the time or read, if she had insomnia, without fear of disturbing him; of letting the books accumulate on his side of the bed, even. Yet now that they had made the decision to part, to lead separate lives, not to lean on each other anymore; now that she had experienced, therefore, a relief that had made her lightheaded for a day or two, euphoric with the feeling that they had come through into a new place—*now*, it seemed, this pain entered, like a new personage in the third act of a play.

24

The decision was mutual, well founded, made soberly and without rancor. The euphoria had been an experience of powerful reality, like the lifting of a weight off the top of one's head or the sudden cessation of a nerve-racking noise. But this waking into dream and into more dream and then into silence and solitude, made it clear that, however much time they had already spent apart, the actuality of separation was only just beginning.

To revoke the decision was hopeless. Even these few days they had just spent together had made apparent again all the complex reasons why for both of them the marriage was untenable. But how strange, she thought, how strange that the *utterance* of that realization, the verbalization of what they recognized must be done, should—after that brief euphoria—so *quickly* have begun to make manifest in dreams the pain of separation. It was the speed of it that astonished her. If it had all been decided suddenly, hastily— but no, it was no new idea, it had been growing for three years, in thought and in talk. Yet now it pounced: it caught her with its claws.

II THE NATURE OF POETRY

Interweavings: Reflections on the Role
of Dream in the Making of Poems

Can I distinguish between dreaming and writing—that is, between dream images and those which come into being while I am in the poem-making state? I'm not sure.

I began writing at a very early age, but the two childhood dreams I remember were beyond my powers to articulate. One of them was a kind of nightmare; and after it had recurred a couple of times I found I could summon it at will—which I did, in much the same spirit, I suppose, as that in which people watch horror movies. Retrospectively, I see it as a mythic vision of Eden and the Fall: the scene is a barn, wooden and pleasantly—not scarily—dark, in which the golden hay and straw are illumined by a glow as of candle-light. And all around the room of the barn are seated various animals—cows, sheep, horses, dogs, and cats. They all sit somewhat the way dogs do, with their front legs straight and their back ones curved to one side, and they look comfortable, relaxed. There's an atmosphere of great peace and well-being and camaraderie. But suddenly—without a minute's transition—all is changed: all blackens, crinkles, and corrugates like burnt paper. There's a sense of horror.

I was not more than six when I first dreamed this, and it frightens me still; can it (I think to myself) have been a prophetic dream about the nuclear holocaust we live in fear of? Then I console myself a bit with the knowledge that it didn't have to be so; I'd already long since been terrified several times by the sight of the newspaper my mother, with astounding rashness, would wrap around the metal-mesh fireguard to make the new-lit coals draw, catching on fire, the charred tatters of it flying up the chimney like flimsy bats. Someone had accidentally dropped a sheet of newspaper over my face when I was in the cradle and apparently

First published in *Dreamworks*, Vol. 1, No. 2, Summer 1980 (New York, Human Sciences Press, 1980).

29

I went into convulsions from the fright of it. I seem to remember it, in fact, though I was only a few months old; and this connected itself to the way a page of the *Times* would burst into a sheet of flame and so quickly blacken. In my dream there were no flames, only the switch from the soft glow in which all the friendly beasts (and I among them) basked and were at peace, to the horror of irreversible destruction, of ruin.

The other dream came when I was eight. I used as a child to love reading the descriptions (often accompanied by small photographs) of country houses for sale which at that time occupied the back page of the *London Times*. They ranged from cottages to castles, and I was not only fascinated by their varied architecture but also by their names. I would furnish each with inhabitants and make up "pretend games" (long, mainly unwritten serial stories within which I moved not so much *doing* anything as *being* one of the people in them—another form of dreaming). Another source of these daydreams was the sample notepaper, embossed or printed with the names of persons or places I presume were made up by the stationer, which my father, as a clergyman, used to receive from time to time. He would give me these advertisements to play with; and from a letterhead such as

Colonel & Mrs. Ashley Fiennes
The Manor House
Rowanbeck
Westmoreland

I could create not the *plot* of a story—I've never been good at that—but a situation and its shadowy children. So—this dream was of a house. When I first dreamed it there were some scenes, events, something of a story or situation in the dream; but those soon faded, and what I remembered (and now still either remember, or remember remembering, so that the picture still has clarity) was the vision of the house itself. It is seen from a hillside perhaps a quarter of a mile away, and it's a Jacobean house with two projecting wings. The stone it's made of is a most lovely warm peach-pink; and the English county it's in is Somerset—lovely name! The mood or atmosphere of this dream is as harmonious and delightful as that of the barn, but this time there's no disaster; it just goes on glowing , beaming, filling the self who gazes from the hillside with ineffable pleasure. Not long ago I realized that the reason I always give my present address as *West* Somerville, which though correct is not necessary for postal purposes, is not from some snobbish concern (East Somerville, like East Cambridge, is a poorer, uglier neighborhood) but because Somerville sounds like Somerset and Somerset is in the West Country. The associations are pleasant; when I say "West Somerville" I evoke for myself the old-rose color of the house in my dream, though plain "Somerville" makes me think of Union Square and its traffic jams. The house of the dream had a name too: Mazinger Hall; and I dreamed it on a Midsummer's Eve. For many years just to think of it could give me a sense of peace and satisfaction. What connection do these two early dreams, which never became poems, have with the images of poetry or with my later activity as a writer? The powerful first one perhaps embodies some basic later themes, of joy and fear, joy and loss. But it's the second one, because of its verbal element—the house *having* a name and an awareness of the sounds and associations of *Somerset, West Country,* being implicit[1]—that links itself to the writing of poems.

Although my first book, *The Double Image,* is full of the words *dream* and *dreamer,* it is daydreaming and the *idea* of dreaming that really prevail in it. It was some years later that I began to write directly from real dreams; "The Girlhood of Jane Harrison,"[2] for instance. I had been reading J. H.'s *Prolegomena to the Study of Greek Religion* and some of her other work, but had not then read her charming autobiographical memoir, later given me by Adrienne Rich because I'd written the poem. My dream is *described* in the poem, but I don't know that the sense, in the dream and in the wake of it, of the symbolic value of the window, indoor

[1]With connotations of *summer* and *sunset* included among them.

[2]From *With Eyes at the Back of our Heads* (1959) which, along with sections of *The Double Image* (1946), is included in *Collected Earlier Poems 1940-1960* (New York, New Directions, 1979).

31

and garden darknesses, the sweetness of marzipan, the naming of roses, the diagram ("like the pan for starcake") of the dance in which Jane Harrison and her *semblances* moved from the central point out towards and beyond the dissolving boundaries of youth's garden, is adequately presented in the text. "Marzipan" is an especially unrealized reference; I myself can only dimly recall what part it played in the dream, and I don't see how anyone else could derive its significance from the poem unaided by any trace of memory. I think it was a word that the figure in the dream murmurs to herself as if its sound and the sweetness and dense texture of the substance so named expressed the feeling of the summer night and its roses. Also it was linked with the "star cake." The garden was a nineteenth century English one, with ample lawns and rosebeds, the surrounding shrubbery backed by taller trees, and a great cedar in the middle distance. Jane leans out of a ground-floor window at first; then she steps into the outdoor space. Though it's dark there's some moonlight, or possibly a glow from the house behind her—enough for trees and bushes to cast shadow. Starting from near the cedar, she begins to dance; and in forming the star figure of the dance, which is a ritual to welcome the autumn that is soon to begin, she multiplies, as if reflected in many mirrors or as if a cluster of identical dancers spread out to the points of a compass rose. She's moved out of the house of childhood, recognized the end of summer, saluted the fall (The Fall from innocence into the vast adventure of Knowledge?) to which her own grown-up life corresponds. Something like that. But as a poem it may be incompletely evolved, or partially unborn. And this is the great danger of dream poems: that they remain subjective, private, inaccessible without the author's gloss. Not only dream material presents this danger, of course; one of the most typical failures of student poetry is the writer's failure to recognize what has actually emerged into the poem and what remains available only to the poet or through explications that are not incorporated in the work. Such nonarticulated material may originate in all kinds of experience; but dream experiences are particularly likely to be insufficiently

32

transmuted into art unless the writer is sensitive to the problem and to its solution.

"Relative Figures Reappear"[3] is another dream-poem I seldom read to audiences. I feel it *describes* a dream but does not evoke it vividly enough for it to stir in others feelings analogous to those it gave to me; and because of this descriptive, rather than evocative, quality its *significances* remain unshared in much the same way as those in the Jane Harrison poem. "The Park" (also from the *Collected Earlier Poems*) on the other hand, in which persons and places of my own life also appear, seems somewhat more evocative—its images have more feeling-tone—and ends with a rather clear statement of intent, specifying the park as the

> country of open secrets where the elm
> shelters the construction of gods
> and true magic exceeds all design.

The dream (and I hope, the poem) gave a sense of the way in which "real magic" may be arrived at by means of illusive modes; or rather that it transcends the trickery or sleight-of-hand it may condescend to utilize. The elm (real, natural, an "open secret") may indeed shelter the construction, by carpenters, of wooden "gods"—but they are real gods! Magic is *happening*, a multi-layered paradox.

Many of my poems of the fifties and early sixties—"Nice House," "Scenes from the Life of the Pepper Trees," "The Springtime," "The Departure," (all from the *Collected Earlier Poems*) for example—may seem to have been dream-derived, but they were not. Rather they are typical examples of the poetic imagination's way of throwing off analogues as it moves through, or plays over, the writer's life. I see a difference between these poems and those of a still earlier period, however: being more concrete and more genuinely related as analogies, metaphors, images, to that life-experience—more rooted, in a word—they are truly poems in a degree that the stanzas of vague talk, unfounded either in actual dreams or in daily waking life, which filled *The*

[3]*Collected Earlier Poems 1940–1960*

33

Double Image, were not. One poem from the early sixties which might easily be mistaken for dream account is "A Happening" (*Collected Earlier Poems*); here a metaphor that expressed for me the trauma of returning to the city after two years in Mexico, proved to be meaningful to many readers. For me it was New York City that was the intractably alien and terrifying place, despite years of residence there and attempts to love it; for others it may have been any other great metropolis. However, the poem includes a conscious irony that I now think is a flaw because of its peculiar obscurity: one of the protagonists (a stranger bird who turns into a paper sack and then "resumes its human shape" when it touches down in the streets of the city) goes uptown to seek the source of "the Broadway river." Now, only someone familiar with New York would know, first, that Broadway does have a river-like meandering course, and second, that in fact it *begins* downtown, where Manhattan's earliest buildings were constructed near the harbor. So the stranger is looking in the wrong direction. That's part of the "plot" of the poem, but it's not fully accessible, and even to a New Yorker can too easily seem merely a mistake on the part of a writer who was, at the time, a fairly recent immigrant. (I had come to the U.S. at the end of 1949, but had spent almost four years out of the country during the fifties.)

In dreams, of course, just such "mistakes" do occur; but the dream *atmosphere* of a poem must be as strongly convincing as a Magritte painting to ensure the reader's not being distracted by its peculiarities from the dynamics of the poem itself. When the images of certain poems (dream derived or not) make one feel one is entering a real dream, it is a sign of their strength, their power. We are convinced, just as, ourselves dreaming, we accept without question situations and juxtapositions our waking reason finds illogical or "weird." Poems "about" dreams which are not well written are as boring or depressing as other shoddy work; and poems which (like my own early work) make constant reference to the dream state but provide no concrete evidence of its existence are at best vaguely pleasant in a

34

melancholy, misty way. When a poem "feels like a dream" it does so by virtue of the *clearness* of its terms (however irrational they may be). When we wake from actual dreams, isn't it precisely the powerful clarity, not any so-called "dreaminess," that speaks to us? It is true that sometimes dream episodes, and figures in them, dissolve or melt into one another and that this witnessed metamorphic process forms part of the dream-drama; but we are not commonly brought to question it while dreaming, any more than we question the transitions of place, mood, and persons we experience while waking.

In the early sixties my husband began working with a Jungian therapist who encouraged him to talk over his dreams with me; and this stimulated me to remember and think about many more of my own dreams than hitherto, both because of our discussions and his account of the therapist's interpretations and because I began to make a practice of writing down what I remembered, and of participating to some extent in the emotional effect of Mitch's dreams as well as my own. Thus, in "A Ring of Changes" (*Collected Earlier Poems*), I wrote,

> I look among your papers
> for something that will give you to me
> until you come back;
> and find: "Where are my dreams?"
>
> Your dreams! Have they not nourished my life?
> Didn't I poach among them, as now on your desk?
> My cheeks grown red and my hair curly
> as I roasted your pheasants by my night fire!
>   My dreams are gone off to hunt yours,
> I won't take them back unless they find yours,
> they must return torn by your forests . . .

It was a time of great pain and a lot of growth for us; looking back I see that the sharing of our dream-life, and of what we were learning about how to *think* about dreams, was what kept us going and held us to one another in those years more than anything else. Whatever conflicts we endured, we nevertheless found ourselves linked in the unconscious; not that, as some have done, we dreamed the same dream or answered dream with dream: yet our common intense interest in our own and each other's nightly adventures in the inner world acted as a powerful bond. After a while I too began to see a therapist and to work more methodically in trying to comprehend the symbolic language. Specifically dream-originated poems of this time are part IV of "A Ring of Changes," "The Dog of Art," the prose story about Antonio and Sabrinus ("A Dream"), and "To the Snake" (all from *Collected Earlier Poems*), as well as some of those previously mentioned: but not "The Goddess," though people have thought so. The daisy-eyes, worked in wool, of the Dog of Art are the "lazy-daisy" embroidered eyes my mother (and later I, myself, when my son was little) used to substitute for the dangerous button-eyes on wire pins with which stuffed toy animals used to be furnished. The dream-images, and consequently the poem, imply relationships between the embroiderer's practical creative imagination and the child's imagination, which infuses still more life into the toy; the functioning of imagination in dream, and the way it incorporates memory; and the way in which artists (of any kind) draw upon all of these things. Daisies suggest the "innocent eye" of art.

Something the Antonio and Sabrinus dream made even clearer for me than it had been before was the urgent tendency of some material toward its medium—in this case prose, not verse. I began telling the story as a poem, but it had been a dream with a very distinct tone or style, a *tale told*; and the slightly archaic diction which was virtually "given," or at least which the dream lay on the very brink of, sounded stilted in verse. (It was in conversation with Robert Bly that the possibility of capturing the tone better in prose rhythms emerged, I remember—unlikely as that seems, for Bly has never, in my opinion, really understood the sonic aspects of poetry, which is why, focusing almost exclusively on the image, he has felt free to translate such various poets. Had he been concerned with ear and voice he would have been daunted by auditory problems he has simply ignored.) The stanzas of verse which conclude "A Dream" began, I think, as the opening of the subsequently abandoned first version. I had a similar experience of material "wanting to be" prose in writing the nondream experience of a tree-felling, the story "Say the Word."[4] One must learn to listen to the form-needs of events; and dream material often seems to make this necessity specially clear.

This retrospective evaluation of my own relation, as a poet, to dreams reveals so far two main points. One is the difficulty of adequately conveying not only the mood of the dream, and of not only describing or presenting its facts, but also—along with mood and facts combined—of capturing within the poem itself a sense of its significance. For the poem to work, this significance may be narrowly personal only if a sufficient context is provided for that personal meaning to justify itself as a dramatic component. For example, in "A Sequence"[5] it is possible (though I am not certain of it) that the tense situation presented in the first four parts of the sequence provides a sufficiently novelistic context for the dream references of part five, tenuous though their meaning may be, to have some impact. One can at least comprehend that the dream joke (which, as often happens, doesn't really seem all that funny when one wakes and looks for the point of it) does in fact give a crucial moment of relief to the protagonists. And perhaps this puts it on a less narrow, more universal level: one accepts the laughter and relief (I speak now as reader, not writer, for the poem was written so long ago) not because one shares the joke but because one has witnessed the characters' previous misery, and also because one is probably familiar with the way in which such tension can at last be broken by something simply silly.

The other point revealed is that the attempt to render dream into poem is potentially an excellent way to learn one's craft, for if the difficulties inherent in that process can be surmounted, those attendant upon the articulation of

[4]From *O Taste and See* (New York, New Directions, 1964).
[5]From *The Jacob's Ladder* (New York, New Directions, 1961).

other experience seem less great. Moreover—and this perhaps is a third and separate point—consideration of dream-images, in which the imagination has free play, or at least a play less censored, than it has in the waking mind, provides valuable models of possibility for the too-deliberate, cautious, and thus "uninspired" writer. (Or perhaps I should say, for the writer temporarily in an uninspired, over-intentional phase; for if a poet's sole experience of being *taken over* by the imagination took place in dreaming, could one consider him a poet at all?)

There is a certain kind of dream in which it is not the visual and its associations which are paramount in impact and significance, but rather an actual verbal message, though a visual context and the identity of the speaker may be important factors. The first dream I can recall having written into a poem ("The Flight," *Collected Earlier Poems 1940–1960,*) was dreamed in London in 1945 but not composed until several years later, probably in New York. The encounter with William Blake—who was sitting on the floor, his back against a wall and his knees drawn up, and whose prominent, unmistakable eyes gazed up at me as he spoke— was so memorable that the lapse of time has scarcely blurred it. And it coincided with the "real life" fact of a bird's getting caught in my room that night and at dawn, when I pushed down the top half of the sash window, shooting unhesitatingly out, calmed by the sleep into which it had sunk when I turned out the light. But it was the extraordinary Blakean words, "The will is given us that we may know the delights of surrender," that made the dream an artistic whole which seemed to ask only for transcription. Yet if I'd tried to write the poem at the time of dreaming I would not have had the craftsmanship to accomplish it, and it would have been lost to me, because once crystallized in an inadequate form it would almost inevitably have become inaccessible to another attempt.

Then there are verbal dreams whose visual context vanishes upon waking, or never appeared at all, the dream having consisted purely of words. The context may arrive later, in the world of external events. "In Memory of Boris

Pasternak" (*The Jacob's Ladder*) exemplifies this latter eventuality. In its second section I wrote about the way in which a great writer can impart to scenes of one's own world a character they would not otherwise have had—in other words, can give one new or changed eyes to see through. It was while I was working on the poem, in a field in Maine, looking about me at the barn and woods and clouds, that I found and buried some dead fledgelings among the wild strawberries; and as I was doing so, a dream I'd lost track of re-entered my consciousness. When I had woken from it two nights before, I'd not associated it with the recently-dead poet; but now this verbal dream, a disembodied voice saying, "The artist must create himself or be born again," came clearly into the constellation of images and experiences clustered around my feeling for Pasternak; and the dictum seemed not only directive but also a comment on how, for the poet, "self-creation" consists in attaining, in a lifetime's practice of the art, the ability to reveal the world, or a world, to others. The dream words are syntactically ambiguous; do they mean, "If the artist fails to give birth to himself (to his creative potential) he must undergo reincarnation until he does so"? Or is the syntax appositive, i.e., "The artist must create himself, or in other words be born anew in each work of his art, as in Christian theology the New Adam takes the place of the Old"? As the dreamer, my sense is that both meanings are implicit. Indeed, one of the most important lessons a poet can learn from dreaming is that, just as in dreams we effortlessly receive images and their often double significances, rather than force them into being by a process of will, so in writing (whether from dream or non-dream sources) the process is rather one of recognizing and absorbing the given than of willing something into existence. But this "given" is not the taken-for-granted reality of superficial, inattentive, moving through life, but the often disregarded reality that lies just beyond or within it.

A dream that exemplifies the verbal message without visual or other sensuous context is this one, in which the following proposition was presented to the intellect (presumably in much the same way as solutions to mathematical problems have occurred to people during sleep):

"Trauerzucker = Zauberzucker"

The dream consisted of these equated possible German compounded words (which would mean "mourning sugar" and "magic sugar") and of the awareness (a) that (in the dream world) there exists a funeral rite in which lumps of sugar are distributed to guests at a wake, and (b) that this was understood to signify "out of sorrow comes joy." Thus, a ritual of sorrow and death, in which sugar is handed out to sweeten the bitterness, turns out to have an intimate connection with or even to be identical with (as shown by the equal sign) the rituals of (favorable, "white," or "good") magic— so that (it was implied) the sugar cubes don't just alleviate, but *transform* the sorrow (into joy).

A curious point was that the word "trauer" was misspelled, so to speak, in this non-visual dream, as "trauber," a word that doesn't exist; however, the word "traube," meaning a bunch of grapes, does, so that "traubenzucker" would be "grape-sugar" (as in Trauben-saft, grape-juice).

Often a dream presents a ring from which to hang the latent questions of that moment in one's life. "The Broken Sandal"[6] was such a one. As it states, I "dreamed the thong of my sandal broke." The questions that follow—from the most literally practical ones about how I'm going to walk on without it over sharp dirty stones, to the more abstract ones

Where was I going?
Where was I going I can't go to now, unless hurting?
Where am I standing, if I'm to stand still now?

—arise (gradually waking) from the initial event. The dream demanded of the dreamer that some basic life-questions be asked. That was its function. In becoming poem, the organic process begun in dream continued, statement and questions

[6]From *Relearning the Alphabet* (New York, New Directions, 1970).

40

giving the poem its necessarily terse form; and the mode of the questions was provided by the dream's sandal-thong metaphor, so that "Where am I (is my life) going?" is given concrete context, a matter of bare feet, of hobbling, of hurting. Finally the dreamer-writer is brought to enquire the nature of the place that is the poem's present. This type of dream-experience and poem-experience is not hampered by the intrusion of the ego and its so often untransferable trappings, but translates seamlessly into the reader's own "I". I wish that happened oftener. Yet perhaps a poetry devoid of the peculiarities of individual, even subjective experience might seem bland; occasionally such a poem may have some degree of stark force precisely because it is unusually simple, but a whole book of such poems might make one suspect the author of deliberately aiming at universality in the manner of gurus and greeting-card rhymesters. The hope is always that, when autobiographical images occur in a poem, readers will respond with the same combination of empathy and of a recognition of their own equivalents with which they would receive a novel, a play, a film. For instance, in "Don't You Hear That Whistle Blowin. . . ,"[7] the "Middle Door" and the personages named—Steve, Richard, Bo, Mitch—are unknown to the reader, but the theme of the poem is loss and change, and my hope is that the poem clearly expresses this and (because of the givens of the dream source) reinforces that theme with the folkloric, nostalgic, associations of railroad trains.

There is a type of dream that, like the simple image of the broken sandal, virtually writes itself: the kind whose very terms are those of the myth or fairy tale. "The Well,"[8] about which I've written elsewhere, is an instance. More recently the nature of a close relationship was dreamed in what felt like mythic terms; the resulting poem ("A Pilgrim Dreaming"[9]) derived its rhythms and diction partly from the feeling-tone of the dream itself and partly from my waking feelings

[7]From *The Freeing of the Dust* (New York, New Directions, 1975).
[8]From *The Jacob's Ladder.*
[9]From *Life in the Forest* (New York, New Directions, 1978).

41

—rather awestruck—about having dreamed something seemingly from my friend's point of view rather than my own, almost as if I had dreamed his dream. Again, one of the two friends of whom I'd written twenty-five years before in "The Earthwoman and the Waterwoman[10]" (not a dream-derived poem) was visiting me one day in 1978, and after she left I dreamed about her as "The Dragonfly Mother,"[11] the long-ago images of water and blueness reappearing in a metamorphosis that expressed the growth and change in her and also in my response to her personality. Thus the sequence was: impression, first poem, passage of time, new impressions, dream, second poem. And in addition (as recounted in the second poem) her visit affected my actions on that day, making me forego doing something I'd thought it was my duty to do (but which as a matter of fact wasn't important, since it was only a matter of speaking for two minutes at a big outdoor rally, at which I would not really be missed). Instead, I slept, dreamed, wrote a poem I like, and recognized how often the fear of displeasing masks itself as a sense of obligation.

Perhaps it is when dreaming and waking life thus interweave themselves *actively* that we experience both most intensely. When such interaction takes place for someone who is not able to incorporate it in any medium, the recognition of its power remains restricted to that individual. But the poet or other artist, as well as giving to dreams a corporeality that enables others to share them, may also sometimes experience the primary interweaving in the very doing of the poem, painting, dance, or whatever. It is then more than recapitulation, it is of one substance with the dream; and its power has a chance to extend beyond the limits of the artist's own life.

Appendix

Some dreams contain a greater quantity of narrative detail than seems manageable in a poem. An example would be

[10]From *Collected Earlier Poems.*

[11]From *Wanderer's Day Song* (Copper Canyon Press, Port Townsend, Washington).

the following (which I can hardly believe occurred as long ago as 1963, it is so vivid to me: that is, its orientation—the placement of doors or rooms to the right or left in relation to the beholder—is so clear in my mind). I am visiting a mental hospital, or rather a *residential clinic,* in search of a woman who works there in some more or less menial capacity, and whom I have agreed to help move into a new apartment. She is in fact moving into my building but I'd promised to assist her before I knew that, and she still doesn't know—I'm going to surprise her with the information later. I find that this place she works in is so interesting that I want to look at everything for its own sake. I more or less forget about looking for her; the people in her office know I'm doing so, anyway.

It's an old building without "grounds," right in the city, a mixture of City and Country School (a private elementary school in New York City) and the Judson Health Center (a neighborhood clinic in New York City). It works on the principle of keeping promises and by lots of creative occupational therapy. The O.T. rooms occupy almost all the space, unlike the situation in most hospitals. On a womans' floor I learn that troubled housewives can come for short periods (e.g., a week) and immerse themselves in doing painting or sculpture or whatever. On a door is a sign about "perpetual counsel"—I open it, not expecting to find anyone there during the lunch hour, but sure enough, there is: promise kept. Likewise on the children's floor is a door saying "The Friendly Lady" will be there at all times: and I look in, and she is.

Also on the children's floor is a special quiet library-room, quite small, rounded or vaulted in shape, in which there are four mural panels—silvery-white designs on milky-pale-blue background—of subjects "from the Zohar,"[12] showing constellations and kingly figures on horseback rising from, *and composed of,* stars; all prophetically tending towards the Stable of Bethlehem which can be seen afar as if amid the nebulae. A theme here is of reassurance—promises *are* kept,

[12]A group of Jewish Cabalistic texts.

the "Friendly Lady" is actually there, "counsel" really is perpetual. There is a sense of consolation and grace akin to that in the idea of the Madonna, The Holy Mother. And the final scene, with the magical starry mural has its own evident symbolism, with powers and principalities moving towards the humble stable. (That the Zohar enters into this certainly pertains to my father's work on Jewish mysticism and Christian faith.)

Another dream "told itself" (in the immediate writing down) in what, with a little crafting, might approximate to the style of the Grimms' *Household Tales*. It's only an amusing anecdote, however; I enjoyed dreaming it but it could not impel me into trying to make a work of art of it: A little girl had longed, as many do (I did, passionately) for the inanimate to speak. To find one of her dolls actually addressing her one day! But as she grew older she of course became more and more aware it probably wouldn't happen. Then one day, when she was about ten years old, it *did* happen!—though it was not a doll that spoke. This is what occurred: Her parents took two newspapers, one conservative, one radical, and the latter was lying on a couch or bed when, as she looked at it, it raised itself up on *its elbow*, so to speak, and began to address her. In delight and excitement she exclaimed, "How I've always wanted this to happen!— And before, it never did, no matter how much I longed for it!" "Ah," said the newspaper (whose name was *The Emancipator*), "I'll tell you the secret of how to get us Things to speak—" And just then I woke up.

Yet another type of dream, verbal but not poetic, is illustrated by the following:

I am at Yale for a reading. A professor points out how many Black college Fellows (as the term is used at Oxford, or in Harvard's "Society of Fellows") are in the hall. I say, ironically, "Oh yes—angels on the point of a needle, right?"

The dream that follows suggests to me two literary possibilities: one would be, to reenter the dream imaginatively and draw forth from it some further elements of story—this would tend to become prose fiction. The other possibility is that since the dream-experience becomes as much a part of one's memory-bank as any other, its images (rather than the fictional situation) may come into play unbidden in the course of some later poem. With another girl (Jean Rankin, my childhood friend) I come to the edge of the sea. (We are about eleven and twelve years old). There seem to be shelves, or levels, of sea, and the whole expanse is cluttered with wrecked tankers, some floating, some half-beached, as far as the eye can see. It's a dank, dark-green, eerie seascape but the water's not cold and we have come to swim. We swim aboard the decks of the nearest wreck—stanchions and bits of companionway all awash and covered with eely seaweeds. We have fun swimming in and out of it all; we don't scrape or hit against anything. There is absolutely no living creature in sight and the shore is a vague sedgy marsh. After a long time, though, we realize that the boat is free of the bottom (and of the ridges or reefs of dark tufa-like rock) and has drifted out with the tide. We become troubled and decide to make our way (wading along the half-submerged decks to the end nearest land) back as far as we can without swimming, and then swim to shore before we get carried out any further. But even then it looks like a long swim—can we make it? Jean thinks we *must*; I am hesitant, thinking it might be better to risk staying on board the many hours till the next high tide washes us inshore again. We are perplexed—especially since it's so hard to judge the distance and the variable depth. Looking out to sea, the other levels stretch away and away, faintly gleaming, thick with wrecks. We might get wedged so that our particular wreck would *not* wash in with the next tide—or, half submerged as it was, it might sink, further out than we were already. On the other hand, the distance we were already out at sea looked greater than any we had ever tried to swim. No one to whom to signal. Woke in perplexity.

An Approach to Public Poetry Listenings

Listening to "live" poetry, from being the peculiarity of an odd few, has come to be accepted (as it was long ago) as an unsurprising thing to do, and one which a good many people have increasing opportunities to experience. For several years now the poets of America have been on the road from college to college, from city to city. As with migratory birds, their times of greatest travel activity are spring and fall; but in the big cities there is not a month in the year when the poetry buff can't find some reading to go to.

The return to an awareness that poetry is to be heard as well as read silently is an important occurrence—indeed, it is a recognition essential to the health of poetry, both for reader and writer. Especially is it important in its contemporary development, in which it is not the actor, the reciter, the elocutionist, who is sought after, to dramatize the poem and read into it his stereotype of what is "poetic," but the poet himself, whose voice, even if he stammer, is individual and authentic.

But notwithstanding the increased audience for poetry read aloud, notwithstanding the good will and apparent enjoyment of the average audience, I believe many listeners are hampered by poor listening habits.

I am not speaking of lack of attention, of poor concentration; indeed, being one of those whose thoughts are apt to wander, I am often admiringly surprised at the quality of attention many poetry audiences seem able to maintain. The trouble is not the attention itself but the level at which it is directed, the area of the poem with which it can make contact: namely, the level of *ideas,* and of the rational appositeness of images—the level, in fact, of that part of poetry which may, if any may, be paraphrased. Although these readers enjoy what they hear, although they are some-

---

Published in *Virginia Quarterly Review*, Vol. XLI, Summer 1965.

times moved by it, they are too often unaware of further elements in it which they are not experiencing.

The moments during a reading when an appreciative murmur buzzes through the listeners are most often those at which some rational point has been strikingly, perhaps neatly, made. There is an historical reason for this. As we know, the critics, almost from the beginning of this century, have been in reaction to a view of poetry as a warm bath for the vaguer emotions, which first set in, I suppose, at the jaded tail-end of the eighteenth century and which somehow prevailed throughout the nineteenth century despite the great poetry that got written in the face of it. From T. E. Hulme and Eliot and Pound, through Richards, Leavis, Tate, Ransom, Winters, Blackmur, et al., down to the writers of textbooks, twentieth-century critics in their different ways and degrees have attempted to train readers of poetry to think as they read, to use their minds. But in thousands of classrooms for a number of decades this necessary intention has been overextended by millions of students and their earnest teachers: with the result that the conscious understanding of poetry has been increased (and the public for it likewise, perhaps) at the cost of a severe underdevelopment in certain areas of response. Not a few poets are themselves involved in perpetuating the partial, overrational point of view. Unconfident of the poem as an existence, created and having its own life and power, they talk about it beforehand as if to conjure it into being. They tell you what it is about, out of what circumstances it arose, what it "tries to say." By the time the poor poem itself gets read, it seems merely a metrical paraphrase of anecdotes already related. Worst of all, there are poets—sometimes good poets in other particulars—who have so little respect for the poem as a total composition that they will interrupt their reading to make explanatory remarks!

Just what is it that is missing in most people's poetry listening? Muriel Rukeyser said one must bring "all of oneself" to poetry. But it is this "all" that the contemporary

47

listener—and not only the listener but the silent reader too—seldom brings to a poem. Let us not speak of the absolute all, the all of mystical experience. I am talking about the "all" that is readily available (or could be) to most people, the bringing into play of sensuous apprehension as a means of receiving the poem, either along with rational intelligence or in some cases as a way through to it. The great majority of good poems can be apprehended intellectually as well as empathically and sensuously, but when the faculties work together, undivided—that is, when we bring more of ourselves to the poem—the poem will yield more of itself.

The tremendous popularity of Dylan Thomas showed that the neglect of such areas of response was intuitively recognized by many people; for though Thomas's images do make nice meat for the exegetists, especially along Freudian lines, yet their mass appeal was not intellectual. The fervor they inspired indicates the existence of an unacknowledged hunger for that in poetry which is not apprehended by the reason but sensuously or subliminally. (On the other hand, the popularity of Allen Ginsberg's "Howl" was due less to its rhetoric, its emphatic pulsing movement, than to the fact that it said things people agreed with, thought were true; when they heard:

I saw the best minds of my generation destroyed by madness, starving hysterical naked

or:

What sphinx of cement and aluminum bashed open their skulls and ate up their brains and imagination?

they assented; it said for them something they had felt but had not been able to express. This is a variant of the intellectual approach, even though many of those who made it thought otherwise. It was a response primarily to content, and only secondarily to the incarnation of content in form.

Ginsberg's "Kaddish," probably as good a poem—in some respects better—never achieved the same popularity because it does not speak for the collective in the same degree.)

Educated readers today, whether college students or older, typically concentrate their attention on what they can quickly verify with the reason, including the poem's sentiments, with which they can "identify"; or if they listen to the sounds as to music, it is as a separate activity. The degree to which sounds, the actual physical existence of the poem as waves in air, can carry content, and *must* carry it in a well-written poem, is something they seem not to realize. This is self-deprivation. Not only are they missing much of what the poem could release to them, but they are quite cut off from some kinds of poems. For there are poems—good poems—which simply are not initially accessible to the intellect. One does not auscultate with a telephone receiver, one does not catch fish with a hammer. We must learn the use of our faculties as we learn the use of tools.

The poems I am thinking of are not the deliberately surrealist poems in which the images alone carry the poem, nor some of the recent dilutions of surrealism in which the visual is given prime importance. The visual image, however strange, is fairly generally acceptable. (Perhaps the wide dissemination of cheap reproductions has something to do with that. Chiricos, Klees, Picassos, have long hung on many a wall where some modern poetry would not be understandingly received; and dim reflections of such images have also filtered into advertisements.)

The poetry I have in mind is rather that in which the sounds—the vowels and consonants, the tone patterns, the currents of rhythm, not the paraphrasable ideas nor yet the visual images (though certainly these are present)—are the chief carriers of content. It is this poetry which is most inaccessible to readers trained to bring, not the whole of themselves, but their wits, or alternatively their emotional opinions, to a reading.

Let us take a specific example, the poem "Grain" by Barbara Moraff:

49

grain/woodfibers arrangement or the grain of love
    groinfibers arranged to skygrowth & irregular monies
    or the swirling clouds that blister slow blister rain
    into earth the face of the lake growth
                      superseding the rain ball
    linked thread of waves each wave that waves the weights

     rains threading gestures
    grain or the arrangement of woodfibers in the marriagebed
    crustacea long fairly horizontal waves regular in the tissue
    of seasons—arch reflecting heat darkened by use
    the marriagebed sift of sapphires the bodies
                     brightened by use
    the loves that parade the sheets depart with coign of
                        rain for eyes
    grey undulations the arrangements woodfiber,
                    crossed venetian
    blinds of the tribe marriage to the tree/whose
                   head pouts clouds
    weight of rains
freelight
  or the grain of arranged loves, pale clouds of the lake thread
    tissue/amoebic grain
  grain as a tree & limbs expand as may twist when snake
    slough his skin, full moon opulence twisting crotch wood
    whose figure's focus is the marriagebed the bed whose cup
    of cloudy markings tells where next a tree spring
    up thru the subtle wood
     o sleep on that wood
      where the trunk forks
    upward into 2 large branches
    crotch wood fibers pressured, crushed caught
     in flow twists flows from division
     into inverted like man's love

    & down the roots where worms room the thing contorts
    for eyes/o let us be sight climbing this tree, defy
    the cold disease which marriage beds

        & at our root the shores of sun
          & up the beach of skin the marriage bed
          let sea stags run it down

The schoolroom approach, that one-sided intelligent alertness, will get us nowhere here. And by the same token, nor
will the expectation of "emotional opinions" with which to
"identify."[1] Yet I am convinced it is a valuable poem.

Relax. Recall the sense of the word "intelligence" as
"news," and suppose that the poem brings to us, not we to it,
some news we can't get any other way; its intelligence is
something we must experience, something we must let happen to us, not something we are compelled to reach out and
grasp by force, as if we were something that must happen to
the poem. Put aside your resistance, your alertness, go off
alone somewhere and read this poem aloud to yourself. (A
good resonant bathroom is a fine place to read aloud if you
are unused to doing so. You can turn on all the taps full blast
and no one will overhear you.) Let the sounds of the poem
surround you. Listen to the pattern of *a*'s and *i*'s and *gr*'s in

    grain/woodfibers arrangement or the grain of love
        groinfibers arranged to skygrowth. . . .

Let that lead you into the winding dance of such patterns
as the poem continues. Feel the almost hypnotic recurrence
of certain words, sounds that knit the undulating lines into a
fabric. Musically the poem coheres. Hearing the poem as a
sound-structure is the way into its world. Once inside it,
once accepting it as a locus, the poem begins to be accessible in other ways. Its vocabulary is almost entirely natural,
physical, elemental—wood, earth, water. The theme of the
marriage bed relates not solely to the place of human sexual
consummation and of sleep and dreams but to the "bed" in
its geographical and horticultural connotations. Something

[1]By "emotional opinions" I don't mean opinions fervently adhered to but
the abstracted, unconcrete, expression of "feelings."

is being said, being given to us, concerning the state of marriage, not in philosophical or moral terms but in dream-subtle images of correspondence that convey a feeling of the state, in all its deepness, perilousness, and fluctuation. That at least is a hint of what the poem communicates to me; and I would defeat my own hope—which is to bring you to experience this poem for yourself, experimentally—if I were to proceed further in glossing it.

Again, try an unthinking, sensuous, dreamy, or drowsy rereading of poems you have already admired intellectually; you may find unsuspected pleasures, new kinds of perception. I am not advocating anti-intellectualism as such. A sense of history, of historical placement; an understanding of allusions; a consideration of technical means; and a pondering—all these are among the ways of establishing rapport with a poem, and one or another of them is often absolutely necessary. The intellect is a part of the whole, the "all of oneself" that must be brought to the poem. But I believe it has been too much favored. I would like to see the lives of those who already care about poetry still further enriched by learning to listen more openly, less tensely and selfconsciously, and without trying to quickly paraphrase the poem as they listen.

One way in which a general change in listening habits might be brought about would be if more teachers—at whatever age level—would give their students fuller opportunities to have poems befall them, as direct experiences, before they begin to analyze them. Visiting poets are asked for permission to tape their readings, but it seems to me that these tapes are seldom used in the classroom later; more often they go into immediate retirement in the college library. I would like to see an extensive use in poetry classes of tapes and records, as well as of "live" readings by visitors, teachers, and the students themselves. This would by no means substitute for eye-reading; it would complement it. And a generation which at school and college had heard more poetry would tend to make its eye-reading less silent—that is, would form the good habit of reading not much faster than the voice speaks, because what they were reading with the eye their inner voice would be sounding out to the alert inner ear.

Another way of correlating ear and eye reception that is sometimes proposed is that the audience should be provided with a text. I don't think this works, because the eye habitually outpaces the voice, so that in effect listening ceases. And even if it doesn't, the rustle of concerted page-turning is distracting and unaccountably absurd. The use of a screen on which the words are projected is agreeably silent, but similarly has the effect of taking the attention away from, and ahead of, the speaker's voice. A more useful possibility would be that the poem be first read, then projected on the screen in silence, then read again while remaining visible. Perhaps the ideal audience might be one which, like some music audiences, had studied the score beforehand. But it should always be remembered that the first meeting with a poem should be aural, open, and rather passive than active.

The special value of hearing poems read by their authors, whether or not they are "good" readers, is that what we hear is the poem itself, not an imposition of "personality" upon the poem, which is what happens when most actors read poetry. In the case of the writer himself, such "personality" as gets into his "delivery" is already in the poem anyway; his voice will clarify, not distort. This doesn't mean that poems should be read aloud only by their authors! But if tapes of the poets themselves were more often available, readers would learn to distinguish better between the true form of the poem, read as written, with line-breaks, punctuation, every typographical device functioning notatively,[2] and the distortions of poetry that occur in many quite popular commercial recordings (and theater evenings) by professional actors who do not understand that the poem is not a vehicle for displays of vocal virtuosity. Emily Dickinson's poems

[2] I was more optimistic, or less critical, in 1965 than I am in 1981. Alas, many poets disregard the structure of their own poems, even if they do not mumble.

53

are often singled out for this type of unwitting abuse. The theatrical school of reading tries to add to the poem. The poet-reader, if he is any good at all—that is, if he is a good poet, never mind his voice timbre—aims at revealing the poem.

Listeners are sometimes disturbed by unexpected pauses between words of a poem, pauses which are not syntactic. For example, I have known many people baffled by such lines as Robert Creeley's:

> God is no bone of whitened contention.
> God is not air, not hair, is not
> a conclusive concluding
> to remote yearnings. He moves
>
> only as I move, you also move to
> the awakening, across long rows, of beds,
> stumble breathlessly, on leg pins and crutch,
> moving at all as all men, because you must.

Why, readers puzzled by the punctuation here ask, didn't he do it like this:

> . . . He moves
> only as I move, you also move
> to the awakening, across long rows of beds,?

There is a rather simple explanation. I think. This is a poetry based on speech rhythms and on the way speech affects, and is affected by, thought rhythms. Listen attentively to your own and others' normal speech: you will notice that there are in it countless hesitations, rallentandos, "rests," taken entirely for granted. (In speech we "fill in" many of these spaces with um's and er's. In poetry, which draws more upon the inner than the outer voice, these um's and er's are, happily, not customarily reproduced.) If the individual poet's inner voice does not have smoothly running speech patterns, the written structure of his poem purposely reflects the fact. I say "purposely" rather than "inevitably" because there are of course poets who deliberately re-form their thought patterns in determined channels. Those who, however, like Creeley and like myself, are interested in discovering the "inscape" of experience—the form and pattern inherent in it—regard the accurate notation of thought and feeling-patterns, in line breaks and other pauses in the poem, as a positive value. Often such pauses—counterpointing the syntactic pauses—imply the unspoken question to which the next word is the answer. Writing of one of the indirect visual intimations of what was happening in the world outside which I used to receive in a somewhat prison-like New York City kitchen whose window was closely abutted by the wall of the next building, I said:[3]

> On the kitchen wall a flash
> of shadow:
> swift pilgrimage
> of pigeons, a spiral
> celebration of air, of sky-deserts.

I believe that the implications, the thought-movement, the actual sequence and interplay of perceptions and realizations, would be lost (and with them the point of the poem) had I written it like this:

> On the kitchen wall
> a flash of shadow:
> swift pilgrimage of pigeons,
> a spiral celebration
> of air, of sky-deserts.

It sometimes happens that a curious question is asked: What makes poets willing to expose themselves by reading in public? This question arises out of a misconception of what poetry readings are all about, I think. Many people were led by the cult of personality that grew up around Dylan Thomas to think of poetry as something you went to

---

[3]"*The World Outside*," from *The Jacob's Ladder* (New York, New Directions, 1961).

see being read. At a reading in New York in which I participated along with five other poets, one member of the audience was actually scanning us with binoculars![4] The "exposure" in fact, however, especially if the poet is resolutely
nonflamboyant, is not of the poet but of the poem. If we are
to ask what makes the poet—or any artist—reveal himself,
inevitably, in his work, we must enter upon a discussion of
the creative impulse itself, which is not the province of this
article. And the willingness to expose the poem to aural
reception is not, as I see it, of a different order from the
willingness to print it.

Having listened to poets, the eager home reader, his book
wilting somewhat in the steamy bathroom (though his receptive faculties, we hope, are crisper than ever) and the
roar of his domestic Niagara protecting him from his fear of
ridicule, (if need be) will have gained a better sense of how
typography functions in indicating far more than mere logical syntax. And the envelopment by the poem (out of which
intellectual apprehensions may arise naturally, instead of
being insisted on unripely) which he experiences in solitude
may be brought back, in time, to public listenings.

[4]This was in 1965.

"News That Stays News"

Thinking about the significance of *periplum,* that word
Pound often uses—

> periplum, not as land looks on a map
> but as sea bord seen by men sailing

—I see its applicability to the experiencing of numinous
works of art from the mobile vantage point of one's own
growth and change: the different angles and aspects of the
work thus perceived, and the new alignments with its historical context, and also with the context of the perceiver's
personal history.

As a coastal city might come, at a certain moment of
sailing past it, into the most perfect, harmonious, and dramatic alignment with the mountains behind it and the sweep
of its bay, so a supreme moment may be reached in one's
own reception and appreciation of a novel, a poem, a string
quartet. That does not mean all subsequent sightings of it
will be a decline. The memory of that supreme vision will in
some degree illuminate each subsequent look one takes.

There's an analogy to the *periplum* concept in a movie
camera's slow panning across a scene. Indeed, one obtains a
similar effect in a car or train, especially when viewing a
downtown skyline from a bridge or elevated highway. But
while these analogies may give to the reader who has never
travelled by boat some physical sense of *periplum*'s literal
meaning, their speed (in comparison to the slowness of a
ship) does not allow for the kind of changes in the beholder
that contribute to new perceptions. All the accrued life-
experience which accompanies one on return visits to works
of art is only sketchily symbolized even in the metaphoric
description of time and change provided by the image of

Written *c.* 1978.

watching the coastal towers and mountains realign to the eye as the observer—perhaps going through changes of mood the while—moves past them in a half-becalmed sailboat from dawn to dusk, a whole long day, and finds them next morning still visible beyond the wake, as if floating between sky and sea.

A friend said to me, as we talked about the experience of discovering, in a supposedly familiar work, fresh and unexpected meanings, "So then one is reading a new book?" But no: if the work truly has the living complexity I term "numinous," it is rather that by one's own development, by moving along the road of one's own life, one becomes able to see a new aspect of the book (or other work of art). The newly seen aspect, facet, layer, was there all the time; it is our recognition of it that is new.

Sometimes an artist's technical consciousness directly, deliberately, contributes to the multi-aspected nature of a work; for example, in Henry James one finds, as well as projective references (back-and-forth cross references), certain "scenes"—in James's particular sense of pivotal, revealing moments—which work by means of the participation of the reader, who has previously been given enough knowledge of the characters to realize what must be passing through their minds at the moment of the "scene" itself. But there are works of a much simpler design which also provide different consecutive experiences to the reader, listener, or viewer who returns to them periodically, bringing his or her new modifications of need or ability. The degree to which the originating artist was conscious of the manifold import of a work does not determine its actual multifariousness: the great work of art is always greater than the consciousness of its author.

Returning from that statement to the *periplum* metaphor, one may say, then, that although the architect of the city may have attempted to plan how it would look from all points of the compass as well as from among its streets and squares, he or she could not have foreseen every effect of light, of weather, or of exactly how, in time, certain trees would grow tall, hiding certain buildings, and others would fall, and small new ones be planted. Nor could the architect guess which surrounding hills would become bare from erosion, while others were terraced into new fields, or covered over with villas in a style wholly different from the style of the city; and even less predictable was the city's appearance to the eyes of strangers from distant places, who one day would look across the water from their passing ship and see the towers pass behind one another and emerge, and again pass and emerge, now in a mountain's shadow and now catching the light of the rising sun, as if dancing a pavane.

All this the architect cannot know. But if the city is beautiful and alive in its own logic (the logic of what the architect *could* know) then each perceived arrangement, each revelation of further correspondence between the parts of the city, and between the whole city and its site, is implicit *in* that logic.

Poetry is a way of constructing autonomous existences out of words and silences.

All words are to some extent onomatopoeic.

Though nonsonic (purely visual) poems do exist, the mainstream of poetry is sonic. It utilizes the visual to notate the sonic, (i.e., the deployment of the printed word on the page is a notation for sonic effects just like the written score of musical works).

Poetry makes more use of silences in its structures than prose does, though good prose is far more rhythmically organized than most readers—especially, alas, most teachers—seem to recognize.

Most poetry is more *directly* derived from the unconscious than most prose.

The didactic has a place in poetry, but only when it is inseparable from the intuitive—e.g., opinion is not a source of poetry, but the poetry of political anguish is at its best both didactic and lyrical.

In our time, a political poetry untinged with anguish, even when it evokes and salutes moments of hope, is unimaginable.

Yet—because it creates autonomous structures that are imbued with life and which stir the life of those who experience them—poetry is, in process and in being, intrinsically affirmative.

Written 1975.

Not only hapless adolescents, but many gifted and justly esteemed poets writing in contemporary nonmetrical forms, have only the vaguest concept, and the most haphazard use, of the line. Yet there is at our disposal no tool of the poetic craft more important, none that yields more subtle and precise effects, than the linebreak if it is properly understood.

If I say that its function in the development of modern poetry in English is evolutionary I do not mean to imply that I consider modern, nonmetrical poetry "better" or "superior" to the great poetry of the past, which I love and honor. That would obviously be absurd. But I do feel that there are few poets today whose sensibility naturally expresses itself in the traditional form (except for satire or pronounced irony), and that those who do so are somewhat anachronistic. The closed, contained quality of such forms has less relation to the relativistic sense of life which unavoidably prevails in the late twentieth century than modes that are more exploratory, more open-ended. A sonnet may end with a question; but its essential, underlying structure arrives at *resolution*. "Open forms" do not necessarily terminate inconclusively, but their degree of conclusion is—structurally, and thereby expressively—less pronounced, and partakes of the open quality of the whole. They do not, typically, imply a dogmatic certitude; whereas, under a surface, perhaps, of individual doubts, the structure of the sonnet or the heroic couplet bears witness to the certitudes of these forms' respective epochs of origin. The forms more apt to express the sensibility of our age are the exploratory, open ones.

In what way is contemporary, nonmetrical poetry exploratory? What I mean by that word is that such poetry, more than most poetry of the past, incorporates and reveals

Published in *Chicago Review*, Vol. 30, No. 3, 1979.

the *process* of thinking/feeling, feeling/thinking, rather than focusing more exclusively on its *results;* and in so doing it explores (or can explore) human experience in a way that is not wholly new but is (or can be) valuable in its subtle difference of approach: valuable both as human testimony and as aesthetic experience. And the crucial precision tool for creating this exploratory mode is the linebreak. The most obvious function of the linebreak is rhythmic: it can record the slight (but meaningful) hesitations between word and word that are characteristic of the mind's dance among perceptions but which are not noted by grammatical punctuation. Regular punctuation is a part of regular sentence structure, that is, of the expression of completed thoughts; and this expression is typical of prose, even though prose is not at all times bound by its logic. But in poems one has the opportunity not only, as in expressive prose, to depart from the syntactic norm, but to make manifest, by an intrinsic structural means, the interplay or counterpoint of process and completion—in other words, to present the dynamics of perception *along with* its arrival at full expression. The linebreak is a form of punctuation *additional* to the punctuation that forms part of the logic of completed thoughts. Linebreaks—together with intelligent use of indentation and other devices of scoring—represent a peculiarly *poetic*, alogical, parallel (not competitive) punctuation.

What is the nature of the alogical pauses the linebreak records? If readers will think of their own speech, or their silent inner monologue, when describing thoughts, feelings, perceptions, scenes or events, they will, I think, recognize that they frequently hesitate—albeit very briefly—as if with an unspoken question,—a "what?" or a "who?" or a "how?"—before nouns, adjectives, verbs, adverbs, none of which require to be preceded by a comma or other regular punctuation in the course of syntactic logic. To incorporate these pauses in the rhythmic structure of the poem can do several things: for example, it allows the reader to share more intimately the experience that is being articulated; and by introducing an alogical counter-rhythm into the logical rhythm of syntax it causes, as they interact, an effect closer to song than to statement, closer to dance than to walking. Thus the emotional experience of empathy or identification plus the sonic complexity of the language structure synthesize in an intense aesthetic order that is different from that which is received from a poetry in which metric forms are combined with logical syntax alone. (Of course, the management of the line in *metrical* forms may also permit the recording of such alogical pauses; Gerard Manley Hopkins provides an abundance of evidence for that. But Hopkins, in this as in other matters, seems to be "the exception that proves the rule"; and the alliance of metric forms and the similarly "closed" or "complete" character of logical syntax seems natural and appropriate, inversions notwithstanding. Inversions of normal prose word order were, after all, a stylistic convention, adopted from choice, not technical ineptitude, for centuries; although if utilized after a certain date they strike one as admissions of lack of skill, and indeed are the first signs of the waning of a tradition's viability.) It is not that the dance of alogical thinking/feeling in process *cannot* be registered in metric forms, but rather that to do so seems to go against the natural grain of such forms, to be a forcing of an intractable medium into inappropriate use—whereas the potential for such use is implicit in the constantly evolving nature of open forms.

But the most particular, precise, and exciting function of the linebreak, and the least understood, is its effect on the *melos* of the poem. It is in this, and not only in *rhythmic* effects, that its greatest potential lies, both in the exploration of areas of human consciousness and in creating new aesthetic experiences. *How* do the linebreaks affect the melodic element of a poem? So simply that it seems amazing that this aspect of their function is disregarded—yet not only student poetry workshops but any magazine or anthology of contemporary poetry provides evidence of a general lack of understanding of this factor; and even when individual poets manifest an intuitive sense of how to break their lines it seems rarely to be accompanied by any theoretical comprehension of what they've done right. Yet it is not hard to demonstrate to students that—given that the deployment of the poem on the page is regarded as a score, that is, as the visual instructions for auditory effects—the way the lines are broken affects not only rhythm but *pitch patterns.*

Rhythm can be sounded on a monotone, a single pitch; melody is the result of pitch patterns combined with rhythmic patterns. The way in which linebreaks, observed respectfully, as a part of a score (and regarded as, say, roughly a half comma in duration), determine the pitch pattern of a sentence, can clearly be seen if a poem, or a few lines of it, is written out in a variety of ways (changing the linebreaks but nothing else) and read aloud. Take, for instance, these lines of my own (picked at random):[1]

> Crippled with desire, he questioned it.
> Evening upon the heights, juice of the pomegranate:
> who could connect it with sunlight?

Read them aloud. Now try reading the same words aloud from this score:

> Crippled with desire, he
> questioned it. Evening
> upon the heights,
> juice of the pomegranate:
> who
> could connect it with sunlight?

Or:

> Crippled
> with desire, he questioned
> it. Evening
> upon the heights, juice
> of the pomegranate:
> who could
> connect it with sunlight?

Etc.

[1] From "Four Embroideries: (III) Red Snow," *Relearning the Alphabet* (New York, New Directions, 1970).

The intonation, the ups and downs of the voice, involuntarily change as the rhythm (altered by the place where the tiny pause or musical "rest" takes place) changes. These changes could be recorded in graph form by some instrument, as heartbeats or brain waves are graphed. The point is not whether the lines, as I wrote them, are divided in the best possible way; as to that, readers must judge for themselves. I am simply pointing out that, read naturally but with respect for the linebreak's fractional pause, a pitch pattern change *does occur* with each variation of lineation. A beautiful example of expressive lineation is William Carlos Williams' well known poem about the old woman eating plums:[2]

> They taste good to her.
> They taste good
> to her. They taste
> good to her.

First the statement is made; then the word *good* is (without the clumsy overemphasis a change of typeface would give) brought to the center of our (and her) attention for an instant; then the word *taste* is given similar momentary prominence, with *good* sounding on a new note, reaffirmed—so that we have first the general recognition of well-being, then the intensification of that sensation, then its voluptuous location in the sense of taste. And all this is presented through indicated pitches, that is, by melody, not by rhythm alone.

I have always been thrilled by the way in which the musicality of a poem could arise from what I called "fidelity to experience," but it took me some time to realize what the mechanics of such precision were as they related to this matter of pitch pattern. The point is that, just as vowels and consonants affect the music of poetry not by mere euphony but by expressive, significant interrelationship, so the nuances of meaning apprehended in variations of pitch create

---

[2] "To a poor old woman," *Collected Earlier Poems* (New York, New Directions, 1938).

significant, expressive melody in the close tone range of speech, not just a pretty "tune."

One of the ways in which many poets reveal their lack of awareness about the function of the linebreak is the way in which they will begin a line with the word "it," for instance, even when it is clear from the context that they don't want the extra emphasis—relating to both rhythm and pitch—this gives it. Thus, if one writes,

> He did not know
> it, but at this very moment
> his house was burning,

the word "it" is given undue importance. Another example is given in my second variant of the lines from "Red Snow." The "it" in the third line is given a prominence entirely without significance—obtrusive and absurd. When a poet places a word meaninglessly from the sonic point of view it seems clear that he or she doesn't understand the effect of doing so—or is confusedly tied to the idea of "enjambement." Enjambement is useful in preventing the monotony of too many end-stopped lines in a metrical poem, but the desired variety can be attained by various other means in contemporary open forms; and to take away from the contemporary line its fractional pause (which, as I've said, represents, or rather manifests, a comparable minuscule but affective hesitation in the thinking/feeling process) is to rob a precision tool of its principal use. Often the poet unsure of any principle according to which to end a line will write as if the real break comes after the first word of the next line, e.g.:

> As children in their night
> gowns go upstairs . . . ,

where *if one observes the score* an awkward and inexpressive "rest" occurs between two words that the poet, reading aloud, links naturally as "nightgowns." X. J. Kennedy's definition of a *run-on* line (*Introduction to Poetry*, 1966) is that "it does not end in punctuation and therefore is read with

66

only a *slight pause* after it," whereas "if it ends in a full pause—usually indicated by some mark of punctuation— we call it *end-stopped.*" (My italics on "slight pause.") Poets who write nonmetrical poems but treat the linebreak as non-existent are not even respecting the traditional "slight pause" of the run-on line. The fact is, they are confused about what the line is at all, and consequently some of our best and most influential poets have increasingly turned to the prose para-graph for what I feel are the wrong reasons—i.e., less from a sense of the peculiar virtues of the prose poem than from a despair of making sense of the line.

One of the important virtues of comprehending the func-tion of the linebreak, that is, of the line itself, is that such comprehension by no means causes poets to write like one another. It is a *tool,* not a style. As a tool, its use can be incorporated into any style. Students in a workshop who grasp the idea of *accurate scoring* do not begin to all sound alike. Instead, each one's individual voice sounds more clearly, because each one has gained a degree of control over how they want a poem to sound. Sometimes a student scores a poem one way on paper, but reads it aloud differ-ently. My concern—and that of his or her fellow students once they have understood the problem—is to determine which way the author wants the poem to sound. Someone will read it back to him or her *as written* and someone else will point out the ways in which the text, the score, was ignored in the reading. "Here you ran on,"—"Here you paused, but it's in the middle of a line and there's no indication for a 'rest' there." Then the student poet can decide, or feel out, whether he or she wrote it down wrong but read it right, or vice versa. That decision is a very personal one and has quite as much to do with the individual sensibility of the writer and the unique character of the experience embodied in the words of the poem, as with universally recognizable rationality—though that may play a part, too. The outcome, in any case, is rather to define and clarify individual voices than to homogenize them; because *reasons* for halts and checks, emphases and expressive pitch changes, will be as various as the persons writing. Comprehension of the function of the linebreak gives to each unique creator the power to be more precise, and thereby more, not less, individuated. The voice thus revealed will be, not necessarily the recognizable "outer" one heard in poets who have taken Olson's breath theory all too literally, but rather the inner voice, the voice of each one's solitude made audible and singing to the multitude of other solitudes.

Excess of subjectivity (and hence incommunicability) in the making of structural decisions in open forms is a problem only when the writer has an inadequate form sense. When the written score precisely notates perceptions, a whole—an inscape or gestalt—begins to emerge; and the gifted writer is not so submerged in the parts that the sum goes unseen. The sum is objective—relatively, at least; it has presence, character, and—as it develops—needs. The parts of the poem are instinctively adjusted in some degree to serve the needs of the whole. And as this adjustment takes place, excess subjectivity is avoided. Details of a private, as distinct from personal, nature may be deleted, for example, in the interests of a fuller, clearer, more communicable whole. (By private I mean those which have associations for the writer that are inaccessible to readers without a special explanation from the writer which does not form part of the poem; whereas the personal, though it may incorporate the private, has an energy derived from associations that are shareable with the reader and *are* so shared within the poem itself.)

Another way to approach the problem of subjective/objective is to say that while traditional modes provide certain standards for objective comparison and evaluation of poems as effective structures, (technically, at any rate) open forms, used with comprehension of their technical opportunities, *build unique contexts* which likewise provide for such evaluation. In other words, though the "rightness" of its lines can't be judged by a preconceived method of scansion, each such poem, if well written, presents a composed whole in which false lines (or other lapses) can be heard by any attentive ear—not as failing to conform to an external rule, but as failures to contribute to the grace or strength implicit in a system peculiar to that poem, and stemming from the inscape of which it is the verbal manifestation.

The *melos* of metrical poetry was not easy of attainment, but there were guidelines and models, even if in the last resort nothing could substitute for the gifted "ear." The *melos* of open forms is even harder to study if we look for models; its secret lies not in models but in that "fidelity to experience" of which I have written elsewhere; and, in turn, that fidelity demands a delicate and precise comprehension of the technical means at our disposal. A general recognition of the primary importance of the line and of the way in which rhythm relates to melody would be useful to the state of the art of poetry in the way general acceptance of the bar line and other musical notations were useful to the art of music. A fully adequate latitude in the matter of interpretation of a musical score was retained (as anyone listening to different pianists playing the same sonata, for instance, can hear) but at the same time the composer acquired a finer degree of control. Only if writers agree about the nature and function of this tool can readers fully cooperate, so that the poem shall have the fullest degree of autonomous life.

A lot of people write in what have come to be called "open forms" without much sense of why they do so or of what those forms demand. Or if they do think, it seems mainly to recognize that they are confused. They are sailing without the pilots and charts that traditional forms provide. If one is interested in *exploration* one knows the risks are part of the adventure; nevertheless, as explorers travel they do make charts, and though each subsequent journey over the same stretch of ocean will be a separate adventure (weather and crew and passing birds and whales or monsters all being variables) nevertheless rocks and shallows, good channels and useful islands will have been noted and this information can be used by other voyagers. But though people have been exploring open forms for a long time now, from the free verse pioneered by Whitman and picked up later by Sandburg or the very different free verse of the Imagists through to the various modes of the last two decades (so that nowadays it is rare to find a college freshman writing in traditional forms) there has been a curious lack of chart-reading, so that people not only have their personal and proper adventures with the infinite variables, the adventures which make it all worthwhile and exciting, but also they keep bumping unnecessarily into the same old rocks, which isn't interesting at all. (And incidentally, when they do attempt traditional forms, college students often reveal an inability to scan that in turn reveals how untrained their *ears* are even in the simplest repetitive rhythmic structures.) Because, judging from my experience as a teacher and also as a reader, this general confusion seems to me to be so prevalent, I'm going to try to note some common problems of technique, of getting the written score of nontraditionally

---

A "Craft Lecture" presented at Centrum, a writing conference at Port Townsend, Washington, Summer 1979.

formed poems down on the paper efficiently. Because there's no consensus about some of the tools of scoring—just as up till the eighteenth century there was virtually no consensus about musical scoring techniques—I believe I can detect uncertainty and a hit-or-miss approach to these matters even in some of the major poets of our time. When I speak of consensus I'm not suggesting that people should write alike—only that it would be helpful if more poets would consider what typographical and other tools we do have at our disposal and what their *use* is. To point out that a carpenter's plane is not designed to be used as a knife sharpener or a can opener is not restrictive of how someone planes their piece of wood; and to indicate that objects specifically designed to whet knives or open cans do exist is not to dictate what shall be cut with the knife or whether the can to be opened should be of beer or beans.

Obviously the most important question and the one about which there's the most uncertainty is, what is the line? What makes a line be a line? How do you know where to end it if you don't have a predetermined metric structure to tell you? If it's just a matter of going by feel, by ear, are there any principles at all to help you evaluate your own choices? The way to find out, I believe, is to look at what it is a line *does*. Take a poem and type it up as a prose paragraph. Type it up again in lines, but not in its own lines—break it up differently. Read it aloud (observing the linebreak as roughly one-half a comma, of course—it is there to *use*, and if you simply run on, ignoring it, you may as well acknowledge that you want to write prose, and do so). As you perform this exercise or experiment you will inevitably begin to *experience* the things that linebreaks do—and this will be much more useful than being *told about* them. However, I'll list some of the things they do which you can listen for:

Unless a line happens to *consist* of a whole sentence, the linebreak *subtly interrupts* a sentence.

Unless a line happens to consist of a complete phrase or clause, it *subtly interrupts* a phrase or clause. (Though lines may also *contain* whole sentences, phrases, or clauses.)

71

What is the function of such interruptions? Their first function is to notate the tiny nonsyntactic pauses that constantly take place during the thinking/feeling process— pauses which can occur before any part of speech and which, not being a part of the logic of syntax, are not indicated by ordinary punctuation. The mind as it feels its way through a thought or an impression often stops with one foot in the air, its antennae waving, and its nose waffling. Linebreaks (though of course they may also happen to coincide with syntactic punctuation marks—commas or semi-colons or whatever) notate these infinitesimal hesitations. Watch cats, dogs, insects as they walk around: they behave a lot like the human mind. This is the reason why Valéry defines prose in terms of the purposeful (goal-oriented) walk, and poetry as the gratuitous dance. If linebreaks function as a form of nonsyntactic punctuation, for what purpose do they do so? In order to reveal the thinking/feeling *process*. What does that imply? I think it implies that the twentieth century impulse to move away from prescribed forms has not always been due to rebellion and a wish for more freedom, but rather to an awakened interest in the experience of journeying and not only in the destination. This statement doesn't mean to denigrate the great works of the past, which do, as a rule, focus on the achieved goal, not on the process of reaching it. All I mean is that just as a sentence is a complete thought so a traditional form— the sonnet, the villanelle, etc., even blank verse—is a complete system; and though a great poet can bring about marvellous surprises within it, yet the expectations set up by our previous knowledge of the system are met, and we get a great deal of our gratification in reading such poems precisely from having our expectations met. And that's somewhat like receiving the fruit of the Hesperides without having travelled there—some other traveller has brought it back to us. But there's something in the twentieth century consciousness or sensibility that wants to share the travails of journeying; or we want at least to hear the tale of the journey. The poet-explorer heading for Mount Everest flew to Bombay or Delhi, what was it like? How did he or she get from there to Tibet? What were the Sherpas like? What about the foothills? Did you still want to get to Everest by the time you first saw the south face of the western peak? And so on. We are as interested in process and digression as in an ultimate goal.

At this point it strikes me that I seem to be making a statement about *content,* which was not my intention. I do not mean that I think we want every poem to be digressive, even meandering. There can be poems, good poems, that are so (as long as each digression ultimately contributes to the needs of the composition), but I'm by no means holding any special brief for them, and it is not content that is in question, but structure. Perhaps I should switch metaphors: let's compare poems to paintings: the analogy would be that, if we choose open forms in which the movement of lines can record the movement of the mind in the act of feeling/thinking, thinking/feeling, we have, as it were, an interest in seeing the brush strokes; we like to experience the curious double vision of the scene represented *and* the brushstrokes and palette knife smears and layers of impasto by which it is produced. In the process of giving us this experience by incorporating into the rhythmic structure of the poem those little halts or pauses which are not accounted for by the logic of syntax, a second essential effect is produced, and that is the change of pitch pattern inevitably brought about by observation of linebreaks. I've written elsewhere on this[1]—the way in which *melody* is created not only by the interplay of vowels *within* lines but by the overall pattern of intonation scored by the breaking, or division, of the words *into* lines, and about how this melodic element is not merely an ornamental enhancement but, deriving as it does from the mimesis of mind process, is fundamentally expressive.

Let us look now at another "tool": indentation. Why do some poems seem to be all over the page? Indentations have

---

[1]See previous essay, "On the Function of the Line."

several functions: one of them has to do with the fact that eye-ear-mouth coordination makes looking from the end of a line all the way back to the starting margin a different experience from that of looking from the end of a line to the beginning of an indented line—the latter is experienced as infinitesimally swifter. This registration of a degree of swiftness conveys, subliminally, a sense that the indented line is related to the preceding one with especial closeness. For example, I used indentation in these lines,

> up and up
> > into the tower of the tree

because if I had put all the words on one line I'd have lost the upstretching sound of the first half line—it would have dissipated. And if I'd gone back to the margin, I'd have lost the ongoing *into*-ness that stretches mimetically up into the tower of the tree. The other main function of indentations is to clearly denote lists or categories for the sake of clarity— but this too functions not only, by way of the eye to the brain, *intellectually* but also, by way of the eye to the ear and the voice, *sensuously* and thus expressively. Through changes of tone and pitch elicited subliminally, the score provides a more subtle emotional graph than it could without them.

If you will take a look at "A Son" in my book *Life in the Forest* you'll see a score that uses carefully consistent degrees of indentation: sub-categories of content within the whole syntactic composition are assigned specific degrees of indentation. The first line presents the subject—flame-plumage-blossom-monster. The succeeding nine lines alternate between attributes and actions, and are enclosed by dashes which open in the middle of the first line. (The first line needed to be simple although interrupted by the dash which sets off the subsidiary clause, in order to link the monster firmly to her attributes.) The last line of the stanza goes back to the margin to complete the sentence: "a flamey monster/bore a son." The second stanza begins with an

74

indented line because the subject of it is uncertain; a question opens the stanza and the person is described as half man and half monster. So the placing of the whole stanza on the page is somewhat wavering. Stanza three, beginning "The son," repeats the logic of stanza one, except that because it speaks of the son deriving characteristics from both parents—feathers of flame from both of them and also something magically transformational from the mother and something of basic human goodness from the father—the last line is centered: "a triple goodness." Stanza four is all on the margin side because it follows syntactically directly from the first skeletal, or scaffold sentence,

> A monster
> bore a son.
>
> If to be artist
> is to be monster,
> he too was monster.

But after the "But" statement there comes another indented passage—indented because it is descriptive, as the lines immediately preceding it are not. The last stanza starts with an indentation that is centered, because that centering on the page suggests (again, in a subliminal way, physiology conspiring with comprehension) a blending or meeting which is what the poem is talking about. The alternations of the concluding three lines echo those in stanzas one and three, but now I feel that this entire stanza should have been indented: that's to say centered, with its existing indentations intact; and it was a failure of craft-logic to leave it at the margin.

Another matter about which there is a vague consensus but for which few people seem to know a *reason* is, what do initial capital letters do and why have they been abandoned by so many twentieth century poets? Well, they stop the flow very slightly from line to line, and if one is using the kind of careful and detailed scoring devices I've been illustrating then their sheer unnecessariness is a distraction. Some people, however, like them for the very reason that they *do* stop the flow a tiny bit—so they can be *made* to function. What about using lower case initials throughout? Personally I dislike this practise because it looks mannered and therefore distracts the attention—especially lower case I (i); and I don't see any function in the absence of a capital letter to signal the beginning of a sentence—especially the very first sentence of a poem. But more important than whether you do or don't use capitals is whether you are consistent about it within any given poem. If you are not consistent in your use of any device, the reader will not know if something is merely a typographical error or is meant to contribute—as everything, down to the last hyphen, should—to the life of the poem.

These seem the principle technical points about which large numbers of people are confused. But I'd like to throw in a concept that doesn't have to do specifically with open forms—the idea of what I call *tune-up*. It involves diction. Obviously we all want to avoid clichés, except in dialogue or for irony; but sometimes even when we're not writing in actual clichés, and even though we may be devoted to the search for maximum precision, it seems as if we don't constantly check over our words to see if our diction is tuned-up to the maximum energy level consistent with the individual poem. Of course, our whole feeling about some poems may be that their tone should be relaxed. But how often a subject's inscape and our own experience of instress in confronting it (which then becomes an integral part of the poem's inscape) could really be sounded out more vibrantly! The technical or craft skill of tuning up is not the same as the process of revision. Major revision is undertaken when structure, whether of sequence, storyline, plot, of rhythm and melody, or of basic diction, has major ailments. But tune-up is something you do when you feel the poem is complete and in good health. It's sometimes a matter of dropping a few *a*'s or *the*'s or *and*'s to pull it all tighter—though beware you don't take out some necessary bolt or screw! But sometimes, more creatively, it's a matter of checking each word to see if, even though it has seemed precise, the correct word for the job, there is not—lurking in the wings of your mind's stage—another exotic, surprising, unpredictable, but even *more* precise word. Startle yourself. Before you leave the well-wrought, honest poem to set off on its own adventures through the world, see if with one final flick of the wrist you can shower it with a few diamond talismans that will give it powers you yourself—we ourselves—lack, poor, helpless human creatures that we poets are, except at the moment of parting from the poems we have brought forth into daylight out of caverns we don't own but have at times been entrusted to guard and enter.

Address to New York City High School Prizewinners

I was asked to talk about the life of a poet. Some of you will
not find poetry at the very center of your lives though no
doubt it will go on being a profound resource—both writing
it and reading it. Others will find that it is indeed a dominant
force in their lives—it has been for me. I started very young.
The primary impulse for me was always to make a structure
out of words, words that *sounded* right. And I think that's a
rather basic foundation of the poet's world. Of course, one
also is motivated by the desire or need to "express one's
feelings"—and it is essential that the poet has something he
or she passionately wants to say—or rather, to sing, since
poetry is closer in its essential nature to music than to exposi-
tory prose. But without the impulse to make a *thing* out of
words, as a sculptor makes a freestanding thing out of clay
or wood or stone, a poem will remain *only* self-expression.
Poetry is an art, not a form of therapy, and if a person with
a love of poetry, a love of language, recognizes this early, it
helps. Because then that person's natural gifts will be put at
the service of the art, instead of the art being put into
bondage and utilized as a "vehicle" for opinions or emotions. The arts are not vehicles, they are not like bicycles or
bomber planes!

I was lucky—as you are—in starting early, because when
you begin to write early you avoid some of the self-
consciousness that people who only begin later in life tend to
suffer from. You just plunge in, not knowing what you're
doing, and find that you've done something, made something. It's exciting and encouraging to take oneself by surprise like that. But even a strong talent needs nourishment:
don't ever feel that if you read other people's poetry you'll
lose your originality. You have to trust it—your talent. If it
could be so easily destroyed it wouldn't be worth much

Given at Washington Irving High School in April 1979 to an audience of
students from all over New York City.

anyway. It's useful to be influenced—after a while an influence will be absorbed into your own style. Read widely and deeply. But also, use your eyes and ears. Try to avoid vague general statements about your feelings, and instead practice accurate description of things you see.—You will find that because you are seeing them through your emotions, as if through tinted glass—blue or rose!—the way you evoke a picture of your street or your friend or the sky will convey more about your feelings than any statement can. And thus another person reading it will feel what you feel instead of just being informed *about* how you feel.

When one discovers that one has a gift for writing poetry it's a solemn and also a deliriously exciting moment. Maybe many moments—because sometimes you don't believe it and then you discover it over again. One feels chosen—and if one has an adequate recognition of poetry being something larger than oneself, one feels a sense of dedication to the calling of poet. It's a secret feeling and you don't have it all the time, but it's there. And because of this dedication a poet learns to revise, to work at his or her poem until it is as perfect as it can be. Not in order to show off, to compete with others, to demonstrate personal cleverness, but for the sake of poetry itself. You can't *make* a poem happen, but once it begins to happen you can help it become complete. It's a little bit as if the poet were a sort of photographic developing medium, which makes the mysterious hidden image appear from the negative and become clearer and clearer. (You've probably watched a Polaroid photo appearing as if by magic while you look. . . .) This task of working at and with the poem is what really grabs one. I think the people who go on writing all their lives are those for whom that process is itself utterly fascinating. For the poet, not *having written* a poem, but the experience of writing it, is what matters. And somehow, if your gift goes on growing and making its demand on you, you will try to find the ways of living that will be most suitable for you as individuals to go on doing your work in poetry—you will find your talent giving shape to your lives.

Anne Sexton's death some weeks ago saddened a great many people. In addition, it startled those who had assumed that, despite all the troubles of which her poetry told, she had come to the long stretch of middle age with some reserves of strength; though—I am told—the friends who knew her best were confirmed in their fear that her determination towards suicide had not really been deflected. My own sadness at the death of a fellow poet is compounded by the sense of how likely it is that Anne Sexton's tragedy will not be without influence in the tragedies of other lives.

She herself was, obviously, too intensely troubled to be fully aware of her influence or to take on its responsibility. Therefore it seems to me that we who are alive must make clear, as she could not, the distinction between creativity and self-destruction. The tendency to confuse the two has claimed too many victims. Anne Sexton herself seems to have suffered deeply from this confusion, and I surmise that her friendship with Sylvia Plath had in it an element of identification which added powerfully to her malaise. Across the country, at different colleges, I have heard many stories of attempted—and sometimes successful—suicides by young students who loved the poetry of Plath and who supposed that somehow, in order to become poets themselves, they had to act out in their own lives the events of hers. I don't want to see a new epidemic of the same syndrome occurring as a response to Anne Sexton's death.

The problem is not, however, related only to suicide *per se*. When Robert Lowell was at the height of his fame among student readers (his audience nowadays is largely an older one) many of them seemed to think a nervous breakdown was, if not imperative, at least an invaluable shortcut to artistry. When W. D. Snodgrass's *Heart's Needle* won the

---

Originally published in the *Real Paper*, Boston, Massachusetts, 1974, and reprinted in *Ramparts*.

Pulitzer Prize, young couples married and divorced, it seemed, especially in order to have the correct material to write about.

I am not being flippant. Innumerable young poets have drunk themselves into stupidity and cirrhosis because they admired John Berryman or Dylan Thomas and came to think they must drink like them to write like them. At the very least it is assumed that creativity and hangups are inevitably inseparable. One student (male) said to me recently, "I was amazed when the first poet I met seemed to be a cheerful person and not any more fucked up than anyone else. When I was in high school I got the idea you *had* to be fucked up to be a real artist!" And a young English teacher in a community college told me she had given up writing poetry because she believed there were unavoidable links between depression and anxiety and the making of art. "Don't you feel terrible when you write poems?"

What exactly is the nature of the confusion, and how has it come about? The mistake itself lies in taking what may possibly be an occupational hazard as a prescriptive stimulus to artistic activity. Whether artists as a class are in fact more vulnerable than other people, or whether their problems merely have more visibility, a serious and intelligent statistical study might perhaps tell us. It makes no difference: the point is that while the creative impulse and the self-destructive impulse can, and often do, coexist, their relationship is distinctly acausal; self-destructiveness is a handicap to the life of art, not the reverse.

Yet it is the handicaps themselves that so often allure the young and untried. The long lives of so many of the greatest artists, sometimes apparently uneventful, sometimes full of passion and suffering, but full too of endurance, and always dominated by love of their work, seem not to attract as models. Picasso, Matisse, Monet, Cezanne, Pissarro, Corot, Rembrandt, Titian, J. S. Bach, Stravinsky, Goethe, William Carlos Williams, Stevens, Pound, Neruda, Machado, Yeats, Shakespeare, Whitman, Tolstoi, Melville. . . . There is romance in their tenacity, their devotion, but it is overlooked.

Why is this? There are topical reasons, but their roots are in the past, their nature historical and political.

In summary, western culture began, during the Renaissance—only recently, that is to say, in the calendar of human history—to emphasize individuality to a degree merely foreshadowed in Greece and Rome or in the theological dramas of the Old Testament. Geographical and scientific discoveries spurred the sense of what humanity on its own could do. The "Elizabethan world picture" had wholeness and consistency; but it held the seeds of an expanded view of things. And as feudal social systems underwent economic changes with the rise of the merchant class and the growth of banking procedures, so, too, the social and economic circumstances in which art was produced underwent changes that heightened the new sense of individuality.

The relationship of the artist to other people rapidly altered. The people began to become "the public," "the audience," and the poet, set aside from that "public," began to become more private, more introspective. When his work (or hers—but it was a long time before there were women poets in any numbers) was printed it was increasingly a revelation to the public of the highly personal, rather than being to a large degree the voice of the people itself which it had been the bard's task, in earlier times, to sound forth. The value put on individual expression, the concept of "originality," and ultimately even upon individualism as a creed, had been pushed further by the time we reach the period of Romanticism, which developed alongside the Industrial Revolution and was in part reactive to the prospect of facelessness presented to the prophetic eye by that phenomenon.

Twentieth century alienation is another phase of the reaction. What began as a realization of human potential, a growth of *individuated* consciousness (to use Jung's useful term) out of the unconscious collective, became first a glorification of willful, essentially optimistic individualism, echoing the ambitious, optimistic individualism of its capitalist context, and then, as that turned sour and revealed more and more of greed in its operations, led to the setting of a high esthetic and moral value upon alienation itself.

But alienation is of ethical value, is life-affirmative and conducive to creativity only when it is accompanied by a political consciousness that imagines and affirms (and works toward) an alternative to the society from which it turns away in disgust. Lacking this, the alienated person, if he or she is gifted, becomes especially a prey to the exploitation that characterizes capitalism and is its underlying principle. The manifestations—in words, music, paint, or what have you—of private anguish are exploited by a greedy public, a public greedy for emotion at second hand because starved of the experience of community. Concurrently, for the same reasons, a creative person—whether a pop star or a Sylvia Plath, a John Berryman, or an Anne Sexton—internalizes the exploitive, unwittingly becoming *self*-exploitive.

And if the public is greedy, the critics, at their worst, are positively ghoulish, or at the least, irresponsible. I feel, for instance, that it is irresponsible for one local[1] columnist, in a memorial eulogy, to have written of Anne Sexton, "The manner of her death is at once frightening and fascinating to those who responded to her poetry, sharing as they do many of the same fears and insecurities she articulated so well. Her death awakens those fears and insecurities, the way some of her poems did, it raises them up from where they hide, buried by ordinary, everyday things." It is irresponsible because it is a statement made without qualification or development in a context of praise, and without, therefore, helping readers to see (as I suppose the writer herself does now see) that to raise our fears and insecurities into consciousness in order to confront them, to deal with them, is good; but that if the pain is confused with art itself, then people at the receiving end of a poem describing a pain and insecurity they share are not really brought to confront and deal with their problems, but are instead led into a false acceptance of them as signs or precursors of art, marks of

[1] i.e., Boston area.

83

kinship with the admired artist, symptoms of what used to be called "the artistic temperament."

Again, when I read the blurbs on the back of the late John Berryman's prizewinning *Delusions, etc.*, and see what A. Alvarez wrote of Berryman's work and death, I feel that a poisonous misapprehension of the nature of poetry is being furthered. "For years," Alvarez says, "I have been extolling the virtues of what I call extremist poetry, in which the artists deliberately push their perceptions to the very edge of the tolerable. Both Berryman and Plath were masters of the style. But knowing now how they both died I no longer believe that any art—even that as fine as they produced at their best—is worth the terrible cost."

At first glance this statement might be taken as being in accord with my own viewpoint; but its effect (since it is obvious that Alvarez believes their art to have been of the highest possible quality, perhaps the best poetry of their time) is still to extol the pursuit of the almost intolerable, the deliberate driving of the self to extremes which are not the unavoidable, universal extremes imposed by the human condition, but—insofar as they are deliberately sought—are luxuries, or which, if part and parcel of individual mental illness, should rather be *resisted* than encouraged in the name of art. In assuming that the disasters of those writers' lives were a form of payment for the virtues of their art, Alvarez, even while he says he has come to feel it is not worth the cost, perpetuates the myth that confounds a love affair with death with a love affair with art.

Thus it is that long lives devoted to the practice of art seem lacking in allure, and young would-be artists, encouraged by people older than themselves but equally confused, equally apt to mistake handicap for power, model their lives on the lives of those who, however gifted, were vanquished by their sorrows. It is not understood that the greatest heroes and heroines are truly those who hold out the longest, or, if they do die young, do so unwillingly, resisting to the last.

An instance would be the young guerilla poets of Latin America, so many of whom have been killed so young. (At least one of them, Javier Heraud, of Peru, would surely have been a major poet. He was shot down at the age of 23.) They were not flirting with death, any more than Victor Jara, the extraordinary and beloved Chilean musician and poet who was murdered in the Stadium in Santiago just over a year ago. They died politically conscious deaths, struggling for a better life, not just for themselves but for their people, for The People. Their tragedy is very different from the tragedy of suicide; they were conscious actors in dramas of revolutionary effort, not helpless victims.

Anne Sexton's struggle has its political dimensions too—but hers is the story of a victim, not a conscious participant. Anne Sexton the well-to-do suburban housewife, Anne Sexton in Bedlam, Anne Sexton "halfway back," Anne Sexton the glamorous performer, Anne Sexton timid and insecure, Anne Sexton saying she had always hoped to publish a posthumous volume, Anne Sexton in her garage breathing in the deadly fumes, was—whatever the clinical description of her depression—"caught in history's crossfire." Not because she was a woman—the problem is not essentially related to gender or to sexual stance. Not because she didn't have radical politics—god knows they are not a recipe for great art or for long life (though I can't help feeling that a little more comprehension of the relation of politics to her own life might have helped her). But because she herself was unable to separate her depression and her obsession with death from poetry itself, and because precisely her most enthusiastic readers and critics encouraged that inability.

The artist, the poet, (like Hokusai, who called himself "the old man mad about painting" and felt that at seventy he had begun to learn, at ninety would have some command of his powers, and at a hundred would begin to do justice to what he saw in Nature) needs the stamina of an astronaut and the energy derived only from being passionately in love with life and with art. "This is this world, the kingdom I was looking for!" wrote John Holmes. And "You must love the crust of the earth on which you dwell. You must be able to extract nutriment out of a sand heap. Else you will have lived in vain," wrote Thoreau.

Such purity, integrity, love, and energy—rarely fully attained but surely to be striven for—are undermined by our exploitive society, which romanticizes its victims when they are of a certain kind (thus distracting us from the unromanticizable lives of the suffering multitude). It romanticizes gifted individuals who have been distorted into an alienated individualism, a self-preoccupation, that is *not* individuation, *not* maturation.

Anne Sexton wrote in *Wanting to Die,*

> Suicides have already betrayed the body.
> Stillborn, they don't always die,
> but dazzled, they can't forget a drug so sweet . . .
> To thrust all that life under your tongue!—
> that, all by itself, becomes a passion.

Too many readers, with a perversity that, yes, really does seem to me to be bound up with white middle-class privilege and all its moral disadvantages, would sooner remember, and identify with, lines like those than with these, which (in *The Death Notebooks*) she also wrote:

> Depression is boring, I think
> and I would do better to make
> some soup and light up the cave.

To recognize that for a few years of her life Anne Sexton was an artist *even though* she had so hard a struggle against her desire of death is to fittingly honor her memory. To identify her love of death with her love of poetry is to insult that struggle.

These are excerpts from a long paper prepared for a series of symposia on "Literature and Medicine" which I attended in the mid-seventies. The topics were chosen from a number of themes to which all participants were asked to address their thoughts. I've now eliminated most of the special references to the possible role of literature in the curriculum of medical and nursing schools, as well as the allusions to papers presented by other members of the study group, but I decided to call this cluster of statements "Talking to Doctors" because it was more particularly the medical profession I had in mind as my audience, than those participants who, like myself, represented literature. There were, of course, some doctor-writers at the symposia—hybrids in a most honorable tradition; but I was thinking beyond those meetings to the nonliterary members of the Society for Health and Human Values who presumably would have access to our proceedings sooner or later.[1] And this had an effect upon the analogies I found myself using, as may be noted. Despite this preponderance of pointedly physiological metaphors, I believe the statements may be of use to the general reader.

1. Art and Therapy

There exists in the late twentieth century a frequent identification of Art with self-expression. The logic of this misconception is as follows: (1) Everybody has feelings. (2) Feelings demand expression. (3) Failure to express feelings is akin to constipation—blockage and toxicity of the system results. (4) The means of expressing feeling are common to everyone, and among the most useful are the arts. (5) The arts are not, or should not be, the exclusive possession of an élite. (6) The arts must be enlisted for social use as mild laxatives.

---

[1]These proceedings are now in fact available (University of Illinois Press), including an unrevised version of this piece.

This series is obviously faulty, though it contains elements of truth. Yes, everybody has feelings, and feelings demand expression—but they demand expression in the sense of articulation, not of expulsion, of pushing-out-in-order-to-get-rid-of. To articulate is "to utter distinctly," "to set forth in distinct particulars" (that's where its relation to the joints, as of a hand, for instance, becomes clear) "to be systematically interrelated," "to speak so as to be intelligible." To articulate feelings, to make them intelligible, does not involve intellectualizing them out of existence, even less is it a matter of convulsive ejection. The aim is not elimination but absorption. The arts are, indeed, modes of articulation; but though I deplore deliberate, exclusionary élitism, my experience as an artist *and as a receiver of art* causes me to doubt that *the doing of art* can be part of everyone's experience; and I certainly object to the commandeering of the arts as utile means of self-expression, for it mistakes the nature of art and takes a part for the whole.

As a receiver of art I know that the articulation of feeling can be experienced vicariously. In experiencing art, we not only are stimulated to empathic realizations, living, let's say, the hopes and fears of a fictive person as we read, even though those hopes and fears do not correspond to actual events in our own lives (e.g. one need not be an old man treated harshly by his children to feel with, as well as for, King Lear)—we also find in art the expression of our own emotions. We turn to love poems when we are in love, to elegies when we mourn. The gaiety of one song speaks for our own light hearts on a lucky morning, or the sadness of another for our loneliness at a different time. Access to these essential resources must indeed not be confined to an élite; the moral quality of a culture may be judged by their availability.

It is also possible for everyone to partake in some degree in the experience of *using the materials of the arts*, whether the visual and tactile arts, dance, music, theatre, or the writing of poetry or imaginative prose. This experience will be life-enhancing, both in itself and as a means to better

88

reception of works of art made by others; undoubtedly, where therapy is needed, it can be a therapeutic activity—whether or not it is "self-expressive" in the getting-it-off-your-chest, letting-off-steam sense. *But it will not necessarily lead to the creation of works of art.*

For while art subsumes in its nature the self-expressive; and is a form of articulation, that is, of setting forth experience, a making intelligible, and so, absorbable, of feelings otherwise unassimilable; it is nevertheless not circumscribed, not to be defined *as* those qualities and those actions. *Art as process* is undertaken by artists (as distinct from persons seeking a means, more or less therapeutic in intent, of self-expression) for its own sake, from an instinctive desire and need to *make,* to form things in a particular medium; and they have towards that medium—be it language, or visual form, or whatsoever—a marked preference not of the intending will but of the sensibility, indeed I would say of the nervous system, which makes them more sensitive not morally or emotionally, but *aesthetically,* at least in regard to their own medium (and frequently *only* in regard to their own medium) than others. Even in cultures productive of more popular and anonymous art than are modern Western cultures, there are degrees of talent, and the occasional supreme artist stands out above the rest. To the artistic sensibility, process is of intense interest, and though the goal is the finished work, the passion and the pleasure—however much the pleasure may be compounded with struggle and even with pain—is in the making of the work and not in the having finished it. Like God in the book of Genesis, the artist does not wait long in contemplation of what he or she has made, but begins on the next day's work.

This presents a contrast to the attitude of the self-expresser, whose satisfaction is typically in the relief of *having expressed,* rather than in the activity of making (which includes self-expression). David Jones, the British writer and artist, called the artist's work *the gratuitous setting up of altars to the unknown god.* Those who would utilize the arts for therapeutic purposes often fail to understand this. They encourage the setting up, in hope of benefit or blessing, of altars to the gods of mental health, self-improvement, or what have you.

I don't mean to suggest that the use of poetry, or music, or painting, or any art, as an activity which may help sick people get better or feel happier, is *wrong*. Two people I know have talked to me very movingly of their work with poetry in such circumstances—one of them working with patients in a psychiatric hospital, one in a rehabilitation program for drug addicts. I also know a number of people, some of them prisoners themselves, who have worked in jails teaching writing and painting. I appreciate the value and importance of such programs (and sometimes buried talent can emerge in them). They can make all the difference to people whose lives are grim and hopeless. Writing or painting is not going to solve the problems that put people in mental hospitals or in jails, nor keep the terminal cancer patient from death; but it can help people grow, and to feel better about themselves because they are *articulating* in some way; and to live more fully, as long as they *are* alive, than they would have done if they had not written or painted. All that is incontrovertibly good. What is not good is that those who introduce these possibilities, not only in institutions but in schools and colleges and thousands of Creative Writing workshops, frequently fail to make any distinction between the activities they promote and art itself. The manipulation of materials and the relief experienced through articulation, though both are factors in the making of works of art, are only factors and not the thing itself; it is misleading to let students suppose they are doing art when in fact they are only taking steps toward doing so. Unless they have that natural, unteachable bent toward a particular medium, and that instinctive drive to make autonomous things, those steps will lead them only to a subjective, private, and temporary satisfaction, not without value, but lower in the scale of possible human experience than it is claimed to be.

I have been speaking of art as process. What of works of

art after the process, what of the reception of art as if affects the self? I believe fervently in the role of the arts as essential nourishment for human beings in good health, and therefore most conclude that they can be potent as therapy likewise. The imagination, the aesthetic sense, the capacity for sensuous pleasure, can atrophy like anything else not used, starve if not fed. And these faculties interact with the emotions and so with moral sensitivity: compassion, as I've said elsewhere, is a function of the imagination. But the *discriminating intelligence* is an essential factor in receptivity to art; without it, a mere appetite can devour shoddy substitutes for real literature (or any other art) just as the body's appetite, in ignorance, and habitually ill fed, can fail to recognize soggy white bread, and franks full of nitrates and nitrites, etc. etc., followed by flavored sugar, and thinks it has had a nourishing meal. And the emphasis on self-expression in process can affect discrimination in reception—or consumption, to follow through the analogy. The presentation to students (including patients in therapeutic programs) of masses of inferior literature merely for the sake of its supposed relevancy is a part of the same problem. The "relevant" in reading material is closely equivalent to the "self-expressive" in writing. I'm not saying it makes sense to present highly complex works in archaic English to barely literate students of narrow experience, for instance; merely that though there can be found work which is both comprehensible and of high quality, too often familiarity of scene or subject is made the standard of relevancy, in an extension of the principle of self-expressive process: identify, establish previous acquaintance, and proceed to *spew forth*. "Identify" as I'm using it here has both its meanings: in a self-expressive act, the person's own emotions are identified; in a receptive act, what is described is identified *with*. Both are useful, necessary, affirmative in potential; the trouble lies in assuming them to be ends, not means; or rather, that they are assumed to be means for attaining elimination instead of absorption and transformation.

Transformation! Yes, that is probably the key word. *To*

spew forth is not to transform; neither is *to state*. Both actions are of use; both may be necessary under certain circumstances. Both may be included in the process of making a work of art. But works of art transcend these and other factors, *transforming* them, along with the raw material of experience (factual or emotional) into autonomous creations that give off mysterious energy. Not everyone has the form-sense and the impulse to *make things out of a particular medium* that distinguish the artist; therefore not everyone can effect transformation of raw material (and most artists in one medium—say language—cannot effect transformation in another, such as paint or clay). Everyone, however, has the potential (however undeveloped) to experience works of art made by others, and partake of that transforming communion. What does the nonartist working in an art medium experience that is of value, then? I think they can experience deeper self-understanding, clarifying articulation, and emotional release. Surely they do not have to be deceived into supposing they are creating works of art in order to experience those benefits. And when they are so deceived, their ability to receive the transforming power of actual works of art is adversely affected, because they are not able to distinguish the shoddy from the authentic: if in their own writing or painting they learn no structural and aesthetic standards, evaluating what they and their peers do purely on a basis of how "self-expressive" it is, how can they develop the ability to respond to the great works which will give them the deepest, most transforming, powerfully enlivening experience? Instinct and intuition can be warped, diverted, corrupted. They will turn for succour to the substandard, for its very familiarity.

The great power of art is to transform, renovate, activate. If there is a relationship between art and healing it is that. But its power cannot manifest itself if the arts are pressed into servitude and reduced to mere means to an end. The more clearly the self-expressive is defined as usefully that and no more, and the less confusion there is between expulsion and transformative absorption, the more can art act in human lives, making them fuller, more active, more human.

2. Disembodied Language

When Emerson said that language was "fossil poetry" he meant to remind us that even words seemingly created to expressly convey abstractions still embody concrete images. This is what intellect forgets or denies whenever it is too exclusively cultivated, to the neglect of the sensuous, esthetic, emotional, or instinctive elements. As a college teacher one often (alas) sees misspellings of a type that reveal a lack of recognition of the image within a word or phrase, even though usage is not incorrect. A few common instances:

> "reprecussion" for "repercussion"
> "forward" for "foreword"
> "peturbed" for "perturbed"

Any of these shows that the writer's sense of the word is abstract: the embodied metaphor—the sound of drums and cymbals banging and clanging far and wide—is absent from the familiar phrase, "causing widespread repercussions," when it is thus misspelled; the short introduction to a book is not realized as being *a word before the text*; and the prefix *per,* meaning *throughout,* (as in permeate and pervasive, as one would hope the student might recognize) is lost from "peturbed," while almost certainly there is no recognition, either, of the relationship of the second part of the word to disturbed, turbine, tumult, turbid, a cluster descending from turba, a multitude, and turbo, a wheel, whirling, etc., and all having to do with commotion. One does not have to know Latin (or Greek, or Sanskrit) to find out these connections. I do not; and while I rather wish I did, I can testify to the compensatory efficacy of curiosity plus a good dictionary or two as tools of investigation.

Another example—amusing in its way—of how a term or phrase can become a mere convention, unrelated to its origins, (a process which accounts for most mixed metaphors of the unacceptable variety, as distinct from the poetic conceit or surreal image that establishes its own veracity) is provided by a writer's assertion that "a wide variety of

93

beautiful wildflowers were growing cheek by jowl beside the path." I have also encountered "lost allusions" and "frequent illusions"! Perhaps best of all is a student's praise for a poet's "effective use of illiteration. . . ."

The unthinking use of "negative and positive" is a curious case; and one that is—unfortunately—too well-established to admit of revision. Doctor and patient are relieved when a test proves *negative*; both are sorry when it is *positive* (though I cannot help supposing that many a diagnostician with a hunch has been more gratified—for a moment, at least—at finding his guess was correct, than distressed at the implication for his patient: if, that is, he is one of those physicians whose ability to empathize is stunted.) As for the "patient," how many doctors stop to reflect upon the nuances of that word, which are easily to be found in the OED or other etymologically profuse dictionaries?—nuances relating to endurance, passivity, subjection to the actions of others, pain and forebearance?

Poetry, even more than good prose (because more condensed) depends for its very life on an awareness of these root meanings. It is not poetry's *only* vital organ, this awareness, any more than the heart or the liver is a human body's sole vital organ; but like them, it is genuinely indispensible. Yet when I speak of awareness I do not mean that the poet is necessarily constantly conscious of etymology, or that he or she need have made a special study of it; rather that the poet's feeling for language must provide an acute sensitivity to verbal interconnections, and enough concern to investigate and verify the history of relationships intuited by the ear. How does this affect the reader? Again, not necessarily by demanding of him or her a consciousness of every nuance, but rather that he or she be receptive to the effects brought about through the writer's awareness, open to the total experience. Yet the attentive reading of poetry habituates the reader to a precise, concrete, sensuous employment of language, so that when sloppy, ineffective, lifeless language is encountered it is less likely to be tolerated. Lifeless language simply does not function with full power even in the most routine ways—or to put it another way, it tends to make actions *routine* that should be continually refreshed: actions anyone may perform, and need to describe, as part of their daily work. It is in such considerations that one may perhaps see a relationship between ethics and the demanding and sophisticated "ear" developed by the study of poetry. Beyond the value it can have for any person or category of persons, poetry can have, for those whose attention is apt to be intensely focused on a narrow or discrete area, an especial usefulness through its stimulation of the imagination, its revelation of analogies, and by its redirection of the sensibility to the underlying dynamics of language as manifested in concrete, sensuous, image-rooted vocabulary.

For a doctor or nurse, for example, this greater sensitivity to language might well mean the development of a keener ear for the emotions and sensations which patients, however restricted their means of articulation, may be trying to express. By the same token, language-sensitive physicians and nurses might be enabled, by careful and imaginative word-choice, to impart more efficiently to patients and their families and to co-workers the information they need. This more accurate and flexible comprehension and utilization of language is not separable from the awakened and functioning imagination. Empathy and compassion, functions of the imagination, lead to the "inspired" word or phrase, the verbal accuracy, "hitting the nail on the head," which leads to further enlightenment, and in turn to a deeper comprehension of the situation.

3. On Responsibility to the Self Versus Responsibility to the Community

Goethe said, "In order to *do* something one has to *be* someone." He was not talking about status and power (or rather, not about the power of status). He was talking about the necessity for self-development, for individuation, as a vital accompaniment to effective action. As a poet who is also, at least sporadically, a political activist in a minor way, I feel strongly that internal and external work, the self-directed or introspective and the publicly-directed or extroverted, must be concurrent, or at least rhythmically alternating. They are complementary, and neither can be substituted for the other. When an individual puts all of his or her eggs into a single basket, whether it is the self-cultivation or the working-for-the-cause basket, what does one see? In the first case, one sees attrition set in sooner or later. It may not have been true in all times and places; but in our own time and place those who turn away from concern for the commonweal to cultivate their own gardens are found to have lost touch with a nourishing energy. Better a bitter spring than no irrigation at all. Ivory towers look out over desert landscapes. In the second case, we see people who burn out, whose zeal—often noble—leads them into a habit of self-neglect that after a while makes their political work curiously toneless and ineffective; or, while it may be superficially effective, that is, productive of immediate results, imparts a sense of hollowness and rigidity, so that one says, "What good would a revolution be that was dominated by such *selfless* zeal! Out of the fire, into the frying pan. . . ." The true heroes and heroines of political radicalism are those who maintain a rich inner life—Rosa Luxembourg, A. J. Muste, Ho Chi Minh. If this is true in the field of social action, it must be true too for the medical profession (whose work of course must necessarily be a form of social action likewise, whether their particular concern is with individual patients or with Public Health). The self will surely suffer if egotism leads a person away from the experience of the Human Communion. And the commonweal, as surely, suffers if those who work for its betterment are hollowed-out self-neglecters whose imaginations are atrophying.

4. The Nature of Objectivity

In poetry (and I would venture to say in painting and other visual arts; or maybe even more generally, "the arts") "objectivity" is never—or never usefully—"cold." It may be objected that this is untrue in the case of satire—but a moment's thought will remind one that satire, which is never very far from caricature, is in fact not objective anyway, or that its objectivity is necessarily mixed with passion. The truly sardonic cannot be indifferent, and cold objectivity implies an indifference. There is, it is true, such a thing as *icy contempt*—but ice burns; icy contempt is twin to *burning indignation*. Cold objectivity, in art—and, I suspect, in medicine or other sciences—is self-defeating; it is subject to a law resembling Heisenberg's Law: the intention of objective regard must be correct knowledge of the thing regarded; but when cold, that regard is a basilisk stare, which shrivels what it would see, and so never does see it in its natural state. Rilke said that, "If a thing is to speak to you, you must for a certain time regard it as the only thing that exists, the unique phenomenon that your diligent and exclusive love has placed at the center of the universe, something the angels serve that very day upon that matchless spot." This formula is not applicable to every situation. Its context was particular; when he spoke of Things, Rilke most frequently meant, specifically, the inanimate—mineral, vegetable, or man-made—and by extension, sometimes, inarticulate, though animate, creatures. He did not mean, I am sure, that a pathologist must look with *love* upon a tumor. However, a *concerned attention* given by the diagnostician to the whole person—not merely as a body but as a social organism—seems to me not very different from the poet's attention to the inscape, the *gestalt* of his theme. It involves objectivity, but it is an objectivity that arises from respect; that is, from the recognition of an identity, a life having its own integrity separate from one's own and no less than one's own. To give the respect of recognition is a form of love; it is one level, one expression, of what Martin Buber termed *confirmation of being*, and said was the best gift one human being could give another.

The aspect of thinking about death that I would like to
speak about is summed up in a phrase of Rainer Maria
Rilke's—the phrase "unlived life, of which one can die."
These words have been a part of my thinking and feeling
for thirty years, and I have quoted them in more than one
poem as well as in prose writings. If I have anything to
contribute to this series of discussions it is not because of the
biographical fact that I am a writer who once was a nurse—
for a while, in my youth—and therefore saw many deaths
take place, and learned that old-fashioned laying-out of the
body which is now, in this country at least, no longer undertaken by nurses, since bodies are immediately put into the
waiting hands of an avid funeral industry. No, it is not
because of this fact, which has not been of central importance among the events of my life at all, but rather because,
being a poet, I have spent a lot of my time in the celebration
of life, of living. When Rilke—within a poem—is asked,
what do you do? he answers, not for himself alone but for
the archetypal Poet, "I praise." But this praising does not
mean a disregard of negatives, a kind of pollyanna insistence on the affirmative. Praise, rather, is rooted in a recognition of fragility, transience, mortality:

I Praise[1]

O, tell us, poet, what you do?
                I praise.
But the deadly and the violent days,
how do you undergo them, take them in?

Talk given at the University of Delaware in 1975 to an audience that included many members of the health professions who had been participating
in a course on "Death and Dying."

[1]Translated by Denise Levertov.

98

> I praise.
> But the namelessness—how do you raise
> that, invoke the unnameable?
>   I praise.
> What right have you, through every phase,
> in every mask, to remain true?
>   I praise.
> —and that both stillness and the wild affray
> know you, like star and storm?
>   Because I praise.

In the poetry of William Carlos Williams, which I began to read almost as long ago as Rilke's letters and poems, there is a recurrent, indeed I sometimes feel even a dominant theme, rarely if ever spelled out but covertly present in poem after poem (and in some of his prose too)—the praise of intense, bold, essentially death-defying acts and attitudes and the sense of the paradoxical dependence of this beauty, which resides in intensity, upon the very brevity of life and the inevitability of death—upon *having* a mortality to defy. Maybe this smacks of the Manichean heresy, of Zoroastrian dualism—but it is not quite that; its praise is not for life as *opposed* to death but for the synthesis, life/death or death/ life, the curious embrace and union of positive and negative that is the human condition and indeed the condition of all creation—although we can perceive the condition most readily as conflict, not as synthesis.

The experience of the tension within that synthesis, however, is productive of aesthetic pleasure, whether we feel that pleasure through Nature directly, as when we recognize the poignance of a flower's brief perfection, a poignance intrinsic to its beauty; or witness the swiftly changing splendor of a sunset sky; or whether we feel it through art, which mediates comparable experiences or presents them in its forms.

Many of the Williams poems that speak to me of the beauty of life-intensity, and therefore of a defiance of death which yet incorporates the *fact* of death into its very being (or rather which could not occur without a nonevasive recognition of death—without giving death its due, one might say—), do not mention death at all. Here is one (from *The Collected Later Poems*) that is a pure celebration of life: it is called "The Manoeuvre."

> I saw the two starlings
> coming in toward the wires.
> But at the last,
> just before alighting, they
>
> turned in the air together
> and landed backwards!
> that's what got me—to
> face into the wind's teeth.

It celebrates life, but it sees life as requiring adroit manoeuvering. The wind, in the teeth of which the birds perform their body-intelligent act, is not death itself but it is a destructive force. For this beauty to take place there has to be a kind of cooperation between destructive and constructive forces.

Again, in one of a number of poems Williams called simply "The Rose," (this particular one from *The Collected Earlier Poems*), he does not speak of death but he implies that curious, fascinating, poignant tension:

> First the warmth, variability
> color and frailty
>
> A grace of petals skirting
> the tight-whorled cone
>
> Come to generous abandon—
> to the mind as to the eye
>
> Wide! Wider!
> Wide as if panting, until

100

> the gold hawk's-eye speaks once
> coldly its perfection

Generous abandon leads to a perfection which he calls cold—but I don't feel he is using the word *cold* as a negative. Rather he is describing a dynamic process—the changing of the flower from bud to full-blown utterance of itself—and the apogee of that process, the point of rest or of full climax, when all that movement at last reveals, in a poised stillness, the very core of the flower, the gold pistil he speaks of as the eye of a hawk. (And which, in the life cycle of a flower, is the source of new life, though it comes into full view only as the rose opens so wide that we know the petals are about to fall . . . and we say the rose is dying.)

Williams does have poems that speak directly of death. In "To an Old Jaundiced Woman" (*The Collected Earlier Poems*) the feeling recorded is pity.

> O tongue
> licking
> the sore on
> her netherlip
>
> O toppled belly
>
> O passionate cotton
> stuck with
> matted hair
>
> elsian[2] slobber
> upon
> the folded handkerchief
>
> I can't die

[2]This has sometimes been reprinted as "elysian," presumably because it was supposed to be an irony to complement the exclamatory address ("O tongue . . . O toppled belly . . . O passionate cotton"), but I think it is a reference to the "Elsie" of "Spring and All" with her "broken brain."

            —moaned the old
            jaundiced woman
            rolling her
            saffron eyeballs

            I can't die
            I can't die

In the more subtle "The Widow's Lament in Springtime"
(*The Collected Earlier Poems*), he presents another facet of
his attitude, and identifies with the way in which a sensuous
love of nature, of living, becomes a channel (even in negative experience) for the expression of grief and the wish to
die, a parallel with those passionate, erotic addresses to
death that have been made in poetry of past centuries—"I
have been half in love with easeful death," for instance, or
Whitman's ocean so seductively whispering "Death, death,
death."

                Sorrow is my own yard
                where the new grass
                flames as it has flamed
                often before but not
                with the cold fire
                that closes round me this year.
                Thirtyfive years
                I lived with my husband.
                The plumtree is white today
                with masses of flowers.
                Masses of flowers
                load the cherry branches
                and color some bushes
                yellow and some red
                but the grief in my heart
                is stronger than they
                for though they were my joy
                formerly, today I notice them
                and turned away forgetting.
                Today my son told me

that in the meadows,
at the edge of the heavy woods
in the distance, he saw
trees of white flowers.
I feel that I would like
to go there
and fall into those flowers
and sink into the marsh near them.

Here the woman is longing "to cease upon the midnight" or rather full in the light of day—and yet such is her feeling for the palpable, for the sweet drift of blossoms, that essentially she is asking to become one with them, she cannot speak of death except in terms of life. But in "Dedication for a Plot of Ground" (*The Collected Earlier Poems*) it is Williams himself speaking about the dead, telling all mourners, in effect, that they had better recognize the fierce vitality of the lived life and bring that recognition to the dedication of this land, and not their carcasses, their fears and lamentations. The message is the same as in the well-known Dylan Thomas poem, "Do Not Go Gentle into That Good Night," though that is addressed to the dying and this to the living.

This plot of ground
facing the waters of this inlet
is dedicated to the loving presence of
Emily Dickinson Wellcome
who was born in England, married,
lost her husband and with
her five year old son
sailed for New York in a two-master,
was driven to the Azores;
ran adrift on Fire Island shoal,
met her second husband
in a Brooklyn boarding house,
went with him to Puerto Rico
bore three more children, lost
her second husband, lived hard
for eight years in St. Thomas,

ıerto Rico, San Domingo, followed
ıe oldest son to New York,
ıst her daughter, lost her "baby",
ıeized the two boys of
ıe oldest son by the second marriage
ıothered them—they being
ınotherless—fought for them
against the other grandmother
and the aunts, brought them here
summer after summer, defended
herself here against thieves,
storms, sun, fire,
against flies, against girls
that came smelling about, against
drought, against weeds, storm-tides,
neighbors, weasels that stole her chickens,
against the weakness of her own hands,
against the growing strength of
the boys, against wind, against
the stones, against trespassers,
against rents, against her own mind.

She grubbed this earth with her own hands,
domineered over this grass plot,
blackguarded her oldest son
into buying it, lived here fifteen years,
attained a final loneliness and—

If you can bring nothing to this place
but your carcass, keep out.

It is with the recognition of my presumptuousness that I
will turn now to some poems of my own. Williams and Rilke
are hard acts to follow! But since I claim their vision of life
and of death as strong influences on my own history as
person and as poet, I must submit some evidence of that
claim.

In my earliest published poems, the images in which I
spoke of death were abstract, vague, though I was not

ignorant of it as a reality: I spent my adolescence in wartime England and worked, as I have said, as a nurse, first in a special wartime emergency program and then as a regular student nurse. Nevertheless it was not until one of my first American books, *With Eyes at the Back of Our Heads*, about ten years later, that I tried to deal plainly, simply and concretely with death:

The Dead

Earnestly I looked
into their abandoned faces
at the moment of death and while
I bandaged their slack jaws and
straightened waxy unresistant limbs and plugged
the orifices with cotton
but like everyone else I learned
each time nothing new, only that
as it were, a music, however harsh, that held us
however loosely, had stopped, and left
a heavy thick silence in its place.

Among the poems I wrote in the late 1950s and early 1960s were many that concerned Mexico, where I lived for a while. Mexican culture, with its memories of blood-sacrifice in the Aztec and other preColumbian periods, with the fatalism a subject people developed willy-nilly under the brutality of the Spanish conquerors whom they had not the power to throw off, and with, even today, a high infant mortality and relatively short adult life-expectancy—Mexican culture does not keep death in a closet. The funeral parlors in Mexican cities have their coffins on full daily display, indeed I would call them simply coffin shops. These stores, like other stores—shoe stores, groceries, what have you—are open fronted, doorless—they are closed only by rolling down the shutter late at night or on holidays. Mexican drivers tend to take risks and seat belts are still virtually unknown. The fact that standards of sanitation and hygiene

105

are not high is not something to be complacent about, of course—but while it may be deplorable from one aspect, it is from another to be seen as a highly sophisticated way of saying that to die is a condition of to live. The sight and knowledge, the acknowledgement, of butterflies sunning themselves on a dungheap must not scare us if we are to live our lives and know joy. Here's a poem in *The Jacob's Ladder* about, or from, Mexico.

The Weave

The cowdung-colored mud
baked and raised up in random
walls, bears the silken
lips and lashes of erotic
flowers towards a sky of
noble clouds. Accepted
sacramental excrement
supports the ecstatic half-sleep
of butterflies, the slow
opening and closing of brilliant
dusty wings. Bite down
on the bitter stem of your nectared
rose, you know
the dreamy stench of death and fling
magenta shawls delicately
about your brown shoulders laughing.

Perhaps this poem by the Rumanian poet Maria Banus is saying essentially the same thing.

Solstices[3]

Even if this is the longest night of my life,
even if I secretly call like a lost child for its mother, "Why?
    Where are you?"

[3]By Maria Banus, born in Rumania, 1910. The poem is revised by Denise Levertov from an anonymous translation.

even if the forest is full of huge claws,
                and I'm cold in my warmest clothes, which have
                the shape of my threadbare body,

even if I doubt the value of my handiwork, crying out,
                                                        "God!
                What have I done with my days?
                Their end draws near, and I, where have I been?
                My hands have done shoddy work,
                                                and now
                they are stiff with cold . . ."

Though it's my lot that now,
                just when summer's golden water surrounds me—
                        slow-moving delta, solstice of intense laminae of
                        sparklings—
though it's my lot
that the longest night of my life should wave itself here
                                by the sunbathed shore
                                like a mourning cape:

yet I will try to be thaumaturge
                                to my own life.
I will lift up the stained black crape and, swinging it in
                                                        circles,
                                        calmly, quietly,
                over the golden delta where fishes swarm,
                thick grass-tufts and flowers crowd,
                and nests are swinging,
I shall let it softly fall and spread out on the water,
                                                transformed
into a tiny parachute fingers of water shall reach for.

I shall make it seem, or be, or become—who knows
                                the limits of bitter magic's sweetness?
—a lily-pad, serenely, and as if naturally,
                                resting itself on the water,
long-stemmed,
supple, slender,

                    umbilical cord bound to the muddy
                                            riverbed.
And poised upon it I'll set
the white, soothing, uncannily sensual
cup of the lily.

(The people of Asia have *always* held on to that awareness
that water lilies—the ineffable lotus—grow out of the mud.)

   Another poem of mine, in *The Freeing of the Dust,* was
inspired in part by Mexico, but also by the sturdy, the salty,
the unconsciously heroic life of the poorest people anywhere, everywhere, the people whose misery caused William Morris to say he was tired of the way in which his
aesthete friends seemed to occupy themselves with culti-
vating "the fine art of unhappiness"; but who notwithstanding their poverty often wear a flower behind their ear, or
wear a flash of humor like a flower, or have for each others'
lives—lives that do not count to the powerful—a concern
that is communion's very self.

                    The Wealth of the Destitute

How gray and hard the brown feet of *the wretched of
                                            the earth.*
How confidently the crippled from birth
push themselves through the streets, deep in their lives.
How seamed with lines of fate the hands
of women who sit at streetcorners
offering seeds and flowers.
How lively their conversation together.
How much of death they know.
I am tired of "the fine art of unhappiness."

   If this flower of mutual concern is often lacking in our
own violent industrial capitalist society, it may well be due
to the fact that such a society dehumanizes even while in
some respects it raises the standard of living. When I came
back from the still basically preindustrial and—much more
importantly—basically people-oriented socialist society of

North Vietnam, after my visit in 1972, to a United States that had just re-elected Nixon, I felt that, despite all the death and destruction taking place in that small country, I had experienced a fresh livingness there that I could not find here in the United States except in isolated individuals.

Fragrance of Life, Odor of Death

All the while among
the rubble even, and in
the hospitals, among the wounded,
                        not only beneath
                        lofty clouds

                                in temples
                        by the shores of lotus-dreaming
                        lakes

a fragrance:
flowers, incense, the earth-mist rising
of mild daybreak in the delta—good smell
of life.

It's in America
Where no bombs ever
have screamed down, smashing
the buildings, shredding people's bodies,
tossing the fields of Kansas or Vermont or Maryland
                                into the air.
to land wrong way up, a gash of earth-guts . . .
it's in America, everywhere, a faint seepage,
I smell death.

(The Freeing of the Dust)

I want to return, as I get close to the end of my talk, to Rilke. Rilke believed that every individual had awaiting him or her a personal, unique death to which they had a right. He believed it was very important to human dignity and fruition to die one's own death. (He also thought and wrote a lot about premature deaths, the deaths of children and young people, but to try to investigate and explicate his ideas on that would take a whole talk to itself.) Now, the personal death does not mean necessarily a painless death; but it does mean an appropriate death—appropriate not in some crude way, some meting out of what might be perceived by others as justice, but appropriate in a far more subtle, internalized way, as the culmination of trends in the *inner* life of the individual. And Rilke seems to have felt that this kind of death could be *experienced* by the individual, could be truly undivided, undivorced from his or her preceding experience of living. And that however painful, it would be recognized at some level of awareness as triumphantly real—it would be *lived*. The ability to *live one's death*, Rilke implies, depends on having lived one's life; you will remember the phrase I quoted at the beginning, *Unlived life, of which one can die*—that would be a slow and shameful death. But he also thought it depended to some extent upon the dying person not being, as it were, kidnapped into a sterile atmosphere. He did not believe that people ought to die in hospitals, apart from the things that surround us in daily life—familiar things of our homes, or even—if far from home—the lifelong familiar things of unsterile ordinary life. To die in a white room surrounded by starched and masked figures, no tree, no dog, no child in sight, no sky, no sounds from the world outside, only the artificial hush of the intensive care unit—this would have been to him the ultimate indignity and oppression.[4] Perhaps he was too literal on this point, for it is conceivable that the human imagination, in the profoundest sense of the word, could live even in those circumstances, as it lives in prison cells and torture chambers. Williams as an old man wrote,

> Only the imagination is real!
> I have declared it
> time without end.

---

[4]When this talk was given, the "hospice" concept was still virtually unknown.

If a man die
             it is because death
                         has first
possessed his imagination.
             But if he refuse death—
                         no greater evil
can befall him
             unless it be the death of love
                         meet him
in full career.
             Then indeed
                         for him
the light has gone out.
But love and the imagination
             are of a piece,
                         swift as the light
to avoid destruction.

("Asphodel, That Greeny Flower," *Pictures from Brueghel*)

To conclude, a short poem of my own (from *The Sorrow Dance*) which I take to be about the way in which an acceptance of our fragility, of earth's fragility, is what permits that *living in the moment,* truly *knowing* we are alive each instant, that seems to me to be our great, our hilarious, our open secret of paradoxical delight.

Living

The fire in leaf and grass
so green it seems
each summer the last summer.

The wind blowing, the leaves
shivering in the sun,
each day the last day.

A red salamander
so cold and so
easy to catch, dreamily

111

moves his delicate feet
and long tail. I hold
my hand open for him to go.

Each minute the last minute.

III POETRY AND POLITICS

On the Edge of Darkness: What is
Political Poetry?

Destiny
will be changed one morning
when, at the edge of darkness,
they stand up.
. . . About them
it was said
they have nothing to lose but their chains.
—Nazim Hikmet

A good deal of poetry one can call *political* in some way has appeared in this country and elsewhere in recent years. When I asked a young poet who has written some such poems what he would want to hear about in a lecture on poetry and politics, he replied that he'd like some assurance that there was a tradition for political poems, the poetry of social criticism, and that it was not a rootless phenomenon. So I shall begin by trying to trace some precedents.

When we look for a tradition for the political, or polemical poem, we may find ourselves turning first to the epic, since Ezra Pound called the epic "a poem containing history." An unsatisfactory definition, for it leaves out the element of narrative, the presence of a hero protagonist (or a heroine, as in the Vietnamese national epic) whose adventures we follow through a course of historical events. Besides, there are hero tales which are indeed epics but are clearly cosmological, theological, rather than historical; which are epics of the inner, psychological, life of humanity, not of outer events. Valéry's assertion that "An epic is a poem that can be told. When one tells it, one has a bilingual text" is a nice aphorism on paraphrase, but even more unsatisfactory as a definition of epic than Pound's. One can "tell" the story sung in a ballad. One can "tell" the story line of many of Hardy's poems. One can even "tell," for instance, the story line of a George Herbert poem such as "The

---

Presented as a lecture at Boston University, 1975.

Collar" ("I struck the board and cried, No more!")—but this doesn't make any of them epics. In any case it is obvious that the presence of history—or of politics, as we call our immediate social environment when it is critically examined, whether favorably or unfavorably—such presence as an intrinsic factor doesn't make a poem into an epic, though the same factor may inform some epics. A sonnet, a ballad, a satiric epistle, an isolated quatrain or couplet may be as pivoted on historical consciousness, and as charged, or more so, with partisan conviction, as any accredited epic. Shelley's "I met Murder on the way/He wore a mask like Castlereigh," is a small model of the political poem which never fails to give me a *frisson*—to make my hair stand on end or the top of my head seem to rise, according to the well known tests of Housman and Emily Dickinson.

If we concede, then, that historical or socio-political motifs have appeared in poetic modes of many kinds, and cannot be identified with any mode in particular, we come straightway to the more essential question: Can partisan, polemical content, in whatever poetic form it appears, be good poetry? This seems to me strictly a modern question, having its roots in the Romantic period but not really troubling anyone until the late nineteenth century. The Romantic period accelerated the isolation of the poet from the community. Perhaps we may say that this isolation had begun, slowly, long before—perhaps from the time of the first printing presses and the consequent decline in the oral, communal experience of poetry and the growth of a literate élite. But the Romantic period intensified this isolation by seeing the artist as endowed with a special sort of temperament which was not only operative during *the making* of works of art, not only when the poet donned the Bardic mantle, and was actually writing, but which made him at all times supersensitive. Shakespeare had written of "the poet's eye in a fine frenzy rolling"—but let's recall the lines that follow:

The poet's eye, in a fine frenzy rolling,
Doth glance from heaven to earth, from earth to heaven;

And as imagination bodies forth
The forms of things unknown, the poet's pen
Turns them to shapes, and gives to airy nothing
A local habitation and a name.

The description is of a working poet, not of the poetic temperament. I don't know where the "supersensitive" image originated—partially no doubt in the cultivation by poets and artists of a Bohemian style of life out of disgust and boredom with bourgeois alternatives—but in any case, poets, or artists in general, did accept this image of themselves and fostered it. It was an easy ego-trip. The public, predictably, began to think of them as undependable fellows, at best whimsical and capricious, at worst, dangerous madmen, and in any case not responsible citizens. The madness of the poet, as seen by the bourgeois, is not the divine madness of the shaman poets of ancient or primitive societies, but a quotidian foolishness and tendency to exaggerate, not worthy to be taken seriously. Thus a good measure of effectiveness was taken away from the poet by what had *seemed* an elevation of his role: that is, by the attribution to him of more refined sensibilities and profounder passions than those of other people. (My own belief, as I've testified elsewhere, is that a poet is only a poet when engaged in making poems, and has no rightful claim to *feeling* more than others, but only to being able to *articulate* feeling through the medium of language.) Moreover, nineteenth century bourgeois consciousness, as a concomitant of its understandable disrespect for the Romantic version of The Poet, proceeded to de-nature or defuse certain chosen poets (not without the collusion of the poets themselves) by enshrining them in temples of respectability—I'm thinking of the adulation of Tennyson and of what his laureateship did to his gifts; or of the vaporous earnestness (what a combination!) of "Browning Societies." Much the same thing happened a little later on to, of all people, Walt Whitman, who for a time was regarded as a sort of Kahil Gibran-like "philosopher." The question, Can a political poem be poetry? seems to me a wholly modern one. The Romantic

117

image of the poet was above all one which emphasized his individuality—his difference from other people rather than the ways in which he resembled them; and this led to the elevation of the lyric mode as the type or exemplar of poetry, because it was the most *personal* mode. Dramatic, satiric, and epic poetry had had precedence through centuries of Western history; and these modes offer obvious opportunities for the expression of ideas, convictions, and even mere opinions. Even before the lyric—both as a mode and as an element in other modes—came to be more and more highly valued (while its true nature was often misunderstood, e.g., "Gems from Thomas Moore," "Gems from Shakespeare," "The Sir Walter Scott Birthday Book" etc., etc.), the novel had swiftly developed and had taken over many of the subjects previously accommodated by nonlyric poetry. Thus there developed a distrust of the political when it did turn up in verse, since poetry and lyric form became almost synonymous to many people—and still are, as anyone who has taught poetry workshops knows. How often does a student ever attempt a nonlyric mode unless assigned to do so?

However, writers who accepted the lyric as the available mode and whose bent was for poetry, not for prose, nevertheless had a variety of things to say; so that the lyric in the twentieth century, like prose fiction, has become a repository for content previously dealt with in dramatic, epic, narrative, or satiric modes. At this time, in America at any rate, there is no category of content not attempted in what appears, in structure, to be lyric verse. But whereas critics and the public are not dismayed when autobiography, psychological explorations, or at the other extreme, trivia, appear in lyric semblance, yet the political is often looked at askance and subjected to a more stringent examination. The question, *Is it really poetry, or is it just versified ideas?* must indeed be asked; but it should by rights be asked equally of all those poems which present content of all kinds *not* anciently considered the province of the lyric, and not only of political content. And if a degree of intimacy is a condition of lyric expression, surely—at times when events make feelings run high—that intimacy between writer and political belief does exist, and is as intense as other emotions.

Here it seems time to respond to the initial enquiry, Has the political poem a tradition? My answer would be, Yes, and that tradition includes "Piers Plowman," Sir Walter Raleigh's "The Lie," certain of Milton's sonnets and of Wordsworth's, most of Blake and of Wilfred Owen, to skip at random from name to name that instantly come to mind, confining myself arbitrarily to English poets. If I begin to look at other literatures I at once include Dante, Quevedo, Heine; while in our own century we have such poets as Neruda, Ritsos, Brecht, etc. as well as innumerable lesser-known ones or ones who write in languages that are infrequently translated into English. I am not attempting to *catalogue* even the major poets who have written political poems, and certainly not the minor ones. Nor do I want to digress into a discussion of the political stance of individual poets, except perhaps to note that most political poetry, if not actually revolutionary, takes its stand on the side of liberty and not of maintaining the status quo. Even poets whose avowed politics we may justifiably consider reactionary, such as Yeats, Pound, or Jeffers, see in their authoritarian allegiances virtues most of us would certainly not associate with the right wing. The same may be said about Neruda's poems of a certain period when he supposed Stalin to possess humane qualities we are sure he did not have. Political poems typically celebrate freedom and honor even when the poet suffers illusion about where these are to be found. There are poems that, crying out against injustice, call for bloody vengeance against tyrants; but poets who knowingly praise tyranny itself are rare indeed. (D'Annunzio is the only example I can recall.)

So, the poem of political content—even of politically *hortatory* content—does unquestionably have a long and illustrious history. What characterizes its contemporary manifestations? Most, indeed I'd almost say all, of the current poetry on political themes is lyrical in presentation though not necessarily in tone. By lyrical in presentation I mean it consists typically of short, or fairly short, poems written without personae: nakedly, candidly, speaking in the poet's unmediated character, often with actual syntactic incorporation of the first person singular, or sometimes the first person plural; but in any case written from a personal rather than a fictive, and a subjective rather than objective, standpoint. The musicality characteristic of its origins has become, as the lyric has expanded its range of content, something of a Cheshire cat's smile—it appears, disappears, reappears. However, this seems to be just as true where other kinds of content are concerned as it is in political poems. The kinds of political content we see in present-day American poetry are several, though one can say they represent a coalition of issues, united by a common desire for social change, and by an intense recognition of the urgency of struggle for survival itself in a world threatened as never before. Thus, we see bodies of poetry dealing with specific aspects of this struggle—poems about racism and the Black, Native American, Latino and other minorities; Feminist poems; Gay liberation poems; poems from the antiwar, antiarms-race, antinuclear movement and from the environmentalist branch of it; but not infrequently, poems in one such category are written by poets who also contribute to one or more of the other categories. A striking characteristic of contemporary political poetry is that, more than in the past, it is written by people who are active participants in the causes they write about, and not simply observers. It's a reciprocal phenomenon: people who are already poets in any case become involved in some aspect or aspects of these interrelated struggles, and it follows naturally that they write poems concerned with the causes they believe in; these in turn inspire others, both to participation and to the writing of poems. Whether these poems are good or not depends on the gifts of the poet, not on the subject matter. But what is interesting historically is the greater interplay between these poets' actions and their writing.

For many of us who are thus involved, it is possible that our sense of political urgency is at times an almost hectic stimulus. Certainly it is true that when one participates, for instance, in a vigil to commemorate the dead of Hiroshima

and Nagasaki, or attends a teach-in about the nuclear super-
danger we all ignore most of the time, then one's conscious
awareness of these issues is intensified; and if one is led
by a resulting commitment to the attempt to combat what
threatens us, and thus to the experience of comradeship in
actions involving some risk, such as civil disobedience, then
one is living a stirring emotional life which—if one is given
to writing poetry—is almost bound to result in poems
directly related to these experiences, and to the beliefs one
shares with companions who often present a humbling
example of modesty, persistence, and courage.

> "Peace" was our password
> that stung from lip to lip . . .
>
> I shall not forget the light
> of recognition in your eyes
>
> your name is New Beginning
> I love you, New Beginning,

wrote the late Paul Goodman after one of the big demonstrations in Washington during the Viet Nam war, in a poem
that typically does not isolate the personal from the social.

One kind of political poem demonstrates active empathy—the projection of a nonparticipant into the experience
of others very different from himself; for example in Heine's
famous poem about the Silesian weavers, one seems indeed
to hear not Heine's voice but that of the weavers themselves.
Yet at the same time how intimately it expresses his own
bitterness. But more typical of contemporary poetry are the
poems being written about prisons by prisoners; about racial
or sexual injustices by people who suffer them and engage
in struggle against them; about the horrors of war, not only
by soldiers (which is nothing new) but also by activists
against war, and about pollution of natural resources by
people who in their daily lives work at organic farming, at
conservation, or at litigation in behalf of the preservation of
the environment; or who join in antinuclear and other pro-

test actions and civil disobedience. It seems as if the sense of urgency, indeed of desperation, that permeates our lives, has the effect, if it does not paralyze us, of intensifying and diversifying our activities; it is not enough to write *or* act, we feel we must do both. And this means that there's less distance between event and poem, less time for reflection, more immediacy. These are neutral factors in themselves— they may be used to advantage or disadvantage.

The world-famous Turkish poet Nazim Hikmet, who spent more than seventeen years of his life in jail as a political prisoner, wrote a number of powerful poems in his confinement, poems which notably combine the context of oppression with the unquenchable love of life that characterized him.[1] A young Mexican-American, Jimmy Santiago Baca, whose first book[2] was also written in jail, presents another example of a poetry of direct personal experience which is both political and lyrical. Such poems are not didactic in an obvious way, not hortatory; they don't tell one what to do. (Though Hikmet does give advice). But Bertholt Brecht, whose name can't fail to come to mind if one is looking for a tradition in engaged poetry, had no compunction about being didactic. These three writers provide an instructive range of possible approaches: Brecht's poems are dry, crisp, they give one curt warnings, they are marching orders. Hikmet is relaxed, expansive, generous—his confidence not only in himself but in humanity is unshaken by a life that would have embittered or crushed most people. Jimmy Santiago Baca, at twenty-five, exhorts not others but himself; full of a rich, sensuous, romantic talent, his poems let us participate in a process of personal growth and developing consciousness, not without bitterness and rage but not dominated by those emotions. All seem to me to *be* political poems despite their differences.

[1]See *Things I Didn't Know I Loved:* Selected Poems of Nazim Hikmet translated by Randy Blasing and Mutlu Konuk (New York, Persea Books, 1975).

[2]*Immigrants in Our Own Land* by Jimmy Santiago Baca (Louisiana State University Press, 1979).

"I'd like to know if political poems have brought about any changes," said my friend who wanted reassurance that there was a tradition behind him. I don't think one can accurately measure the historical effectiveness of a poem; but one does know, of course, that books influence individuals; and individuals, although they are part of large economic and social processes, influence history. Every mass is after all made up of millions of individuals. Many forces combine to push now one individual, now another, into prominence at certain crucial moments. The flash of a poem onto the mind's screen, a novel imaginatively entered and lived in at an open time in that person's life, certainly can be among those forces. A famous example of the historical impact of literature is that of Turgenev reading *Uncle Tom's Cabin* and, at least partially because he was moved by it, (and with all its flaws it *is* moving), creating *A Sportsman's Notebook*, which in turn was at least one of the factors that impelled the relatively liberal Tsar Alexander to free the serfs. Ford Madox Ford has a little fantasy on this theme. First he notes that,

> It is to be remembered that Alexander ordered the emancipation of the serfs three days after he had finished reading *A Sportsman's Sketches.* . . .

and then he goes on to imagine,

> the humane Tsar lying down on a couch. . . . I don't know why I imagine him lying down . . . perhaps because humane people when they want to enjoy themselves over a good read in a book always lie down . . . the humane Tsar, then, lying down with the *Sportsman's Sketches* held up to his eyes began to read what Turgenev had observed when shooting partridges over dogs . . . with the ineffable scapegrace serf Yermolai at his heels. . . . And suddenly the Tsar was going through the endless forests and over the endless moors. He had the smell of the pines and heather in his nostrils, the sunbaked Russian earth beneath his feet. . . .

Yermolai did not have the second gun as ready as he should; Yermolai had not even loaded the second gun; Yermolai, the serf, had lagged behind; serf Yermolai had disappeared altogether; he had found a wild bees' nest in a hollow tree; he was luxuriously supping honey ignoring the beestings. . . . And suddenly the Tsar himself was Yermolai. . . . He was a serf who might be thrashed, loaded with chains, banished to a hopeless district a thousand miles away, put to working in the salt mines. . . . The Tsar was supping the heather-scented brown honey in the hot sun. . . . He saw his Owner approaching. His Owner was fortunately a softy. Still it was disagreeable to have the Owner cold to him. . . . And quickly the Tsar sent his eyes over the country, through the trees in search of a hut. If he saw a hut he would remember the story of its idiotic owners. He would tell the idiotic story to the Owner and in listening to it the Owner would become engrossed in the despairing ruin of those idiotic creatures and would forget to be displeased and the Tsar would have two undeserved pork chops and the remains of a bottle of champagne that night in the woodlodge.

And so the Tsar would become a woodcutter in danger of being banished for cutting the wrong trees, and a small landowner being ruined by his own ignorance and the shiftlessness of his serfs . . . and a house-serf dressed as a footman with plush breeches to whom his Owner was saying with freezing politeness; "Brother, I regret it. But you have again forgotten to chill the Beaujolais. You must prepare yourself to receive fifty lashes. . . ." And the Tsar would be Turgenev shuddering over the Owner's magnificently appointed table whilst outside the footman was receiving the fifty lashes. . . . And Alexander II would become the old, fat old maid, knitting whilst her companion read Pushkin to her, and crying over romantic passages and refusing to sell Anna Nicolaevna to Mr. Schubin, the neighbouring noble landowner who had fallen incomprehensibly in love with Anna

Nicolaevna. . . . And the Autocrat of All the Russias would find himself being the serf-girl Anna Nicolaevna, banished into the dreadful Kursk district because the incomparable noble landowner Mr. Schubin had fallen in love with her. . . . And the great bearded Autocrat with the hairy chest would be twisting his fingers in his apron and crying . . . crying . . . crying. . . . And saying, "Is it possible that God and the Tsar permit such things to be?"

And so, on the third day, the Tsar stretches out his hand for his pen . . . and just those things would never be any more. . . . There would be other bad things, but not just those because the world had crept half a hair's breadth nearer to civilization. . . .

. . . You may imagine how Turgenev's eyes stood out of his head on the day when he met Mrs. Harriet Beecher Stowe . . . who for her part had never been below the Mason and Dixon line . . . and who was introduced to him as being the heroine that had made the chains to fall from the limbs of the slaves of a continent. . . . He said that she seemed to him to be a modest and sensible person. . . . Perhaps the reader will think out for himself all that that amazing meeting signified.

Still another aspect of the tradition of political poetry is the way in which, just as songs do, it can express and heighten a shared emotion, intensifying morale rather than making converts. "To have embodied hope for many people, even for one minute," said Neruda, "is something unforgettable and profoundly touching for any poet." The response to contemporary engaged poems, I have found, is frequently from readers who find their own experience confirmed in them, and from others who discover in such poems something that culminates a process of thought and feeling already under way, and propels them into some form of action.

I've been talking all this while about poetry that is political; that's all very well, but the question of whether it is poetic remains unanswered. Now we must enquire of our inner Sphinx, What does "poetic" *mean?* To which, of course, our Sphinx will disdain a direct response—yet perhaps a faint smile, a flutter of its eyelashes, a brief passage of Sphinx tongue over Sphinx lips, may indicate that the *senses* are implicated. The Sphinx tail may lash a little—a sure sign that the *aesthetic faculty* is involved.

We are to ask, then, of the political poem (which in our time means relatively brief, and therefore ostensibly lyric, poems that deal nevertheless with social observations and even opinions, such as the lyric used not typically to deal with) that it affect our senses and engage our aesthetic response just as much as one with whose content—spring, love, death, a rainbow—we can have no argument. Children of the twentieth century that we are, the old topics may indeed only exacerbate our *angst,* and we are long used to a wider and gloomier range. Yet we are still inheritors of the Romantic emphasis on the individual and upon individual epiphanies. And in habitually equating the poetic with the lyrical perhaps we are, after all, correct; but we have come to identify the short poem with the lyric *even when it lacks lyricism,* and consequently, often fail to recognize the lyric *spirit* if it appears in company with the didactic. Thus a totally unlyrical poem passes muster, even though it is flat and banal, merely because it is short and deals with a noncontroversial personal experience; whereas the passionate partisanship of a political poem may block the reader from responding to its sensuous and emotive power simply because expectation does not link these elements with political convictions. That is one reaction. More dangerous to poetry is the contrasting assumption by partisan poets and their constituencies that the subject matter carries so strong an emotive charge in itself that it is unnecessary to remember poetry's roots in song, magic, and the high craft that makes itself felt as exhilarating beauty even when the content voices rage or utters a grim warning. The results of this assumption give rise to much understandable distrust and prejudice.

126

No matter how much validity and courage the poet's opinions have, no matter that he or she may have died for them or gone into bitter exile on their account, "unless" (wrote William Carlos Williams), "unless all this is already in his writing—in the materials and structure of it—he might better have been a cowhand. . . . Everything else is secondary, but for the artist *that,* which has made the greatest art one and permanent, that continual reassertion of structure, is first. . . . The altered structure of the inevitable revolution must be *in* the poem, in it. Made of it. It must shine in the structural body of it. . . . Then, indeed, propaganda can be thoroughly welcomed . . . for by that it has been transmuted into the materials of art. It has no life unless to live or die judged by an artist's standards. But if, by imposing . . . a depleted, restrictive and unrealized form, the propagandist thinks he can make what he has to say convincing by merely filling in that wooden structure with some ideas he wants to put over—he turns up not only as no artist but a weak fool."[3]

Political poetry, said Neruda, is never what young poets should begin with. "Political poetry" (he added) "is more deeply emotional than any other except love poetry. You must have traversed the whole of poetry before you become a political poet."[4] Clearly, then, political poetry does not obey special laws but must be subject to those which govern *every* kind of poetry. Paul Valéry was speaking of poetry's essential nature when he said, "Poetry must extend over the whole being; it stimulates the muscular organization by its rhythms, it frees or unleashes the verbal faculties, ennobling their whole action; it regulates our depths, for poetry aims to arouse . . . the unity or harmony of the living person, an extraordinary unity that shows itself when

[3]"Against the Weather" (1939), in *The Selected Essays of William Carlos Williams* (New York, New Directions, 1969).

[4]*Seven Voices,* interview with Rita Guibert (New York, Alfred A. Knopf, 1972).

127

a person is possessed by an intense feeling that leaves none of his powers disengaged."[5]

What those of us whose lives are permeated by a sense of unremitting political emergency, and who are at the same time writers of poetry, most desire in our work, I think, is to attain to such osmosis of the personal and the public, of assertion and of song, that no one would be able to divide our poems into categories. The didactic would be lyrical, the lyrical would be didactic. That is, at any rate, my own probably unattainable goal. . . .

To sum up: (1) Politics is a subject many poets and poems, including some of the greatest, have treated throughout European history. It is no more alien to the medium than any other human concern. (2) The suspicion with which political or social content is often regarded is a modern phenomenon and arises from a narrow and mistaken idea of the poem as always a private expression of emotion which the reader is permitted to overhear, and that therefore the hortatory or didactic is an unsuitable mode of address for poets. (3) The political poetry of contemporary America is more often written by active participants in political and social struggle than it was in the past. (4) Many writers of political poetry persist in supposing the emotive power of their subject alone is sufficient to make their poems poetic. This accounts for a lot of semidoggerel. But the fact of their direct involvement in the situations about which they write may sometimes be an advantage if they are also really poets, imparting a concreteness to their passion and an authenticity to their metaphors. (5) Poetry can indirectly have an effect upon the course of events by awakening pity, terror, compassion and the conscience of leaders; and by strengthening the morale of persons working for a common cause. (6) For political poetry, as for any other kind, the *sine qua non* is that it elicit "the poetic emotion"—that which Valéry describes as a condition "in which . . . responses are ex-

[5]In Paul Valéry, *The Art of Poetry* (New York, Houghton Mifflin, 1939).

changes between all [the reader's] sensitive and rhythmic powers." "The poet's profession," Valéry claims, "is to find by good fortune and to seek with industry the production of those special forms of language" which set up "this harmonious exchange between impression and expression."[6] And political verses attain to that exchange—that is, to the condition of poetry—by the same means as any other kind: good faith, passionate conviction and, in equal measure, the precise operations of the creative imagination which sifts and sorts, leaps and pounces upon, strokes and shoves into a design the adored *words* that are the treasure of a faculty in love with its medium, even upon what Hikmet called the very "edge of darkness."

[6]In Valéry, *The Art of Poetry*.

Poetry and Revolution: Neruda Is Dead—Neruda Lives

Political poetry is more deeply emotional than any other except love poetry.
—Pablo Neruda

People who are "apolitical" or those who deplore Neruda's political affiliations, tend to express their admiration for his lyricism as if it were quite separable from his convictions; while those whose political stance is similar to his applaud the "message" of his polemical poems, and ignore their other elements and all the rest of his work. It is ironic that this is so, for Neruda's genius lay precisely in his having frequently fused the polemical and lyrical impulses into an unusual degree of unity. One may think, in seeking comparisons, of a Ritsos or a Nazim Hikmet; but English-language poets present few relevant examples.

In Ezra Pound, for instance, though one is conscious of a didactic temperament in back of most of his writings, there is frequently the feeling of alternation, of deliberate, antiphonal contrast, not only from canto to canto but within individual cantos, between passages of history recorded and passages evoking the timeless, the world of sky, sea, olive trees. William Carlos Williams' few classifiably political poems, such as "The Mind's Games" or "The Suckers," *are* simultaneously lyrical and polemic, but they represent only a small part of his work (though all of his work is imbued with a social concern).

In the case of Neruda, however, although in most periods of his life one finds examples of individual poems one might place in distinct "lyric" or "polemic" categories, there is typically an interpenetration of the two forces throughout the larger part of his immense *oeuvre*.

Undoubtedly the essential reason why he was able to create "political" poems that are supremely and unassailably

---

Reprinted from the *Real Paper*, Boston, Massachusetts, 1973.

poems, was that he experienced in his own life that lengthy and complex movement towards and preparation for them of which he was himself to write later:

> I would never advise [young poets] to begin with political poetry. Political poetry should emanate from profound emotion and convictions. Political poetry is more deeply emotional than any other except love poetry and it cannot be forced without becoming vulgar and unacceptable. You must have traversed the whole of poetry before you become a political poet. And a political poet must be ready to take all the blame heaped on him for "betraying poetry and literature by serving a definite cause." Therefore political poetry must arm itself internally with enough substance and content and emotional and intellectual richness to defy anything of the sort. It seldom succeeds.[1]

By the time Neruda experienced living in Spain during the two years of the Republic that immediately preceded the Civil War, he was thirty years old and was already a poet of achievement who had been writing since boyhood. In Spain he found a land he loved as he loved Chile itself.

> How, even to tears, how with my soul I love
> your hard earth, your humble bread,
> and your poor—how, in my being's deepest crevice
> there grows the lost flower
> of your age-wrinkled, changeless villages . . .

There he found friends and fellow poets of the closest congeniality—"a brotherhood of poets"—about one of whom he wrote, in "To Miguel Hernandez, Murdered in the Prisons of Spain,"

---

[1] From *Seven Voices,* interview with Rita Guibert (New York, Alfred A. Knopf, 1972). I have inserted the quotation marks I believe Neruda intended, but which, as often happens in the transcription of recorded speech, were omitted.

You know now, my son, all that I couldn't do, you know
that for me, in all of poetry,
you were the blue fire . . .

And there he underwent, before the new Spain was smashed
by war, the experience of a positive, nonalienating society.
After the mere week I spent in Hanoi in the fall of 1972, I
can form some conception of how impressive that must
have been. Indeed, for Neruda—whose time in Spain at the
period of its awakening was so much longer, and for whom,
as a Latin American, Spain was after all the "old country,"
its culture lying in back of his own country's culture, its
language his own language—it was decisive, a turning point
in his development.

Rather than throwing him back into the romantic melancholy of his youth, the disaster of the Spanish Civil War,
following as it did upon that vision of a just society, of
the possibility of the human communion, only made him
tighten the belt and clench the fists of his poetry. From then
on it was a consciously committed—though it never became
a narrow—poetry. (Incidentally, if in "Let the Railsplitter
Awake" Neruda mistook Stalin for a man of nobility and
integrity, so might any of us have done, up to a certain point
in history. It was a mistake Neruda made in generosity of
spirit. Many people, including myself, are willing to forgive
Ezra Pound at least *some* of his lapses from sound judgement and to see, for instance, that at least to begin with, he
really thought Mussolini was a sort of Confucian leader, a
responsible and humane "father of his people"—even if we
ourselves would not want a fatherly leader in any case, and
even if we blame him, a man of such brilliant intelligence in
certain areas, for what can only seem like stupidity in continuing to cling to that belief in the face of so much contrary
evidence.[2] All the more, then, should we avoid self-

[2]This was written in 1973. Things I've read and heard since about Ezra
Pound and fascism make me feel considerably less forbearing towards him.
He seems, alas, to have been much more consciously and viciously in tune
with fascistic thought and practice than I was willing to believe (1981).

righteousness about a misapprehension Neruda shared with many excellent people of his generation.)

Neruda's revolutionary politics is founded in revolutionary love—the same love Che Guevara spoke of. Revolutionary love subsumes a bitter anger against oppression and oppressors.

I do not want to shake hands all round and forget;
I do not want to touch their bloodstained hands;
I want punishment.

I do not want them sent off somewhere as ambassadors
nor covered up here at home till it blows over.

I want to see them judged,
here, in the open air, in this very spot . . .[3]

But revolutionary love is not merely anthropocentric; it reaches out to the rest of creation. Neruda's celebration of animals—

If I could talk with birds,
with oysters and small lizards . . .
If I could discuss things with cats,
if chickens would listen to me!

of vegetables—

The artichoke
soft-hearted
upright in armor
constructs
a small cupola . . .
The cabbage
gives itself over
to trying on skirts . . .

[3]Translation by Robert Brittain, *Masses and Mainstream*, 1950.

of the earth—

> . . . The solitary peace of field and rock,
> the marshy borders of the river,
> the larch tree's fragrance,
> the living wind like a heart pulsing
> in the crowded restlessness
> of the great araucaria . . .

or—

> And suddenly I go to the window. It's a square
> of transparency, a pure distance
> of grass and pinnacles; so I go on working, among
> the things I love: waves, rocks, wasps,
> with a drunken salt-sea happiness . . .

These celebrations are not irrelevant, dispensable, coincidental to his revolutionary convictions, but an integral part of them. Archetypal Man, servant and sufferer, builder and creator, he who moves the stones to build cities and monuments, and outlives them, Juan Coldeater, Juan Naked Foot, is brother to the ox and the panther, to the grain of wheat and the rain.

Desite the deplorable inadequacies of some of the currently available translations (when I participated in a recently presented program, "Neruda/Chile" I found, even with my far from perfect knowledge of Spanish, glaring errors in poems I was assigned to read, and had to make hasty corrections) we have in Neruda a rich source of life—a poetry capable of "increasing the sense of being alive," which Wallace Stevens said was one of the basic things poetry should do. If poetry must "teach, or move, or delight," in Neruda we have a poet who does all three. He teaches us, for instance, who the enemy is—i.e., not merely the U.S.A. but all corporate colonialism: ". . . an empire which sets the table, and serves up the meals and the bullets . . ." And he does so as unequivocally as a film maker—

I think, for instance, of the Costa Gavras film about Latin America, *State of Siege,* which is simultaneously clear, uncompromising, and dramatic. He moves us, with the intensity and depth of his love and grief and compassion:

> . . . Cristóbal, this memento is for you.
> For your comrades, fellow-shovellers
> into whose breasts the acid enters,
> and the lethal gases . . .
>   for all of you
> lighter-men of the bay,
> work-blackened boatmen, my gaze
> goes with yours this workday,
> and my soul is a lifted shovel
> loading and unloading blood and snow
> beside you, lives lived in the wasteland.

And he delights us, awakening our own capacity for seeing the wonder of what lies about us, as he shares his own keen delight in its glorious multiplicity.

> I want all the hands of man
> to pile up mountains of bread
> and gather up
> all the fish of the sea,
> all the olives
> of the olive tree, all
> the love still not awakened,
> and leave a gift
> in each of the hands
> of day.

Neruda is the great political poet *par excellence,* the one who demonstrates that there is no inherent contradiction between the spheres of poetry and (revolutionary) politics, the one who brings home to us that indeed it is their basic relatedness that is inherent: that a profound and generous passion for life, for all of earthlife, is the source of both.

135

From a Torture Cell

This piece was originally accompanied by a list of persons to whom readers could address protests and petitions on Kim Chi Ha's behalf, and included some topical references which have become irrelevant. It should be noted that American PEN and Amnesty International have, since 1975, stepped up their efforts on behalf of political prisoners everywhere. Yet imprisonment and torture continue unabated; and when the situation appears to improve in one country, in another it deteriorates.

D. L., 1981

"Aah. Now I have it," says the King in one of Kim Chi Ha's fables, who can't understand why the people—whose livers he wishes to devour "on doctor's orders"—show no fear of him and even call out "Go to Hell!" and "Stop telling lies" when he demands that they slit their bellies open for his benefit, and pretends that he will eventually give them back—"Aah. . . . Your fearlessness comes from . . . that cursed Jesus,

He pretended to bear all the burdens and agony of human
                                                                    beings.
He was humbly born, a carpenter.
But he was ambitious.
By calling himself the Son of Heaven.
He misled the world and confused the people by means
     of promises and rumors.
He deserved blame and he deserved death.
He lacked due appreciation for the power of Rome.
It's not Jesus the people should depend on, but the six-
                                                                    shooter."

Written for *American Poetry Review,* a literary tabloid.

And he not only fires his six-shooter but brings to bear all his royal rifles, machine guns, cannons, tanks, and planes—yet fails to destroy the bleeding but nevertheless inviolate small statue of Jesus he so fears.

Sometimes, ironically, the distant and exotic seems to act upon the phrenological bump of indignation when home-grown outrages fail to do so. Kim has said of himself, "I'm not a Solzhenitsyn, you know . . ." We have here a person who takes no personal pride and pleasure in martyrdom—yet is being martyred in a bloodiness to which the Solzhenit-syn affair cannot be compared. Perhaps people's will to attempt useful action on Kim's behalf (as distinct from an inactive "sympathy" which will do nothing to save life and limb) may best be stimulated by trying to give some idea of what kind of a writer he is (though of course, as he would undoubtedly be the first to agree, the moral obligation to decry torture, persecution, oppression of all kinds, *ought* to be felt as keenly in behalf of the inarticulate, the obscure and ungifted, as for the most talented).

The English translations in *Cry of the People and Other Poems*[1] are unfortunately the well-meant but somewhat in-ept, and inevitably hasty, work of a group of his supporters who, as they themselves state disarmingly in a prefatory note, "are not poets." The English is, on a basic level, some-what less than adequate—viz., "trouts" for "trout," "Feo-dora" for "Fedora" (hat), an inexplicable "grande" for "grand," "brooch" misspelled "broach," and so on. That several hands undertook the task and did not always work in aesthetic harmony is likewise evident. In a long poem (the title poem) that is uncompromisingly topical, such antique rhetoric as "Frame not the innocent . . ." "Create not inci-dents . . ." etc., are unfortunate renderings. Nevertheless there emerges, to the reader willing to expend a little em-pathic energy on these poems, a voice—the voice of a poet. It is, it seems to me, a rather Mayakovskyan voice, having that tone which, despite equally poor translations of Maya-kovsky, we know as a peculiar blending of lyricism and

[1]Autumn Press, Tokyo.

137

satire: Kim is said to think of himself as a humorist. In disclaiming the role of "a Solzhenitsyn" he said, (in an interview), "my problem is nothing . . . I'm Kim Chi Ha. Not a tragic figure. A comic, like these bad teeth of mine. I feel happy in any situation." But at the same time (1972) he spoke of his "pity, deep pity, for the government. . . . But I think when one cannot manage power, one must give it up." And: "one hundred and seventy of my friends were tortured in March. But that's not new. They tortured them this year and two years ago and five years ago. It's a part of life for those around me. Sunday is my confirmation day and I must forgive them [the government and the Korean CIA] but I can't. Even after I'm dead I'll not be able to forgive them. I want to, but I can't." While Kim, in some poems, appears to fuse the lyrical and satirical elements, he also writes poems that are not in the least satirical. The first third of the book presents "straight" elegiac lyrics which these lines may represent:

> Farewell, farewell
> Passing the low silvery hills,
> Passing the dancing flowers
> In the quivering shade of the grove.
> Vanishing city
> Where my bloody youth was buried,
> Farewell.
> Winds fluttering restlessly
> Among the fallen shacks,
> Among the collapsed fences.
> Sunrays yelling, tearing apart the yellow earth.
> Heavy silence
> Suppresses the crying all around,
> And in the heart, sadness burns . . .

More dynamic, and more indicative of the poet's originality and strength, "The Sun":

The sun was only as wide as a man's foot.
Not a single person knows of the cyclone approaching,

138

In the fields, however,
The leaves dance to and fro in the wind—
The wind has been known to move mountains.
The waves are not quiet for a moment.
Do you know that the blade has at last corroded?
You would not know though the wind howled by.
The sun was only as wide as a man's foot: idiot sun!
The fire-tempered steel melts in the fire;
The water reared city falls asleep in the water.
No one knows, now
On the streets, every night,
People let out cries from their nightmares.
Sometimes people go mad! Do you know?
You probably don't know that the blade has corroded.
Do you know or don't you?
Was there ever a night when you were not whipped?
There was probably never a day when rocks did not fly at
    you.
Never a day, of course! . . .

The second third of the book consists of satirical poems
that often—in these versions at any rate—are formally prose
parables or fables, rather than strictly poems. It is in these
that I see a *fusion* of lyric and satiric—the lyric (aside, of
course, from whatever sonic felicities may exist in the
Korean) residing in the surreal images and situations. In one
such bizarre fable, "The Origin of a Sound," the protagonist,
a kind of easygoing Everyman, "an innocent and decent
man who could live without laws telling him how to behave," but who is consistently luckless, at last is driven to
exclaim, "What a bitch this world is!" and for this well-
justified complaint is arrested, and accused of "standing on
his own two feet and spreading groundless rumors." This
turns out (elaborated upon) to be a crime against the state,
and so the following sentence is pronounced:

That from the body of the accused shall be cut off
    immediately, after the closing of this court,
One head, so that he may not be able to think up or spread
    groundless rumors anymore,

Two legs, so that he may not insolently stand on
        the ground on his own two feet anymore,
One penis and two testicles, so that he may not
        produce another, seditious like himself.
And after this is done, since there exists a great
        danger of his attempting to
resist, his two hands shall be tied together behind
        his back, his trunk shall be
tied with a wet leather vest, and his throat shall
        be stuffed with a hard and longlasting
        voice-preventing tool, and then he shall be
        placed in confinement
for five hundred years from this date.

"No!" he cries out.
Snip
"No, my penis is gone!" snip snap
"My testicles too, no no" crack,
"My neck, oh my neck is gone." hack hack
"No, my two legs also gone" Handcuffs, leather
So they brutally shoved the fellow An-Do
        into a solitary cell.
Clink
The locks are locked . . .

An-Do continues to cry out in protest, and tells the wild
geese to tell his mother that he swears to return, "even if I
am dead . . . whatever happens."

And then An-Do wanted to sing, but he had no
        head. He wanted to cry, but he had no eyes.
He wanted to shout, but he had no voice.
With neither voice nor tears, he cried soundlessly
        day after day, night after night, shedding
        blood-red tears,
Crying soundlessly in the depths of his soul, crying
        no, no, no.
Roll,
Roll your trunk.

140

An-Do rolled over and over,
Back and forth from wall to wall, Kung, back
    and forth from wall to wall, continuously,
    Kung
And one more time Kung and again
Kung
Kung
Kung.

And the poem ends with the revelation that the mysterious sound, *Kung*, which has been troubling all hearers, is made by the endless rolling back and forth of An-Do's headless, limbless, faithful trunk. And those who know this "as they whisper this story in the streets of Seoul, have a strange fire in their eyes."

Finally, there is a title poem, a long didactic piece in two-line stanzas (one wonders if in the original they are rhymed couplets) which strikes me as less aesthetically successful, though it was considered all too successful as political statement and was the cause of his arrest in 1974. In it he deals in detail with act after act of the Park regime; its brutal exploitation of the people and the land is not generalized about merely, but referred to in inexorable specifics. A few examples: the stanza that tells us, "For the export trade in stone/Even tombstones are not sacred" carries a note, "A reference to the Yi dynasty tombstones that have been sold to the Japanese for use in the latter's stone gardens." Others need no notes:

In collaboration with oil men,
Refineries are established;

Expressways are built
To consume more oil

and so on, until

Relying on imported oil,
Our coal mines left to rot;

141

Dependent on imports only,
Our own resources ignored;

Domestic industry lies desolate,
Dependence on foreign capital complete,

Bankrupt industry induced
To suck the blood of labor;

Pollution industries imported
The people choked to death . . .[2]

It is without a doubt a useful piece of writing, though it is
not poetry. And it becomes, towards its end, a rallying cry
that must indeed be an inspiration to those actively engaged
with Kim in a struggle against an oppression so heavy that,
for instance, in 1971, a worker, who had tried unsuccessfully
to organize Seoul's garment workers, burned himself to
death to protest Korean labor's inability to improve its conditions. But if we had only this poem to go by, we would not
think Kim a poet, though we would note his ability as a
polemicist, and appreciate his sheer courage. Fortunately
we have his other work too.

Kim is only thirty-four. He has already become a *voice of
the people*, a spokesman for inarticulate millions. His potential as a writer is strong. He could conceivably become a
world poet, a Nazim Hikmet or a Pablo Neruda. At the very
least, he is evidently a writer of originality, vigor, and that
courage to continue writing under the most dangerous circumstances, the thought of which makes one less than sympathetic to some of the so-called problems of many writers
in—or at least on the borders of—well-cushioned academia.
When one sees a picture of Kim tightly bound—even tighter
than Bobby Seale at Chicago—and thinks of the cruel tor-
tures he is right now enduring and of the great waste of gifts
his death would mean, it puts one in a rage. May all of us

[2]This last does in fact have a note: "The government's desire to promote
the expansion of the heavy and chemical industries has led it to permit
foreign enterprises to pollute the environment without restriction."

142

feel that rage and make it a rage fruitful in action; not one
that merely expends itself in useless internal bitterness. Don't
let Kim's own words fulfill their prophecy:

No going home,
even if you rise,
see the bloodstains on the wall,
hear the shrieks of ghosts come back
and tremble

The room with footsteps
heavy on the ceiling all night long,
back and forth,
faceless, disembodied laughter
comes mocking and arrogant from above.

I shall not return having once stepped into this place.

An Ally's Victim

Kim Chi Ha, the South Korean poet long imprisoned and tortured for his opposition to the brutal government of his country, was released from jail December 11, 1980. His precarious health and the fear that he could be re-arrested at any time (as happened after his "pardon" in 1974) temper one's relief at this good news. It will be important for international public opinion to maintain vigilance in his behalf.

I have written elsewhere about Kim Chi Ha's poetry,[1] which is a powerful contribution to world literature; and many readers will remember that Muriel Rukeyser wrote of him, in the prefatory note to her last major work, *The Gates*, "The poet has written his stinging work—like that of Burns or Brecht—and it has got under the skin of the highest officials." (In 1975, as president of American P.E.N., Rukeyser undertook a journey to Seoul in the hope of securing Kim Chi Ha's release by personally appealing to various officials, including Cabinet ministers and the Cardinal. The attempt failed.) With David McCann's sensitive translations and another volume, *The Gold Crowned Jesus and Other Writings*,[2] Kim Chi Ha's validity as a poet is well established; what I'd like to speak of here is his politics, for they show clearly, I think, the nobility and spirituality typical of the forces that the United States, by its support of regimes of repression and torture, actively helps to repress.

Written for *Worldview*, a weekly magazine of current affairs.

[1]In the preceding article and in the introduction to *The Middle Hour, Selected Poems of Kim Chi Ha*, translated by David R. McCann (New York, Human Rights Publishing Co., 1980).

[2]Translated by Choy Sun Kim and Shelley Killen (New York, Orbis Books, 1978).

Kim Chi Ha, along with other protestors of various religious denominations, had been accused of being a communist infiltrator of religious groups. This was part of the Park regime's policy, which, by labelling all democratic and liberalizing efforts as part of a "communist conspiracy," aimed to frighten any "centrist" or politically naive Koreans and to weaken international (Western-aligned) sympathy for the opposition. The post-Park regime, under Chon Doo Hwan, is obviously only a step from terrible to more terrible, and follows the same path.

What Kim Chi Ha is actually is a remarkably undogmatic Catholic—which is to say, he is a Christian first and a Catholic second. In his "Declaration of Conscience" (included in *The Middle Hour* as an afterword) he has written,

> I will never become fettered by any dogma or creed. Nor ever yield in my mind and soul to intimidation. I am ideologically open-minded. . . . I have never found any single system of thought logically convincing. . . . All human beings have an inherent right to choose their own intellectual and spiritual values and to be guided by their own conscience.
>
> I want to be identified with the oppressed, the exploited, the suffering, and the despised common people. I want my life and my love to be dedicated, passionate, and manifested in practical ways.
>
> I became a Catholic because for me Catholicism nurtures and spreads a valid hope for the redemption of human society. It offers a way in which not only spiritual and material burdens can be lifted from the common people but also a way for oppression to be ended by the salvation of *both* the oppressor and the oppressed.
>
> . . . Democracy is indivisible from an uncompromising rejection of oppression. . . . Democracy upholds the right of revolution . . . the ongoing and inextinguishable possibility of overthrowing illegitimate authority. . . .

I want the fulfillment of real democracy, nothing more, nothing less. In this sense I am a radical democrat and libertarian. I am also a Catholic and one of the oppressed citizens of the Republic of Korea who loathes privilege, corruption, and dictatorial power. This defines "my political beliefs."

But having introduced the theme of revolution, Kim Chi Ha does not side-step the issue of violence. He speaks of it openly and, most importantly, acknowledges his own ambivalence about it—an ambivalence unavoidable, it seems to me, by all who want to see, and participate in, the establishment of peace and justice, but who at the same time recognize the terrible dilemma presented by the use of violent means to obtain those desired conditions—the danger of becoming that which one loathes because the means are not consonant with the end.

When the violence of tyranny sustains oppression, [Kim says] the people's will is crushed, their best leaders are killed, and the rest are frightened into submission. The silence of "law and order" settles grimly across the land. Then an antithetical situation comes into being and the *people's* violence erupts and shatters this deathly "order." To a degree I approve of this kind of violence. No, that is not strong enough. I *must* approve it. I loathe the violence of oppression and welcome the violence of resistance. I reject dehumanizing violence and accept the violence that restores human dignity. It could justly be called a violence of love.

Violence and destruction bring suffering and hardship. But we must sometimes cause and endure suffering. Never is this more justified than when the people are somnolent in silent submission, when they cannot be awakened from their torpor. To preach "nonviolence" at such a time leaves them defenseless before their oppressors. Ghandi and Franz Fanon agonized over this dilemma. Father Camillo Torres took a rifle and joined the people in their armed revolt. He died in battle in their company, his own rifle never fired. I do not know if his beliefs and actions were correct or not, but the purity of his love always moves me to tears.

I welcome the violence of love, yet I am also an ally of true nonviolence. The revolution I support would be a synthesis of true nonviolence and an agonized violence of love. But to arrive at the ultimate revolution, in which nonviolence does not involve cowardly compromise and the people's violence does not dishonor the bonds of love and fall into carnage, humanity must undergo an increasing spiritual renewal and the masses must experience world-wide awakening.

Kim openly acknowledges his consciousness of contradictions:

The more I search for answers, the more contradictory ideas I find. Must revolution reject religion and religion be the foe of revolution? I think the answer is "No." Perhaps by this reply alone I could not be a Marxist-Leninist. But the Marxist dictum that religion is the opiate of the masses is only a partial truth applicable to one aspect of religion.

When a people have been brutally oppressed and exploited for a long time they lose their passion for justice and their affection for their fellow beings. Committed only to self-survival they sink into individualistic materialism. Their near-crazed resentment and rage at social and economic conditions, diverted into frustration and self-hatred, is repeatedly dissipated in fragmented aberrant actions.

[And] the high priests and Pharisees defuse the people's resentment and moral indignation with sentimental charity. The god of philanthropy serves the oppressors by changing the people into a mob of beggars.

Kim writes of his "long arduous search for personal and for political answers" and tells us that he sympathized with efforts to combine Marxist social reform and Christian beliefs in the 1972 Santiago Declaration of Christian Socialism.

The synthesis draws from diverse sources, such as the adaptation of the teachings of Marx and Jesus. Marx's contribution is a structural epistemology which maintains that social oppression blocks humanity's liberation. From the teachings of Jesus is taken a humanism which advocates love for all people and the sanctity of humanity, and an emphasis on spiritual rebirth and truth as the way to liberation.

The synthesis seeks to unify and integrate these concepts. It is not a mechanical process of grafting parts of Marxism onto Christianity. The union produces something entirely new. And this new synthesis is still amorphous, is still forming.

. . . my participation since 1971 in the Korean Christian movement for human rights . . . convinced me that the Korean tradition of resistance and revolution, with its unique vitality under the incredibly repressive circumstances prevailing here, is precious material for a new form of human liberation. This rich lode will be of special value to the Third World. Shaped and enhanced by the tools of liberation theology, our experiences may inspire new forms of *Missio Dei* in the grim struggle of the South Korean people.

This then is the kind of person who is imprisoned and tortured by one of America's allies. If a majority of those who, naively supposing that it will restore buying power to the dollar, voted-in a Congress headed by an ignorant movie sheriff—if these ordinary and for the most part good-natured Americans really understood that the United States, under Democrats and Republicans alike, routinely assists in the destruction of people of Kim's caliber, would they not be shocked? Or am I being even more naive in thinking that they would be? Kim Chi Ha himself has written that, "the common people I have known are trustworthy and admirable. And they are endowed with a vital inherent intelligence." If that is true of the people of the United States also, then their poor political judgement must be attributed to ignorance—an ignorance for which not only the media but "liberal intellectuals," privileged people who have more than average access to varied sources of information, must be considered at least partially responsible. We don't do enough to disseminate whatever better knowledge of current affairs (and other matters) we may possess.

It was in May of 1975 that Kim Chi Ha—thirty-four, the father of a baby boy (he had been pardoned and freed for a while after his earlier imprisonment, only to be re-arrested in 1974 and given a life sentence), and ill with a recurrence of tuberculosis—wrote in a postscript to his *Declaration of Conscience,*

> I am not allowed to receive visitors or mail, or even read the Bible. I have been forbidden to write anything. I cannot move around much. This underground cramped cell is scarcely seven by seven.
>
> I sit here in the dark thinking about the uncertain future. But prison has not dimmed my spirits. These miserable conditions and the endless waiting have made me more determined than ever.
>
> I feel a quiet composure, almost serenity. But I am very anxious about what might happen to the individuals involved in making this statement public. My friends, please help these good people.
>
> Do not grieve for me. We will surely see each other soon.

Kim Chi Ha has been freed; but South Korea's jails are still full, C.I.A.-trained torturers continue to ply their trade there and in other countries; the lists of the "disappeared" grow longer.[3] At a time when, in my opinion, a first priority for any responsible person should be to do all in his or her power to stop the acceleration of the arms race and of

[3]And now (summer of 1981) U.S. arms, advisers, and Green Berets in El Salvador are openly re-enacting the events of the early 1960s in Vietnam in support of a government which massacres its own population.

policies that can only result in global catastrophe, it is vitally important to recognize that these victims of terror and oppression do not constitute an entirely separate issue. The institutionalized violence which condemns them to torture is an expression of the same insane greed for power which develops and stockpiles genocidal weapons and is leading us towards Armegeddon. We cannot hope to find the moral energy to prevent the horrors we dread for the future without also working to eliminate the present hell in which so many languish.

IV POLITICAL COMMENTARY

Solzhenitsyn Reconsidered, 1974

I have hesitated before including this article, written in February 1974 for the Boston weekly Real Paper, *and full of then topical references which now seem positively antique. Yet I decided in its favor, because it does make some points that go beyond its dated particulars. Priorities continue to be ranged irrationally: what people get indignant about is most frequently not what is ethically the worst, nor even what really threatens the quality of their own lives the most. I will not specify what seem to me to be the analogies, seven years later, with the instances I gave in 1974, or this note will quickly seem equally dismissible. But surely readers will not find it difficult to supply their own list of such analogies. I have, however, added a few notes to the text.*

D. L., 1981.

I've been increasingly perturbed lately by what seems to me a new level of ignorance and indifference to certain pressing problems. It's an indifference on the part of people who, during the sixties and until a year ago, were in some degree seriously concerned about civil rights, the war, Third World struggles, etc.

It is no news to any of us, alas, that once the Vietnam Peace Treaty, so called, was signed and U.S. troops and POWs returned, all but the most active and dedicated anti-war activists sighed with relief, over-ready to believe that the war was over. I was made sharply aware of that when, last spring [1973], I put on a mixed media presentation on North Vietnam as a benefit for the Wounded Knee Defense Fund. The presentation had previously drawn rather large and keenly interested audiences, but I suddenly found myself with small, merely polite audiences who seemed to feel Vietnam was past history and the American Indian Movement no concern of theirs. As for drawing any parallels between "pacification" programs in South East Asia and events in Indian history, I could not even get people to argue about it. [*Seven years later, how many people remember that "pacification" was the term cynically used by the Pentagon to describe the attempt to destroy Vietnamese morale by systematically destroying the civilian population? Deforestation, the use of antipersonnel weapons to mutilate in complicated ways (thus requiring many individuals to care for each wounded one), the placing of whole regional populations of peasants in concentration camps, the napalming of villages and their inhabitants on suspicion of their sheltering guerillas—all this was known as "pacification." Certainly college students who were children during the war do not know this. And Wounded Knee? How many, reading this, know what happened in 1973 at the site of the 1890 massacre?*]

Yes, the apathy of this range of people—from McGovern supporters to anarchist artists, from ecology-conscious rural homesteaders to youthful revolutionaries—towards the ongoing fighting in S.E. Asia during the past year ['73–'74] is well known. It is, for instance, virtually impossible to raise any money these days for Medical Aid for Indochina, I'm told.

But despite this new wave of apathy it seems that there is always a certain basic quantity of free-floating indignation among us. What I am especially disturbed about is the way in which even this minimal resource is currently being applied to a problem which does not, by my reckoning, count as a priority: the plight of the Russian dissidents.

Now, I am talking about priorities. I do not for a moment mean to suggest that the troubles of Sakharov, Solzhenitsyn, Chukhovskaya, and many many others whose names we don't know, are unreal or unimportant. And freedom and justice are indivisible. But is it not hypocritical and unexcusably self-righteous for Americans—especially for those segments of American society which are not cut off from opportunities for informing themselves about all and any of the matters I have already mentioned—to put Russian prison camps, Russian censorship, and Russian bureaucratic crassness at the top of their altruistic worry-list, as they appear to be doing?

Solzhenitsyn himself, in reviving the history of Stalin's era of terror, is not claiming that the full horror of the camps has

154

been maintained unchanged throughout the intervening decades: rather he is pointing out that many of those who got their start under Stalin have remained in power and unrepentant (much as many Nazis and "good Germans" have undoubtedly done). No one, so far as I know, has proved that conditions in Soviet prisons and camps today, however bad, are such that it could be claimed they are worse than those in U.S. jails (which are not only brutal and racist, but include the terrifying mind-control programs such as the one at Dannemora, New York, in which all vestiges of the few civil rights a convict has are unequivocally lost). [*Public awareness of prison conditions has possibly increased somewhat since 1974; and there is a good deal of talk about "reforms." But for every small concession made, here and there, to humane values, ten horrors spring up elsewhere. With the acceleration of cuts in social services of all kinds and the still rising cost of living, the crime rate will obviously go up in the 1980s, with the resultant still greater overcrowding of already crowded jails. And a right wing administration will mete out ever harsher punishments, condoning existing conditions and allowing whatever minor alleviations may in some instances have been introduced (such as educational programs or improved visiting conditions) to deteriorate or be "de-funded."*]

And let us look at Solzhenitsyn himself: his hassles include nonpublication in his own country, and internal exile (*this was before his deportation*). These are certainly violations of his human rights. But can they be compared with the sufferings of a Martin Sostre? [*Martin Sostre (see p. 159) finally obtained his release in February 1976.*] And though it is right to protest those violations, would it not be well to remember Solzhenitsyn's point of view a little more accurately before we rush to make him into a culture hero?

In an article printed on the Op-Ed page of the *New York Times* on September 15, 1973 he sneers at guerilla movements, identifying them, rather than the oppressions they struggle against, with terrorism and violence, and adds that "the term 'urban guerillas' in South America almost reaches the humoristic level." He also claims that "the bestial killings in Hue," supposedly by the Vietcong, but never in fact authenticated, were "reliably proved" and that they were "only lightly noticed and immediately forgiven because the sympathy of society [Western in general and American in particular, apparently] was on the other side. It was just too bad that information did seep into the free press and cause a tiny bit of embarrassment of the passionate defenders of that other social system [North Vietnamese communism]."

In his Lenten letter (1972) to the Patriarch of the Orthodox Church in Russia, Solzhenitsyn urged him to promote a spiritual renewal of that body. He failed to mention that it was perhaps inappropriate to speak of a *renewal*, considering the history of the Church under the czars as an instrument of oppression. No regime supported by the Catholic Church at its worst periods, in any country, has surpassed the brutalization, cruelty, and arrogance of which the Russian Orthodox Church was an active part for centuries. The Father Zossimas, the kindly individual village priests, the pilgrim mystics, did not represent the power of the church but were its aberrant exceptions. How can Solzhenitsyn, I wonder, not recognize *as the Christian he claims to be,* the origins of the militant atheism he so deplores?

Solzhenitsyn (in the same letter) referred to the Revolution as "the collapse of Russian life"—implying not merely that the revolution as a great popular movement towards human dignity and comradeship was betrayed by its leaders, but that it was to be regretted in the first place.

In reacting to an incident in North Vietnam, wherein Ramsey Clark received an antiwar letter from an American POW, Solzhenitsyn slanders Clark, not merely calling him "this fluttering butterfly" but asking, "How can anyone believe that he [Clark], after all an Attorney General, simply could not have guessed that the POW who handed him the piece of paper *needed by Clark for his political purposes* [my italics] had just been submitted to torture? Quite understandably, no one reproached Ramsey Clark for it. After all, that was not Watergate."

With amazing naiveté—or could it be disingenuousness?—

156

he claims that "if the Republic of South Africa were to detain and torture a Black leader for four years as General Grigorenko has been, the storm of world-wide rage would have long ago swept the roof from the prison." Would it were true! Is it possible that Solzhenitsyn, who apparently has access to the Western press—viz. his stories about U.S. POWs, Hue, etc.—is unaware of South Africa's systematic barbarities, and of the "liberal" or "free" world's virtual indifference to them? [*He has apparently maintained his invincible ignorance during his years of American affluence. Just weeks after I wrote the article, he was deported from Russia, accepted a Nobel prize, and after a brief sojourn in Switzerland moved to the United States.*]

There is more, but I will not labor the point further. By all means we should defend the right of Solzhenitsyn to his proper rights, including the freedom from fear, the fear of losing still more of them. But let us not exalt this man into what he is not: a hero of humanity and compassion. Let us rather see him more realistically as a man whose trials and tribulations in the camps, followed by subtler persecutions later, have perhaps given him something of a martyr complex. Believing himself to be a writer of the first order (a judgement some would question), he feels his own current problems to be worse than those of other people, and the problems of Russian dissidents as a class to be more severe than those of any other oppressed class—which is simply not true. He therefore is sympathetic to anticommunism anywhere, choosing to ignore the sins of anyone who opposes communism and to slander the U.S. antiwar movement, for instance, even in its more conservative manifestations, because it opposes the professional anticommunists.

Is it not time, half-paralyzed though we may be by long frustrations and the complexities of conscious life in our time and place, to revise our priorities? Is it not too easy to let ourselves indulge in feeling indignant about something for which the United States, for once, is not to blame?

Should we not inform ourselves better about some of our domestic outrages, and also follow up our years of antiwar effort by remembering the overseas victims of U.S. crimes, whether Thieu's prisoners or the victims of our bombs and napalm?

[*At the bottom of the page, in the original "Real Paper" publication, appeared a "box," (accompanied by a graphic of a bound and imprisoned semi-abstract figure) subtitled "Where Our Priorities Lie":*]

Let me enumerate a few of what I do think are priorities— priorities for our emotion, our anger, our actions in behalf of freedom and justice. I shall list them as they occur to me, and not in a graded scale:

• The continuing torture of the more than 200,000 prisoners in Thieu's U.S.-supported regime, with its U.S.-provided tiger cages and what a Canadian Secretary of State has termed "grossly inhuman conditions." [*Substitute the dictatorships which the United States has continued to back with arms, equipment, etc. The world's torturers have studied in the United States special police academy.*]

• The fate of the starving people of Chile, and of jobless Chilean refugees, since the U.S.-engineered coup.

• The murder and imprisonment of Greek students and workers, while U.S. diplomatic ties with Greece, and all they imply, remain normal. [*Greece is in better shape now— but pick a substitute; there's a wide choice. South Korea, Thailand, the Philippines, almost any country in Latin America . . .*]

• The humiliations perpetrated under apartheid in South Africa and Namibia (countries U.S. banks and corporations continue to invest in heavily), where Africans (and whites who dare to aid and abet them) are imprisoned, fined, or whipped for such crimes as learning to read, refusing a job proffered by the Bantu Affairs commissioner, attempting to go on strike for any reason whatsoever, and so on.

• The imprisonment (with fifteen-year sentences) of persons in U.S.-protected South Korea for voicing criticism of President Park's "constitution." [*It did not then seem possible that things could get any worse in South Korea but since*

*Park was assassinated his successor has managed to make
them so.*]

• The continuing martydom of Martin Sostre, a hero if
there ever was one. Sostre, black and Puerto Rican, was
convicted in 1968 on a drug frame-up because of political
activities at his Afro-Asian bookstore in Buffalo. In solitary
confinement for the past year at Clinton Correctional Facil-
ity, New York, Sostre has been denied medical attention
and visitors, and regularly beaten, for refusing to submit to
the rectal search. His forty-one year sentence on phony
charges of assaulting a police officer and selling heroin (the
original political charges, arson and inciting to riot, were
dropped) was recently mockingly reduced by eleven years;
his defense fund is $1,000 in the red. [*As previously noted,
Sostre is no longer a prisoner after eight years in jail.*]

• The wave of political harrassment in North Carolina
during the past year or so. The Charlotte Three (about one
of whom, T. J. Reddy, I have written in the *Real Paper*,)
are black activists accused, in 1972, of burning down a Charlotte riding stable in 1968. On the testimony of two convicted felons, who were offered immunity, they were found
guilty and given sentences of ten, twenty and twenty-five
years. The cases of the Wilmington Ten and the Ayden
Eleven follow the same formula: unfair jury selection; convicted felons offered a deal to testify for the state; lack of
material evidence; excessive bond; excessive sentences.
[*After years of unjust imprisonment and of litigation, these
people too are free today. To that degree, at least, American
democracy does work, albeit creakingly. The formula for
putting social/political activists out of the way, however, is
unchanged—especially in regard to Blacks and other minorities.*]

• The struggle of Native Americans in general, and the
more than three hundred Wounded Knee defendants now on
trial in particular. [*Space does not permit a summary of this
struggle during the past seven years, but health and other
statistics reveal little change for the better. Moreover, the*

159

government has proclaimed a major area of Indian sacred sites in the West to be (because it is rich in minerals, including uranium) a "national sacrifice." Radioactive wastes from mining, and chemical pollutants, have already damaged numerous Native American communities.]

• Conditions and events in U.S. jails across the country—for instance, our local hellholes such as Walpole. And the (apparently no longer newsworthy) fate of the Attica survivors, sixty-one of whom are now under indictment on over 1,300 charges. [*Walpole, Massachusetts, remains a typical hellhole. How many are there in the country as a whole? Attica survivors have by now been pardoned and paroled, but virtually every jail in the United States continues to provide the degrading conditions that caused the Attica uprising.*]

• The struggle of the Puerto Rican people for independence and to save their beautiful island from ecocide. Already suffering from industrial pollution, the island is threatened by plans for a superport-refining-petrochemical complex to be built by the oil companies. The plan would endanger air, water, and wildlife as well as fishing and agriculture; last July 4, [1973] 25,000 Puerto Ricans marched in protest. [*The most "dated" thing about this whole article is the omission of any mention of nuclear arms and nuclear power. The ban on above ground testing (1963) had made many of us who participated in the Ban the Bomb movement of the fifties feel somewhat relieved, and the war in Vietnam had further distracted our attention from that issue. The "atoms for peace" illusion persisted in all but the best informed, and the recognitions which brought together environmental activists and a new manifestation of the radical left in the last few years were still embryonic in 1974. Today no reference to ecocide could omit the threat posed by uranium mining, nuclear power plants, deadly waste. In compiling such a list I would certainly mention the example of corporate imperialism provided by the planned or actual export to Third World countries such as the Philippines (where even such safety precautions as the Nuclear Regula-*

tory Commission requires in the United States would not pertain) of nuclear reactors, which even their proponents admit call for vigilant supervision (just as the most carcinogenic types of cigarettes and other products are shipped off to countries where no health warnings and safety standards are in effect.) And without question I would have to emphasize as the very top of all priorities the need for recognition of the threat to all life of the very existence of nuclear weapons, for passionate opposition to their manufacture and to the obscene consideration of nuclear war as an option.

In the last paragraph of the boxed section I offered to supply, on request, the names and addresses of various defense and support committees and antiwar groups. What I could do in a local weekly I can not repeat in a book, obviously! But I advise those who, as I put it, "want to get back into, or to begin, some useful action," to find their local branch of the American Friends' Service Committee (AFSC), or of The War Resisters' League, and obtain from them a listing of relevant active groups, national or regional.]

With the Seabrook Natural Guard in Washington, 1978

In the summer of 1978 the NRC, after prolonged debate, voted to stop construction of the nuclear plant in Seabrook, New Hampshire. The fact that a month or so later the decision was reversed made this merely an episode in a long story, but the story of the "Natural Guard"—two hundred demonstrators, of whom I was one, who went down from Seabrook to sit-in at the NRC building in Washington for three days while the NRC commissioners were considering the shut-down—remains significant, relevant beyond its brief topicality. Its meaning has to do with the mood and potential of the antinuclear movement. What happened on H Street was ignored by the press; yet it may well have revealed, much more intensely than the Seabrook June 1978 weekend's science-fair atmosphere and large crowds, what the spirit of the 80s has the potential to be.

Underlying everything else was the fact that no one, however frustrated, simply flounced out of a meeting yelling at everybody, followed by his or her entourage. There were, of course, no doors to slam!—and better still, very few entourages. Affinity groups, even when re-formed on an ad hoc basis at D.C., continued to be strong units; and even though some made what was I think the mistake of having permanent instead of rotating "spokes" (spokespersons), there was less sense of élite leadership than in any comparable body I know of. (These terms, "affinity groups" and "spokespersons" perhaps need explication: antinuclear coalitions, such as Clamshell in the Northeast states, for example, have adopted or developed some organizational and procedural guidelines derived from Quaker and other examples. An affinity group averages perhaps twelve to fifteen individuals, and an effort is made to ensure that all

---

First published in *The Literary Review*, Edinburgh.

the people in a group get to know one another informally as well as in formal meetings and actions, thus strengthening bonds of human concern and loyalty and doing much to avoid infiltration by *provocateurs*. The leader or chairperson role is broken down into several parts, such as Facilitator, Notetaker, Time Keeper, "Vibes Watcher," and so on, and these roles rotate so that no individual can become an institutionalized authority. Each affinity group chooses a "Spoke" to represent it at local or regional meetings of assembled spokespersons, and is empowered by the group to make necessarily rapid decisions on its behalf or to bring back to the group the problem to be decided when this does not have to be made in a hurry. Group decisions are made by consensus—a method which, while time-consuming, does have psychological and ethical advantages. The role of the Vibes Watcher is to observe when tensions are accumulating in ways that threaten productive thinking, and to intervene with a few minutes of relaxation.)

What happened on this occasion was that two hundred people spent over fifty-six hours living on a piece of sidewalk in front of the NRC building—eating, sleeping, holding meetings, chanting, singing, or simply sitting. (Dan Ellsberg quoted Ghandi to us at the rally which preceded the sit-in: "Sitting is good. But it does make a difference *where* you sit.") For those of us who also spent long hours on the excruciating steel cots in the holding cells after being arrested on Thursday night the last day was particularly uncomfortable; speaking for myself, my fifty-four-year-old body seemed to develop aching knobs and knots all over, and I couldn't sit, lie, or stand with comfort. Yet we all kept getting another wind. ("This is my eighteenth," someone said at one point.) Despite the seeming squalor (probably none of us had ever been quite so filthy for quite so long) no one seemed to get sick. We shared *everything*—every apple went around five or six people, a bite apiece; every plastic bottle of juice or water belonged to anyone, everyone. The toilets in Lafayette Park did heavy duty, but (with their

163

automatic flushing system) remained decent and useable. (Thank you, D.C. Parks Dept!) These are some notes on the experience written a few days after I got home:

• Flash: Unable to find my bedroll on returning from a spokes' meeting in the other nearby small park, and loath to wake sleepers at 3:00 A.M. to find it, I lie down with Tom and Joe on Tom's outspread sleeping bag, Wednesday night. It is a crowded bit of sidewalk, sleepers' feet near our heads. We are just settling down when I exclaim involuntarily, in a loud whisper, "I just had a toe in my ear!" We get the giggles. Laughter builds trust.

• On Tuesday night, encamped at the Paulist Seminary, which was our "staging area," we had to flee indoors, drenched, from a wild thunderstorm. Each cannonade of thunder and zigzag of lightning seemed virtually simultaneous: the storm was right in the field with us. It was beautiful—but some people hadn't even got their tents up yet. As we sat damply in the candle-lit refectory for the evening's long planning meeting, someone named Eric, from Buffalo, saw me shiver and lent me a flannel shirt. It felt so warm, good, soothing—a maternal shirt. I realized, in its comfort, that in this community of action one did not have to solve every problem oneself: we could rely on each other. Mutual Aid. We might get exasperated in the almost endless meetings as we attempted to reach consensus, but considering the competitive mores we have all learned, the level of reciprocal concern was amazingly high. Of our affinity group, named "Genesis" because we were first in the Boston area to get "trained," (i.e., to obtain the nonviolence training stipulated for participants in the Seabrook demonstration) four people came to D.C. following the Seabrook weekend and the other five members of our present ad hoc group were "strangers." Yet such is the spirit of solidarity, built upon individuals' personal commitment, that in a few hours we all became as close to each other as if we'd lived in common for a long time.

• Flash: Nature study. A pigeon has nested in the top of a

164

tall lamppost near the park toilets so that she has a built-in incandescent egg warmer or chick sitter. More laughter.

• Realization: Throughout the action, no one smoked dope or drank liquor or beer or offered provocation to the police or others or trashed anything. And we left our sidewalk home as clean, or cleaner, than we found it. This was not because anyone came and harangued us or gave us pep talks. Discipline came from within individuals and their affinity groups. How different an atmosphere from the fierce, bitching, trashing, "off the pig"-shouting demonstrations of the late 60s, early 70s! I then got caught up in that behavior myself, but I see the present mode of confrontation as having a far more effective potential. Besides, I've come back to my original belief that, for anything of value to evolve, the means must be consonant with the end, as far as is humanly possible. Of course, the disillusion that followed the assassinations of Dr. King and Malcom X, our seeming impotence to stop the napalming and bombing in South East Asia, the Kent State killings, the hunting down of the Panthers—that disillusion and the nihilistic rage that ensued, could occur again. But the sense of inner, individual change and growth that characterizes the nonviolence of the antinuclear movement does seem to me to promise more staying power. Most of the people involved had no firsthand experience of the violent, frustrated style of the early seventies, and it would seem very alien to them—offensively so. Most of them come from the environmental movement; many have Earth Days and backpacking trips as memories from high school years. They've evolved a gentle, unpretentious, civilized style of daily life, and they seem to me more mature than the people of the same average age—early twenties—that I knew and acted with nine or ten years ago. A lot of them are only beginning to perceive political interconnections; but they are fast learners. The people in my Seabrook affinity group are almost all connected, as present or past students, to Tufts, where the university's South African investments and its acceptance of a million dollars from

165

the infamous Marcos, dictator of the Philippines, have been strongly protested during the past year, and where such issues as the J. P. Stevens Boycott have drawn support. Most of us have been involved in some or all of these causes as well as in the Mobilization for Survival Teach-in and Environmental Action's follow-up to it last fall. Clams and Natural Guards are neither Flower Children nor Maoists nor any of the stereotypes in between. They distrust authority, but are generous listeners to the convictions, or the thinking-out-loud doubts, of others; they are sceptical of presumptuous or pretentious opinion, but open to persuasion if they feel it is coming from a sincere source. I feel I have much to learn from these brothers and sisters.

• Flash: The Die-in. The exact scenario of the die-in—starting with a little skit about the Commissioners conferring, followed by the simulated announcement of a melt-down—was created in Lafayette Park about a half hour before it began. Our press release about it said:[1]

> The horrible death many living beings have suffered and are suffering as a result of nuclear power, and which will be suffered by many more if plant construction is not stopped, will be simulated today at noon in a "Die-in" by a large group of the demonstrators who have been encamped at the NRC since Wednesday afternoon. This is an attempt to dramatize our demand that Seabrook and all other nuclear plants be closed down and solar and other alternative energy resources be developed instead. We feel that due to the NRC's emphasis on profits at the expense of human life, imminent and ever-increasing danger of catastrophe forces us to such forms of protest.

(Question: What happens to all the press releases, radio and TV interviews conducted by roving reporters, statements

---

[1] I quote from a ms. draft. Any changes made later were minimal.

issued on request from jail cells, etc., etc.? I myself, during these few days, participated in at least four such. But they vanish forever into the media's tape recorders, notepads, and files. During the whole action I saw only one good story on it—by Paul Valentine, in the Washington Post—and even that did not *describe* the scene. The "human interest" aspect was everywhere neglected—yet the papers are full of "fillers," photographic and otherwise.)

• This is what it was like to participate: When the "Meltdown" announcement is made, and a siren sounds, we who have decided to be "victims" begin to act out sudden, violent, and increasing pain. "Oh, my eyes! Ach! I'm burning! My skin! Oh God!" etc., etc. We cough, retch, writhe. Moans quickly turn to screams of agony, then to weaker, sobbing moans again. The horror is real. We are all imagining it together, vividly. We identify with people suffering the torture of cancer, leukemia, and unidentified low-level radiation sickness, and with the victims of Hiroshima and Nagasaki. I feel as if I have napalm on my skin, too; it is all one. We know that whether in war or in so-called peacetime there would be death on the streets, mass death very much like what we are pretending. We sink slowly to the ground, falling upon one another or straight onto concrete. Some give a last convulsion. Then we lie there. The moaning gradually dies away. A silence, of which the low monotone humming of our comrades who stand witness on either side of the Die-in area is a part. Into this silence intrudes the muffled sound of a police bullhorn telling us to move on or we would be arrested. We don't stir. The arrests begin—one can hear the sergeant directing his men. And our witness people stop humming and break into song. How strong, how supportive they sound. I know the woman against whom my face and one arm are pressed—it's Sue, from New Haven, I recognize her flowered dress. Nearby I see Don's hand—again, it is by his shirt I know him. Just so might it be if we were really dying. Sweat is running into my eyes. It must be 90°. After a while it seems as if everyone near me has been picked up by feet and shoulders and carried away. Something happens to my sense of space. I feel as if I were in a great desert. My vision is restricted to a small bit of gritty concrete. I know the police, press, and passers-by—including workers returning from their lunch hour—are watching us. I mustn't budge. Though I can still hear our people singing the round, "Love, love, love, love/ People, we are made for love/Love each other as ourselves/ For we — are — one," and it sounds sweet and deep and fine, yet everything that is happening, all other sounds, seem a million miles away. My sun-visor protects one cheek, but the other side of my face is broiling. I feel forgotten—not by my friends, no, but by the police. I get an image of vultures circling above H Street, above the nearby White House, above a Washington self-destroyed by its blind pursuit of power and profit. After what seems an age I am carried over to the shade and plonked down there, still "dead." (My thanks to whichever merciful cop thought I might be getting sunstroke.) And some time later I'm again picked up and taken near the paddywagons to be booked. The tight hand-cuffs and the bumpy ride to jail—our heads bashing against the steel roof of the wagon—are part of another chapter; this one ends with the sisters already in the wagon calling, "Welcome."

In jail, the women, at any rate, gave each other a very real and sensitive kind of mutual support. (The men, later, said this had not been as true for them. Feminism has given women the habit of such support, while men have not yet developed a comparable interrelationship.) We did not divide into factions. If anyone was upset, someone noticed it immediately, and clustered round to console or advise, like whales or dolphins around a wounded member of their tribe. At one point a very young woman who had decided to noncooperate was handled rather harshly by two of the women jailers (the third was glowingly humane, a sister we'll all remember). This was at a point when each of us had to go separately into a small office where we were told to strip and do a couple of knee bends, as well as having yet another mugshot taken. (We'd already been photographed a couple of times, and fingerprinted.) People were very tender with Cindy when she returned in silent tears to the holding pen. I think her tears were for the "common criminals" to whom such humiliations are familiar, rather than for herself. I myself, slightly paranoid from fatigue, got upset about another matter: our affinity group members on the men's side got a legal aide to slip a note of encouragement to Libby and Maggie, but left my name out. (Our fourth woman was a Support Person, and so not in jail.) Instead of recognizing the truth (which was that they had caught a glimpse of the other two, but not of me, as we filed into the arraignment waiting area, and so had concluded I was already released) I let myself feel rejected—a nonperson just because I was older and a well-known writer. *So our comradeship was an illusion?* It was anguish. Of course, it turned out that this was pure fantasy, but while it lasted, people I had not known a few hours before, as well as Libby, whom I knew well, were there with me, picking up on my unspoken feelings just from looking at me, and trying to assure me I must be mistaken. One woman massaged my hands, with remarkable results, taking away a lot of weariness. She also taught us all a song, which went, "I found God in myself, and I love Her fiercely." Every decision—especially the question of bail solidarity—was thoroughly discussed, and no one was put down. A $10 forfeited collateral, which would free us to continue the struggle, seemed eventually the best course of action, and this is what we obtained.

• Flash: A "righteous" date-nut bar I find in the depths of my satchel (a satchel confiscated at the jail but returned to me before arraignment) gets passed around the circle of women, along with water in a plastic bag, in a communion ritual, each taking a crumb and a sip and handing the "sacraments" to the person next to her. Trust and a common purpose make ordinary things holy.

• After we'd been arraigned and released, all of us who'd

169

been in jail overnight went back to H Street and resumed our sit-in. It seemed we'd been gone a long time, though really it was from about one or two o'clock Thursday afternoon till about noon Friday. The others had tidied up the scene somewhat—packs were stacked in one area, water containers in another (this didn't last long) and a literature table had been set up. Quite a few newly released people were prepared to join the next action, another piece of dramatization akin to the Die-in, which was planned to take place if the NRC decision on Seabrook, promised by 4:00 P.M., was that construction should continue.

• The Decision: When 4:00 P.M. went by, and at 6:00 P.M. it was announced that the decision would not come down until 8:00 P.M., my heart sank. I'd always believed that the Commissioners had really made up their minds by Thursday, and would only *announce* their verdict on Friday; I had doubted whether they were really in the building any more at all, and suspected that the announcement might be deliberately delayed so as to defuse any action we might take. The building and the street would be empty of workers, everyone gone home for the long weekend, even the press, and no one but ourselves and the police left. Were my fears coming true? I was so exhausted by 6:30 I thought I couldn't hold out till 8:00. Pat, our Support, had found me a bed to go to and a ride to get to it. But no one else was leaving, and I hung on. There was no general move to escalate or accelerate our action this time; only one man moved silently among us holding a sign with his name on it and an invitation to join him in an attempt to enter the offices. A few demonstrators had been in the building some hours already, in a reading room, but just as the police let our illegal sidewalk-sitting pass, so did that effort go unassailed. No one moved to join this man now. One woman moved over and sat right in front of the main door in a solitary blocking action, but she too was ignored by the police. She remained there weeping. Her distress expressed the feelings of many of us—yet a kind of patient hope prevailed, and kept us

170

quietly waiting until after 8:00 P.M. The songs we sang in those two hours grew quieter, less exuberant; towards the very end we were silent; then the silence filled with a great vibrating OM! AUMMM. And at last one of the Commissioners, heralded by an announcement from the door to tell us that this was indeed he, and that the moment had come, issued from the building, and we held our breath as he made his way to the loudspeaker. A drawn-out moment of pure tension, in which one hardly dared think, "Would he have had the nerve to come into our midst, to speak to such a scruffy rabble, if he had bad news for us?" Then the announcement: *Seabrook construction suspended.*

• JOY! Screams of joy, tears of joy, shaky laughter, leapings up and down, everyone hugging everyone, whooping, arms waving, shrieking, gasping out, "We *did* it, we *did* it!" For a full half hour the whole street is filled with embracing, dancing, ecstatic people. When the cops, from inside and outside the building, line up and begin to leave, they get a cheer and a round of "For he's a jolly good fellow." Most of them are smiling broadly, especially the Blacks. Many, during the sit-in, had given us a friendly word, and all had equalled our own discipline in not offering provocation. They were, of course, obeying orders; someone high up, for one reason or another, had evidently been anxious to avoid a showdown. Was it just white middle class privilege in action? Probably. But the demonstrators' lack of animosity to a bunch of guys just doing their job was genuine, in any case. Later a janitor tells some of us there were scores of other police concealed in the building all week, and two busloads more kept in reserve in a nearby garage. They had been prepared for five hundred of us and a fullscale attempt to enter and occupy. Shall we ever know what would have happened if that had taken place?

• HOPE: In the delirium of that half hour my emotion was accompanied by one thought: "How rare is the experience of victory!" A friend phrased it next day: "The unfamiliar savor of hope." I know that in my political experience

171

I've never before felt a clear sense of having won, though in antiwar days we used to chant "Dare to struggle, dare to win." The Vietnamese won the war, yes, and we could feel we had helped; but all of that occurred in so slow and inconclusive a way. When Saigon was renamed Ho Chi Minh City, I got a small sip of the sensation, but it was more like an aroma than an actual mouthful of food. The extreme and forceful joy on H St., Friday, June 30th, 1978 is without parallel in my life.

• RECOGNITION: The meaning of it: We know we can't take credit for the Seabrook decision as if it were all our doing. The 20,000 at Seabrook, the 2,000 at Manchester, the 200 of us in D.C.—we are only one factor, and perhaps not a major one. But we *are* a factor. We know that without the psychological pressure of our movement as a whole and our presence here, the decision (which took the Commissioners so long to make, and for which they stayed on in their offices for eight long hours later than the Friday noon departure Daniel Ellsberg had predicted as typical for D.C. bureaucrats) might have been different.

We know, too, that the decision is only temporary, a stay of execution which Meldrim Thomson and his like will surely attempt to reverse. (N.B. As stated in the introductory paragraph, this reversal did in fact take place only a month later.) The struggle for and against Seabrook is sure to continue—and the land is full of other nukes. Even in the first flush of triumph we were chanting, "On to Rocky Flats." But perhaps the most important results, for the long run, are (1) that the cessation of construction at Seabrook now does set a precedent which will be educationally useful in our outreach efforts, and (2) that the experience of reward for effort, of gratification, of hope, will take root and spread branches of confidence and determination throughout our ranks. People who were not at D.C. will not feel quite the primal excitement we Natural Guards have known, but surely feel good, too. I'm certain a great many people will show up at Rocky Flats, Colorado, who would not have

172

gone there if we had lost that round. I know *I* mean to go.[2]
We have so much frustration in our lives—a little encouragement can go a long way. The new, positive spirit, clear
about right and wrong but not corroded by hate and cynicism, that I see as the mark of the movement in the on-
coming 80s, is going to be strengthened by such incidents of
hope. One taste of People-power, however qualified, gives
one an appetite for more.

• Flash: 11:00 P.M. Friday. Tom, Joe, Libby, Pat, Maggie
and I (Jill and Mark had to leave earlier, alas) stroll up the
street to buy soft ice cream and Chinese eggrolls. What
luxury! When we get back to "our block," we join in picking
last scraps of paper and an occasional cigarette-end off the
cement. (Few smokers among the demonstrators.) Some
people are meticulously scraping off the remaining bits of
masking tape with which we'd marked a passageway for
passers-by and people who worked in the building. Street
housekeeping. Tired as we are, we linger; we don't like to
say good-bye, even for the night. Tomorrow we'll meet for
a farewell breakfast, then people will head for home or
summer jobs or wherever they are going. But "we are one,"
like the song says—no kidding. "See you in Rocky Flats."

Postscript: December 1980. Now, in 1980, the focus has
rightly changed from nuclear power plants to nuclear arms
and the urgent need to halt the arms race. Rocky Flats is
still, therefore, a focal point, while the need to prevent a
Seabrook being built, or to shut down other plants, though
still important, no longer seems a first priority. It is not, of
course, that this was not true before—just that more people
now have a clearer sense of priorities, and that the urgency
is ever more extreme. At the same time, the Three Mile
Island accident did a good deal (though not enough) to raise
public consciousness of the power plant dangers. The tone
within antinuclear organizations has changed somewhat in
these past three years. Factional disputes have occurred,

[2]In fact I was not able to do so.

some people have given up, others have only recently begun to participate. Most of us are more somber. But the spirit I felt in the Natural Guard action, that new spirit I tried to describe, has not died. It's still there, and is our most basic resource, the locus of my deepest hope. That's why I believe this little document is still topical.

Speech for a Rally on the Boston
Common, September 15, 1979

I wish I felt this had become irrelevant. Unfortunately things have only worsened since this piece was written, and I believe both its warnings and its plea must be reiterated.

D. L., 1981.

1979 . . . the last summer of a decade is over. 1979 . . . ten years ago the strength of the draft-resistance movement had been rapidly and efficiently sapped by legislation giving deferments to anyone who could afford to stay in school. If you were middle class you didn't have to struggle not to be drafted. If you were poor, you couldn't afford to stay in school and you couldn't afford to resist. The draft took you off the street—for a while. If you survived, what did you come back to? What did those parts of you that weren't missing do next, heroes, veterans of a foreign war? Back to the street. 1979 . . . and the martial drums are rumbling again. The very rich go on getting richer. The people in the middle are scared. The people at the bottom wonder about the coming winter when they will have to choose between heat and food. The drums are rumbling. It is inconvenient to have too many unemployed, too many welfare mouths to feed, they mutter. Time for a draft again—always a good way to get the young folk out of the way for a while. Right now the bill has been put aside for further study—but that study will be of the most efficient means to organize and control the draft, not of whether it is morally valid. And behind those rumbling drums are much bigger drums, that have never been silent but now grow louder. "Defense," they say, "Defense." And what do they mean by that? They

---

First published in *Resist Newsletter*, Cambridge, Massachusetts, and reprinted in *Follies*, Los Angeles, California.

mean, "Offense, Attack." "First Strike Capability," booms a kettledrum. And distant but clear you can begin to hear the words "Limited Nuclear War." Are they indeed drums? Or is that sound the sound of a giant machine, a giant engine revving up, getting into gear? The arsenals are full to bursting. At night the great generals lie dreaming of the day when they will really see their new ingenious toys of slaughter in action. The big ones, not mere antipersonnel bombs and the like. A natural law, they tell themselves with a delicious shudder—what exists to strike must at last do so. Destiny. Somehow they themselves will escape. Somehow. And the heads of the great corporations, they too lie awake, figuring, figuring. The sale of arms has always been the world's most profitable business. And the spin-offs of war—ah, beautiful, to a mind in love with multiplication, the way riches upon riches, degree after degree of power, accumulate from war's rich soil. To one who might ask them whether no fear haunts them, of being themselves devoured by the war monster they are bringing to its horrible maturity and preparing to unleash again, they turn the ghastly glitter of obsessed eyes. No, they have fed their fear into the safety of a computer, from which it has emerged as a number, an efficient zombie, words like *radiation-sickness* and *annihilation*, which it used to whisper, erased from it.

1979—and that there is madness stalking the land is very clear. What place is there for military draftees, male and female, actual people, infantry, unskilled privates, in a war that would employ the sophisticated weapons the Pentagon gathers and gathers as pus gathers in a dirty sore? But there is method in the madness. Keep the people still believing war is a matter of armies, of man-to-man combat, of "bravery," a place for people to "test themselves"—and keep using the word "defense." Build up the sense of threat, build up the thought that ordinary people can meet the threat, yes, bring out and brush up the timeworn concept of "military *service*" of "serving your country." It's a time-honored way to deal with unemployment and to control

176

possible rebellion. Do all these things and don't forget, at the same time, to begin showing the Vietnamese war as a "mistake" which after all was "necessary," as proved by the atrocities those nasty little yellow people commit, as you can see any day at the movies . . . Any distinction between fact and fiction is unimportant: people will believe what they are shown. Be very *methodically* mad, and you can go on making superb profits at the top levels, while the people (getting poorer all the time) are prepared—prepared—prepared—first for the diversion of attention to some little new wars, to prove that there can be survivors of nuclear and other technologically conducted wars, and thus to get people into the habit of thinking statistically (so they'll accept the vast numbers of those who get wiped out); and then for the big war, unprecedented ecstatic global blossom of fire and light.

Yes—the draft, which for the moment has been shelved, but will be trotted out again at a convenient moment, is part of that insane but methodical preparation. Soon we will be in the 80s, and the 80s may be all there is of the future. Yes, we've stumbled through the 70s and doomsday hasn't happened. Yet. But make no mistake—if we don't stop the revving up of that monstrous machine, if we don't get together to block the reinstitution of the draft, to stop the arms race, to stop nuclear power (whose function is not only to produce energy in a way so dangerous that it is simply not worth the risk, but to provide bomb-quality nuclear material)—if we don't build a great firewall of refusal to all of these, then we too are mad, then we too are participants in our own destruction. STOP THE DRAFT. STOP THE ARMS RACE. STOP NUCLEAR POWER.

Two Speeches About Survival and a
Message to Children, 1980

I: Address to the Commission on the Environment and Energy at the World Peace Parliament, Sofia, Bulgaria. September 24, 1980

Three thousand people from very many parts of the world—peace activists, trade unionists, writers, ecologists, politicians, teachers, etc., ranging from Latin American guerillas to a New England state government representative, from a New Zealand environmentalist to a Mauritian doctor—attended this gathering (sponsored and paid for by the Bulgarian government)—which went unremarked in the United States press. Bulgaria itself has a burgeoning aware-ness of ecological problems: at present it has only one nuclear power plant, shared with Rumania. My concern was to try to introduce information on the hazards of "peaceful" nuclear use to representatives of countries where this information was even less fully available than it is to the American public, as well as to emphasize that while American radicals must struggle against our own government's provocative and ever-growing arsenal, the peo-ple of other countries—including the U.S.S.R.—should be doing so too. I was given the opportunity to make similar remarks in radio and television interviews while in Sofia, as well as in contributions to several Bulgarian magazines.

We are here to speak about Peace and how to attain it and maintain it, and I believe our discussions will be badly unbalanced unless we recognize that there are three inter-related forms of war. The first is literal—military war. The second is the continual attack on human potential by eco-nomic, social, and racial injustice, which deprives millions of something as basic as adequate protein, as well as of other fundamental rights, and thus perpetuates itself. We all recognize the existence and interaction of these two. But the third form of warfare is less generally acknowledged, al-though it is equally important to do so; I mean the war

178

which all societies, whatever their ideologies, are carrying on against the rest of nature, against natural resources and thus, with an extraordinary and perverse blindness, against themselves, *our*selves; against our own genetic future as well as the elements (air, water, earth) we need for life.

That capitalist countries, dominated by the motive of immediate profit, should gamble with the future by promoting nuclear power and lethal chemical products and by-products, is not surprising, but it is tragic that socialist countries do the same and that the many newly independent countries, with a desperate need to feed their people and develop viable economies, should also hope to obtain what used to be called "atoms for peace" as a means towards progress.

The truth is that as a species we have made some very bad mistakes, and our survival will depend, even if we manage to avoid the horrors of war, on admitting those mistakes and seeking a new road. These mistakes, which have accelerated enormously in the twentieth century, have ancient roots in the anthropocentric view of Man as the natural ruler of the world, whose "manifest destiny" is to "conquer Nature." This universal intellectual and technological imperialism of Man towards the rest of Nature, animate and inanimate, has created weapons which, for the first time in history, make possible the destruction of absolutely everything on the planet, either in one vast unimaginable (but possible) firestorm or by the slower but even more horrible process of a series of "limited" nuclear wars and their aftermath of disease, mutations, and the poisoning of the elements. We know that. But this same anthropocentric arrogance is also waging the third kind of war, under the disguise of raising material standards of living. Just as chemical fertilizers and insecticides produce faster and larger crops for a time, but meanwhile deplete the soil of its minerals and kill the beneficial earthworms, so do the consumer goods of high-energy-use societies, which are desired by nonaffluent societies, offer quick gratifications at suicidal expense. It is difficult for a speaker from an affluent society to express this in a

179

world so full of literally starving people: it may be misunderstood. But consider a few facts:

• In addition to the arms stockpiles of the world's major military powers, which are insanely excessive by any calculation (enough to kill every person on earth many times over) each "peaceful" nuclear reactor in the world produces approximately 400–500 pounds of plutonium, every year; and just one pound of plutonium, if equally distributed, could give lung cancer to every individual on earth.

• Plutonium particles can go on concentrating in the testicles and ovaries of successive generations, passing on damaged genes for 500,000 years.

• Possible theft of enriched uranium for the purpose of making bombs means that, regardless of political philosophy, a nuclear economy leads to a police state.

• Uranium miners and processors are victims of constant overexposure to radiation and radioactive dust. The effects (cancer, leukemia, and genetic damage) can take many years to show up. Such workers are usually not informed of the danger.

• Low-level radiation (even without leaks and accidents) constantly exposes the public, and especially nuclear industry workers, to amounts which are added to the natural "background radiation" which we all experience anyway. Thus the hazardous effects increase year by year, because they are cumulative in the body.

• Nuclear power does *not* create more jobs, whereas the development of safe alternative energy *would* do so.

In order to create a world-wide society of economic, social and racial justice, and a world without war, we must *have* a world in which to struggle. If we are to save our planet and its elemental resources from irreparable damage and destruction, we must revise our self-image and recognize that our task is not to conquer nature but to recognize ourselves as part of a global ecosystem. That means that the superpowers and all high-energy-use countries, without exception, must reeducate themselves towards a less luxurious and wasteful style of life, in which many luxuries that we

180

have mistaken for necessities would be recognized as harmful. And it means that poor countries recognize that the so-called higher standard of living consumer goods represent is eventually disastrous. Hunger must be eliminated, yes, and the right of all to education, housing, health care, and dignified work must be not only recognized but implemented; but those seductive aspects of twentieth century technology which are not ultimately life-enhancing but destructive must be seen as a terrible addiction, like the addiction to heroin.

In all countries, without exception, people must stop leaving decisions to their governments and strive for human survival by individually and collectively saying No. No to the arms race and no to the continued rape of the earth.

I am an American citizen and I use every opportunity I have to urge people in America to resist our government's military policies and the corporate economic policies that act hand in hand with it. I urge people in America to demonstrate and to prepare for an eventual national strike against such policies. But this is not a national but an international problem, a global problem. And so I urge *all of you,* from whatever countries you come, to do the same. Our very survival is in the balance—we should not wait for our governments, however democratically elected, to decide our fate: all of us, ordinary people everywhere, should put pressure on our governments to disarm. And all of us should think deeply about what it means to be a human being, and realize that we cannot attain our beautiful common goals, our vision of justice and compassion for all, by arrogantly violating our Mother, the Earth. Our future depends upon our developing a different sense of values.

II: Address to the International Meeting of Writers Sofia, Bulgaria, September 28, 1980

This three-day meeting took place immediately after the week-long Peace Parliament. Some, but not all, of the approximately two hundred and fifty writers attended both events.

181

Dear Brothers and Sisters,

At times during the Peace Parliament I felt discouraged because I felt that though we all sincerely desired a lasting world peace we were only talking to each other. How can we really change the policies of those who continue to escalate the arms race? But when I read the Appeal launched September 24 I felt more hope, especially when I read these words: "To be concerned is not enough! To be alarmed is not enough! The people have the power to preserve their basic right! Act now!" I believe that as writers we have a special responsibility to ask ourselves exactly what this means and what form *our* contribution to such immediate action ought to take. Every kind of person has that responsibility, but writers, because they have the gift of verbal expression and because they have, in varying degrees, some ready-made access to the public, have even more obligation than those who do not possess those privileges.

These are some suggestions for how we can make our particular contribution:

1. One of the greatest obstacles to peace is the combination of ignorance about the exact nature of nuclear force and its effects with the feeling of powerlessness which most average people experience. Whether they trust their governments and therefore say, "Leave it to the experts, they must know best," or whether they distrust them (probably with very good reason) and therefore say, "What's the use, we ordinary people have no influence," there are millions and millions of people who never assert their basic right, as living creatures, to survive. The role of the writer, as an articulate person, vis-à-vis this phenomenon seems to be (*a*) that we should do our best to inform ourselves both of what the actual physical consequences of technological warfare are, and of the profound immorality and absurdity of even *thinking* in terms of possible "limited" nuclear war; and also of the inextricable interweaving of so-called peaceful use of nuclear power with the process and continued threat of war. (*b*) That we use our verbal gifts to disseminate this knowledge so that it enters the imagination of others in a way

182

which will awaken their determination to take action against the threat of global suicide. We may be able to do this in our poems or fictions, or we may not find the inspiration to do so. It is not useful to create bad art for a good cause, and I do not believe in *forcing* ourselves to write such poems; but what we *can* do is write articles, speak in public whenever we have (or make) the opportunity, incorporate our knowledge of these matters in our classes and lectures if we are teachers, as many of us are, talk to people individually, and utilize whatever prestige and leverage we have as artists (in addition to what we can do in our primary creative work).

2. Because as writers we do have access to readers and listeners, we are in a position to encourage people to remember that all people everywhere have one great nonviolent recourse—the general strike. An international general strike for disarmament—what a magnificent vision! No doubt many of you will reply, "How ridiculously ideal!" Yes, I understand that there are many obstacles to such an event; yet "they" could not kill *all* of us, and the greatest obstacle is the mixture of ignorance, lack of imagination, and lack of self-confidence which we, brothers and sisters of the tribe of the word, can help to alleviate. But we must accelerate our activity, for while the superpowers are engaged in an arms race, *we* are inevitably racing against time.

3. Finally, something which cannot change in a moment, certainly, but which is to my mind very urgent nevertheless, and absolutely fundamental:

> I believe that behind all the truths which we can learn from a study of political science (such as the economic forces behind apparently ideologically motivated events, the structure of capitalist societies, etc., etc.) is something even deeper and more widespread, namely the arrogantly anthropocentric view of life which leads mankind to exploit Nature instead of respecting and harmonizing with Nature. In my speech at the Peace Parliament's commission on the Environment and Energy I used the term "intellectual and cultural

imperialism" of man towards other forms of life and towards the elements themselves. It is this which infects even socialist societies with a consumer mentality. I believe that unless we humans revise this self-image, which is at the root of our competitiveness, aggressiveness, and acquisitiveness as a species, we are on a suicidal path even if we manage to avoid war. We must learn to regard ourselves as one part—not the most important—of a global ecosystem. We must learn to grow and distribute enough food for all people, and to provide the other fundamental rights—housing, clothing, education, and the opportunity to work and live in freedom and dignity—without destroying our very environment in the process. To struggle for justice, we must have a world to struggle in. We must develop all the *renewable* sources of energy, and like the ancient tribal peoples (whose wisdom we have ignored on all the continents while we trampled upon their sacred places and attempted, at various epochs of history, to destroy them altogether) we must recognize again that the Earth is our Mother. If poets cannot understand this, who will? And if we do understand it, then indeed, we have a role to play, a task to perform: we must use our poet's imagination and our gift of language to bring these realizations to others. Let us take very seriously what the manifesto of the Peace Parliament says in conclusion:

"Let our voice be heard as never before!"

III: A Message to Children

Before leaving Sofia, the visiting writers were asked to join with their hosts, the Bulgarian writers, in writing messages to the future children of the world. These will eventually be published in a multilingual edition.

184

Dear Children,
You who are little babies now, or not yet born:

I am writing this to you across the years. At this time, 1980, a long time before you will read this message, the world is in great danger. Foolish and greedy people have invented horrible weapons of war, and threaten to use them in their quarrels. And besides that, other such people (and some people who thought they were doing something good, too—but they were mistaken) have developed all sorts of complicated and unnatural things. Some of these things, such as nuclear power plants, and certain chemicals for producing unnecessary things, or for producing necessary things more quickly, are so dangerous that they would poison the whole earth if we who love life, we who live now, many years before you read this, don't stop them. If you exist, children of the future, who read this, it will mean that we succeeded: that we *did* manage to stop the terrible world war fought with nuclear bombs and laser beams, which would have killed all the people and animals, flowers and trees and butterflies and everything. It will mean that we did manage, as well, to change the stupid, dangerous, ways of living which in our days threatened the health and survival of our home—your home—the earth. So you will understand that I hope with all my heart that you *will* read this message—because it will mean that, long after I and the rest of us who send you these messages have lived our lives, the beautiful world and its children, its poems, its clouds and grass and all its other lovely things, is still there. It will mean that in *your* time people are no longer so foolish and greedy and unkind to each other, but have learned to live in friendship and peace and to be good and happy.

With love from
Denise Levertov

185

V MEMOIRS

Muriel Rukeyser, more than any other poet I know of (including Pablo Neruda) consistently fused lyricism and overt social and political concern. Her *Collected Poems,* which came out just over a year before her death, clearly reveals this seamlessness, this wholeness: virtually every page contains questions or affirmations relating to her sense of the human creature as a social species with the responsibilities, culpabilities, and possibilities attendant upon that condition. And virtually every page is infused with the sonic and figurative qualities of lyric poetry.

Her life presented a parallel fusion. From her presence as a protester at the Scottsboro trial in 1931, when she was eighteen, to the lone journey to Seoul which she undertook in 1975 in the (alas, unsuccessful) attempt—using her prestige as president of PEN—to obtain the release from jail of Kim Chi Ha, the Korean poet and activist, Muriel *acted* on her beliefs, rather than assuming that the ability to verbalize them somehow exempted her from further responsibility. The range of her concern expressed the fact that she went beyond humanitarian sympathy to a recognition of interconnections and parallels: she had a strong, independent, personal grasp of politics, and just as she blended the engaged and the lyrical, the life of writing and the life of action, so too did she blend her warm compassion and her extraordinary intelligence. To list some of the subjects of her poems is also to allude to events of her biography, and vice versa: Spain during the civil war; the working conditions of West Virginia miners in the 1930s; the unhating, profoundly civilized spirit of Hanoi, 1972; war-resistance and jail in D.C.—these are a few instances that come to mind. Whether working with schoolchildren in Harlem or

---

Written for *In These Times,* a socialist weekly, March 1980.

learning to fly a plane; whether experiencing single-parenthood or researching the life of the sixteenth/seventeenth century mathematician, explorer and alchemist Thomas Harriot, Muriel never placed the objects of her attention in the sealed compartments of sterile expertise, but informed all that she touched with that unifying imagination that made her truly great.

Something that especially moves me about Muriel Rukeyser is the way in which her work moved towards greater economy and clarity in her later books. There are marvellous early poems, but sometimes her very generosity of spirit seemed to bring about a rush of words that had not the condensed power she eventually attained. Clarity of communication was not easy for her because her mind was so complex, causing her conversation often to be hard to follow as she leapt across gulfs most of us had to trudge down into and up the other side; but she did attain it—a luminous precision—time after time.

I had known Muriel for many years before she and I and Jane Hart went to Vietnam together in the fall of 1972. That journey bound us in a deeper friendship. Among my recollections are two small incidents from that trip that seem expressive: one is her painful embarrassment at having to receive medical attention in a Hanoi hospital—she felt that, among so many war-injured Vietnamese civilians, an American with an injured toe was grossly out of place. (In fact, the matter was serious because of her diabetes.) The other is the look of distress I suddenly noticed on her face when I, in answer to a question from one of the Vietnamese writers we met, described New York City in extremely negative terms. She was a New Yorker born and bred and though she knew all about its terrors and tragedies, she loved the city and saw its possibilities, looking upon it with passionate hope, as upon a troubled but beloved person.

It would be inappropriate to memorialize her, however briefly, without mentioning her humor. (She included in her last book the two-line squib,

I'd rather be Muriel
than be dead and be Ariel,

under the title *Not to be Printed, Not to be Said, Not to be Thought*.) Equally inappropriate would be omission of a reference to her lifelong interest in science and to the fact that she wrote not only poetry (including translations) but notable biographies, children's books, and two other uncategorizable prose works, *The Life of Poetry* and *The Orgy*. Then, too, there was her life as a teacher, for many years, at Sarah Lawrence, where the tutorial system demands of faculty an unusual degree of dedication.

The loss of this person, this poet, and for some of us this wonderful friend, is a great one. Her work and her example remain to sustain us—an ongoing source of life-affirmative energy. In the preface to her *Collected Poems* she wrote of "the parts of life in which we dive deep and sometimes—with strength of expression and skill and luck—reach that place where things are shared, and we all recognize the secrets." Muriel Rukeyser had that strength, that skill, that luck—and she did reach that place.

II: About Muriel, August 1980

I first met Muriel at a dinner preceding a reading in New York City. We were both to read. I was very late because I got lost on the Columbia campus and didn't have with me the exact location of the event. It was a wild, windy night and I wandered about confused and anxious. When I finally got to the right building and right room my impression was of a crowd of dark-suited irritable middle-aged men holding sherry glasses and looking at their watches. From the midst

---

Written for a collection, as yet unpublished, of memories by many friends of hers.

of them broke the tall and quite massive woman who was Muriel—she came welcomingly towards me on thin legs, like a large waterbird, and exclaimed in a deep voice (not really so much deep as rich) "Ah, you've come at last! I've been terribly bored, waiting to meet you!" I'm sure that in fact there were nice and interesting people there, but Muriel so outshone them all that the effect for me resembled the cinematic technique which puts all but one character out of focus and concentrates the spectator's awareness wholly on that central personage. I was nine or ten years younger and much less known than she, but Muriel at once treated me as an equal and assumed that we would be friends.

A few years later (1965) I wrote of something which occurred during the reading on that same night:

> Two or three years ago Muriel Rukeyser was answering questions from audience after a poetry reading at Columbia University. A man in, I judge, his late twenties—perhaps older—spoke up. "Maybe this question I'm going to ask will strike you as foolish . . . I'm not a writer myself, not an English major . . . in fact I'm an engineering student" (idiot laughter from unidentified sources) "but I *am* eager to read poetry. . . . And the question I want to ask is, to get the most out of one's reading, what should one bring to a poem?" Muriel Rukeyser is a tall, leonine woman, a genuinely sybilline presence. She rose and stood silent while she brooded over what had been asked; her arms hung by her sides, she was quite obviously unaware at that moment of the other people sitting on each side of her, or of the large audience awaiting her reply. Then she lifted her head and spoke directly to the questioner: "It's *not* a foolish question. It's a question everyone has to ask, all of us. And I think what must be brought to a poem is what must be brought to anything you care about, to anything in life that really matters: ALL of yourself."

192

When the deep voice, sure of what it felt, ceased to speak there was a long quietness. Then people rose to their feet to clap. It is not often that the answer to a question is thus applauded.

My son must have been about twelve when I began to know Muriel, and her son was two or three years older. We arranged for the two boys to meet, but children rarely take to one another when they are supposed to, and they did not develop a friendship as we had hoped. But Muriel always took a special interest in Nikolai, writing him recommendations for Putney and The Rhode Island School of Design which helped his acceptance at both places, and from time to time exchanging letters with him. This feeling for Nik was personal and particular, but it was also an instance of her great love for children and indeed for all kinds of beginnings, seeds, images of growth. Over the years our friendship, though we saw one another rather rarely, continued to grow. I dedicated a poem called "The Unknown" to her because it seemed to be about a kind of revelation Muriel's imagination exemplified: the way the unconscious works at a different pace from our willful intentions, and surfaces—bringing us clues, keys, rewards—only after strenuous efforts have been put aside and replaced by a surrender that is receptive. Muriel's conversation often dipped beneath the waters of consciousness and reemerged at unexpected points as a diving bird does; to understand her one had to swoop after her, like some following, smaller bird alert to her subaqueous movement.

Going to Vietnam together (with Jane Hart) in 1972 of course consolidated our friendship. One of my residual impressions of that trip is of how firm and strong a presence she was, how unflappable. She saw and felt everything so deeply but while Jane, I think, relied (at first) on a certain scepticism to protect herself from some of the impact of what we experienced, and while I tended to seesaw between euphoria and despair, Muriel stood rocklike in the

193

midst of what we all knew to be American shame and Vietnamese courage, never losing either her compassion or her humor. Her sensibility was so well tuned that she could derive from it sound and balanced intellectual conclusions without going through a laborious reasoning process. Of course, she was at the same time highly intellectual and passionately interested in ideas and in science; but her intellect was fed to an unusual degree from intuitive sources. Another poem of mine, "Joy," (which also quotes from a letter of my mother's about the rediscovery of joy after its long absence) refers to an experience of Muriel's when she was hospitalized in the mid sixties and the accidental breaking of old scar tissue released in her a new flow of psychic energy.

With all her intelligence, energy, and humor, she was nevertheless terribly vulnerable to feelings of shame and embarrassment. She was also, like everyone else, not free of feelings of jealousy and hurt pride in certain situations, but what was so marvellous and loveable in her was the way in which she could admit them. No one I've ever known was more generous.

After my mother died in 1977, when I told Muriel forlornly that I felt myself to be a middle-aged orphan, she said, "Oh, I'll adopt you. You'll be my Adopted Something." She meant that and I felt it, felt warmed and strengthened. She was the same age as my late sister, but I don't think we felt like sisters—a truly sisterly relationship must be based on a closely parallel childhood and youth. Muriel and I were colleagues who became friends—fellow votaries of Poetry who were also mothers and political allies. Her "adoption" of me gave a further depth to that relationship, and she was a source of strength to me although she herself was declining in physical strength.

Muriel's last word to me was a phone call she made to Arkansas to tell me I'd been elected to the American Academy of Arts and Letters. I was much more impressed at her kindness in doing so than by the honor itself, which I didn't fully understand. But a few weeks afterwards, when Grace Paley called to tell me Muriel had died that day, I realized that my election and Grace's, both of which Muriel had evidently worked for, unknown to us, constituted a kind of bequest from her. She lives in her work and in our memories; but life has less resonance without her.

Some Duncan Letters—A Memoir and a Critical Tribute

In the early spring of 1948 I was living in Florence, a bride of a few months, having married American literature, it seemed, as well as an American husband. Both of us haunted the U.S.I.S. library on the via Tornabuoni—Mitch to begin rereading at leisure the classics of fiction he had been obliged to gallop through meaninglessly at Harvard, I to discover, as a young writer of the British "New Romantic" phase of the 1940s, the poetry of what was to be my adopted country. I had read at that time a minimal amount of Pound (anthologized in a Faber anthology) and Stevens ("discovered" in Paris a few months before when Lynne Baker lent me a copy of *The Blue Guitar*). William Carlos Williams I had found for myself in the American bookstore on the Rue Soufflot, near the Sorbonne, but though I knew with mysterious certainty that his work would become an essential part of my life, I had not yet heard enough American speech to be able to hear his rhythms properly; his poems were a part of the future, recognized but held in reserve. The rest of American poetry was *terra incognita,* except for Whitman (in the William Michael Rossetti edition of 1868) and a few poems by Emily Dickinson, Robert Frost, and Carl Sandburg—again, anthology pieces only. I had read Eliot; but like most English readers at that time, I thought of him as an *English* poet (and of course, the fact that it was possible to do so was precisely what made Williams so angry with him, as I later understood). Also I had read and loved, at George Woodcock's house in London a year or so before, a few poems from Rexroth's *Signature of All*

From *Robert Duncan: Scales of the Marvelous*, ed. Robert J. Bertholf and Ian W. Reid (New York, New Directions, 1979). (Written in 1975)

Things.[1] Those were the limits of my acquaintance with U.S. poetry.

The American library was not, to my recollection, rich in poetry; but among my findings were some issues of *Poetry,* Chicago; and in one of these, a review by Muriel Rukeyser of Robert Duncan's *Heavenly City, Earthly City.* Both these people, then just names to me, were to become, in varying ways, close friends who influenced my history—as did Dr. Williams. Thinking back from the present (1975) I realize how destiny was sounding the first notes, in that cold Florentine spring, of motifs that would recur as dominant themes in the fifties and sixties (and in the case of Muriel Rukeyser, with whom I visited Hanoi in 1972, into the seventies) and which, indeed, are so interwoven in my life that whatever changes befall me they must be forever a part of its essential music.

In Muriel's review of *Heavenly City, Earthly City,* she quoted:

> There is an innocence in women
> that asks me, asks me;
> it is some hidden thing they are
> before which I am innocent.
> It is some knowledge of innocence.
> Their breasts lie undercover.
> Like deer in the shade of foliage,
> they breathe deeply and wait;
> and the hunter, innocent and terrible,
> enters love's forest.

These lines, and the whole review, so stirred me that I convinced myself no one in Florence needed that particular issue of *Poetry* more than I did, and I not only kept it out for

---

[1]Rexroth had struck up a correspondence with me at that time, for he was editing *New British Poets.* He was the first American writer I knew personally—but I had not met him except through letters.

months but, when we left for Paris, took it with me . . .

Retrospectively, I see that I was drawn to Duncan's poems of that period not only by their intrinsic beauty but because they must have formed for me a kind of transatlantic stepping stone. The poems of my own first book (*The Double Image*, 1946) and those that Rexroth included in *The New British Poets* (New Directions, 1949) belonged to that wave of Romanticism which Rexroth documented, an episode of English poetry that was no doubt in part a reaction against the fear, the drabness, and the constant danger of death in the daily experience of civilians as well as of soldiers in WWII. While the subject matter of the poems of the "New Romantic" movement may often have been melancholy and indeed morbid, the formal impulse was towards a richly sensuous, image-filled music. When the war ended, English poetry quickly changed again and became reactively dry, as if embarrassed by the lush, juicy emotionalism of the forties. But though not many individual poems of the New Romantics stand up very well to time and scrutiny, they still seem preferable to the dull and constipated attempts at a poetry of wit and intellect that immediately succeeded them, for their dynamic connected them with a deeper, older tradition, the tradition of magic and prophecy and song, rather than of ironic statement. And it was to that old, incantatory tradition that Duncan, then and always, emphatically (and, as I did not then know, consciously) belonged. So here, I must have intuited, was an *American* poet whose musical line, and whose diction, were accessible to me. It must have made my emigration, which I knew was not far distant, seem more possible, more real.

In a 1964 letter, after talking about a then new poem of mine called "Earth Psalm," Duncan says it caused him to reread "To Death," a poem in my 1946 volume.[2] "I began to conjure" he said, "the Tudor, no Stuart (something between

<hr/>

[2]Now reprinted in *Collected Earlier Poems* (New York, New Directions, 1979).

King James's Bible and Bunyan) dimension (a fourth dimen-
sional of you) with figures from a masque. . . . Haven't
we, where we have found a source, or some expression of
what we love in human kind, to give it a place to live today,
in our own gesture (which may then speak of nobility or
ardour)—Well, if Orpheus can come forward, so, by the
work of the poem, Death and His Bride in brocade—"

"How many correspondences there are," he goes on to say,
"between your *Double Image*, 1946, and my *Medieval
Scenes* written in 1947. In this poem 'To Death'—'brocade
of fantasy': in 'The Banners' where the 'bright jerkins of a
rich brocade' is part of the fabric of the spell; or in 'The
Conquerors' compare 'The Kingdom of Jerusalem'. . . ."
And after a few more lines of comment he begins, right *in*
the letter, the poem "Bending the Bow":

> We've our business to attend Day's
> duties, bend back the bow in dreams as we may,
> til the end rimes in the taut string
> with the sending . . .
>
>   I'd been
>
> in the course of a letter—I am still
> in the course of a letter—to a friend,
> who comes close in to my thought so that
> the day is hers. My hand writing here
> there shakes in the currents of . . . of air?
> of an inner anticipation of . . . ? reaching to touch
> ghostly exhilarations in the thought of her.

But here, noting the life-loom caught in the very act of its
weaving, I anticipate. In 1948 I had nothing of Duncan's but
those quotations in *Poetry*, fragments congenial and yet
mysterious; and when I arrived in New York for the first
time in the fall of that year I was too passive, disorganized,
and overwhelmed by unrecognized "culture shock" (the

term had not yet been invented) to do anything so methodical as to try and find his book or books: so that when I did happen upon *Heavenly City, Earthly City* on the sale table outside the Phoenix Bookshop on Cornelia St., just a few blocks from where I was living, it seemed an astonishing, fateful coincidence—as in a sense it was.

The book enlarged and confirmed my sense of affinity and brought me, too, a further dim sense of the California of fog, ocean, seals, and cliffs I was by then reading about in Robinson Jeffers.

> Turbulent Pacific! the sea-lions bark
> in ghostly conversations and sun themselves
> upon the sea-conditiond rocks.
> Insistent questioner of our shores!
> Somnambulist, old comforter!

Duncan wrote in the title poem; and:

> Sea leopards cough in the halls of our sleep.
> swim in the wastes of salt and wreck of ships,

and:

> The sea reflects, reflects in her evening tides
> upon a lavender recall of some past glory,
> some dazzle of a noon magnificence.

Much, much later—in 1966, it must have been, when I visited Carmel and Monterey—there was possibly some recall of those lines in a poem of mine, "Liebestodt": "Where there is violet in the green of the sea . . ."

But the impact of Duncan's rich romanticism was perhaps less powerful by the time I found the book, for I was also beginning to get a grip on William Carlos Williams's sound by then, able to "scan" it better now that I was surrounded by American speech, no longer baffled by details like "R.R."

(railroad—in England it is railway) or obstructed in reading by the difference in stresses (e.g., the first American menu I saw announced "Hot Cakes" which I ordered as "hot *cakes*").[3]

Now I was quickly, eagerly, adapting to the new mode of speaking, because instinct told me that to survive and develop as a poet I had to; and Williams showed me the way, made me listen, made me begin to appreciate the vivid and figurative language sometimes heard from ordinary present-day people, and the fact that even when vocabulary was impoverished there was some energy to be found in the here and now. What I connected to, originally, in Duncan, was a music based in dream and legend and literature; and though my love of that music has proved to be enduring, it was not uppermost in my needs and pleasures just then when I was seeking a foothold in the realities of marriage, of keeping house in a tenement flat, raising a strenuous baby, buying groceries at the Bleeker Street Safeway.

Meanwhile Duncan, unknown to me still, was changing too, on the other side of the continent. There was of course this big difference in us, a thread of another texture in among those that we held in common: he had a sophistication in which I was quite lacking, which gave to his romanticism an edge, not of the type of wit academics of the period cultivated anxiously—like a young man's first whiskers—but of an *erotic irony* such as Thomas Mann adumbrates in his essays on Goethe and elsewhere. He was not only a few years older than I: he had already an almost encyclopedic range of knowledge, had studied history with Kantorowitz, had read Freud; and he lived in a literary and sexual ambience I didn't even know existed. Whatever he wrote was bound to include an element of complex consciousness; indeed, I can see now that while my task was to

[3] And, as in this instance, the different perception of parts of speech, the English retaining *hot* as an adjective, and Americans creating a compound noun, hotcakes.

develop a greater degree of conscious intelligence to balance my instincts and intuitions, *his* was, necessarily, to keep his consciousness, his diamond needle intellect, from becoming overweening, violating the delicate feelings-out of the Imagination; and it was just because his awareness of every nuance of style, of every double meaning, was so keen, that he has, through the years, been almost obsessively protective of the gifts of chance, of whatever the unconscious casts upon his shore, of "mistakes" which he has cherished like love-children.

My first direct contact with Duncan came in the early fifties and was almost a disaster. By this time I had become friends with Bob Creeley and *Origin* had begun to appear. Mitch and I had gone back to Europe on the G.I. Bill in 1950, when our son was just over a year old, and in 1951 the Creeleys came to live a mile or two away from us in the Provençal countryside. Sitting on the ground near our cottage, by the edge of a closely pruned vineyard under the slope of the Alpilles, Creeley and Mitch would talk about prose, and Creeley and I about poetry: Williams, Pound, Olson's "Projective Verse" which had just come out, how to cut down a poem to its sinewy essence—pruning it like the vines. I learned a lot; and am not sure what, if anything, I gave in exchange, though I know I was not merely a silent listener. Duncan had not yet met or been acknowledged by either Olson (with whom Creeley was corresponding) or Creeley,[4] and though he had not been dislodged from my mind I don't recall mentioning him. After I was back in New York, and just at about the time Cid Corman included some poems of Duncan's in *Origin* (1952) I received a communication from a San Francisco address signed only "R.D." It was a poem-letter that (I thought) attacked my work, apparently accusing it of brewing poems like "stinking coffee" in a "staind pot." When the letter spoke of "a great effort,

[4]Robert Duncan had, however, sent *Medieval Scenes* to Olson as early as 1948.

202

straining, breaking up all the melodic line," I supposed the writer was complaining. How I could have misread what was, as Duncan readers will recognize, "Letters for Denise Levertov: an A muse ment"—how I could have so misinterpreted his tribute, it is difficult now to imagine. I've never been given to paranoia; perhaps it was simply that the mode of the poem, with its puns, lists, juxtapositions (more Cubist than Surreal) was too sophisticated for me to comprehend without initiation. I had at the time not even read half the people he mentions in the poem as sources, or at any rate as forming an eclectic tradition from which I thought he was saying I had unwarrantably borrowed (but to which, in fact, he was joyfully proclaiming that I belonged): Marianne Moore, Pound, Williams, H.D., Stein, Zukofsky, Bunting, St.-J. Perse. Of these, I had by then read only Williams, Marianne Moore and Perse in any quantity; I knew Pound's *ABC of Reading* pretty well but had not tackled the *Cantos*. Of H.D. I knew only the anthologized Imagist poems of her youth, and of Stein only "Melanctha"; of Zukofsky and Bunting, nothing. Duncan also speaks in the poem of Surrealism and Dada: and I was at least somewhat acquainted with French Surrealism (and the English poet, David Gascoyne's book about it) but with Dada not at all. So much of the corresponding intellectual background, in the simplest sense, was lacking in me as a recipient of the letter.

I wrote to "R.D." enquiring plaintively why he had seen fit to attack me for a lack of originality, for I took phrases like

> Better to stumb—
> ll to it,

and

> better awake to it. For one
> eyes-wide-open vision
> or fotograph
> than ritual,

203

as stern admonitions, when, of all the names he cited, only Williams was to me a master, and from him I believed myself to be learning to discover my own voice. I concluded my letter by saying, in all innocence, "Is it possible that the initials you signed with, R.D., stand for Robert Duncan? You don't sound like him!—But in case that's who you are, I'd like to tell you I loved *Heavenly City, Earthly City*, and therefore hope it's not Robert Duncan who dislikes my poems so much." I quote from memory, but that's a pretty close approximation. It is a wonder that Duncan was not furious at my stupidity; especially at my saying he did not sound like himself. If he had been, I wonder if our friendship would ever have begun? Certainly if it had not, my life would have been different. But luckily he responded not with anger (or worse, not at all) but with a patient explanation (on the envelope he added the words, "It is as it was in admiration") of his intent, including his sense—central to an understanding of his own poetry—that "borrowings" and "imitations" were in no way to be deplored, but were on the contrary tributes, acts of faith, and the building stones of a living tradition of "the communion of poets." This concept runs through all of Duncan's books. It is most obvious in the Stein imitations, or in his titling books *Derivations*, or *A Book of Resemblances*, but is implicit in every collection, though not in every poem; and it is closely tied to his recognition of poetry (and of all true art) as being a "power, not a set of counters" as he put it in a section of "The H.D. Book" that deals with H.D.'s detractors, the smart, "bright" critics. If Poetry, the Art of Poetry, is a Mystery, and poets the servers of that Mystery, they are bound together in fellowship under its Laws, obedient to Its power. Those who do not recognize the Mystery suppose themselves Masters, not servants, and manipulate Poetry's power, splitting it into little counters, as gold is split into coins, and gaming with it; each must accumulate his own little heap of manipulative power-counters—thus so-called originality is at a premium. But within the Fellowship of the

Mystery there is no hoarding of that Power of Poetry—and so-called borrowings are simply sharings of what poetry gives to Its faithful servants.[5] By the light of this concept we can also understand Duncan's often criticized "literariness," i.e. his frequent allusions to works of literary and other art and his many poems that not only take poetry itself as theme but overtly incorporate the "languaging" process into their essential structure—as he does even in this very first "Letter" in the sections subtitled "Song of the Languagers," and later in such poems as "Keeping the Rhyme," "Proofs," "Poetry, A Natural Thing" or "The Structure of Rime" series, and so many others.

Some readers—even deep and subtle ones—object to poems about poems (or about the experiencing of any works of art) and about writing and language, on the grounds that they are too inverted; I have never agreed (except in regard to conventional set pieces "about" works of art, those which seem written in fulfillment of commissions or in the bankrupt manner of British poets laureate celebrating Royal weddings). If much of a poet's most passionate and affective experiences are of poetry itself (or literature more generally, or painting, etc.) why should it not be considered wholly natural and right for him to celebrate those experiences on an equal basis with those given him by nature, people, animals, history, philosophy, or current events? Poetry also is a current event. The poet whose range is confined to any single theme for most of a working life may give off less energy than one who follows many themes, it is

[5]This does not necessarily imply that the poet should erase his signature from his works nor that poetry, or other art work, is best undertaken communally. To me the sense of chronology, the cumulative power of a lifetime's work, is of profound importance; and it can only be experienced if authorship and sequence are known. As for "group poems," I find them superficial: each individual needs solitude in order to bring his or her experience in life and language to fruition in the poem, and it is through communion with ourselves that we attain communion with others. Duncan's own practice seems sufficient evidence that he would agree.

true—and if any single thing characterizes those whom we think of as world poets, those of the rank of Homer, Shakespeare, Dante, it is surely breadth of range. But Duncan, although in tribute to the Mystery he is avowedly and proudly "literary," cannot be accused of narrow range, of writing *nothing but* poems about poetry.

It was in 1955 that I first met Duncan. He spent a few days in New York on his way, with Jess, to spend a year in Europe—chiefly in Majorca, near to Robert Creeley with whom he had by this time entered into correspondence but still not met. I am not able to locate the letters that preceded this joyful meeting, nor do I remember our conversation. But the tentative friendship that had begun so awkwardly was cemented by his visit, and I recall with what a pang I watched him go down the stairs, he looking back up the stairwell to wave farewell, I leaning over the landing banister.[6] I gave him a notebook for his journey; he used it as a drawing book and gave it back to me full of pictures a year later; and still later I wrote captions for them.

Whatever had passed between us before that time—and Duncan years later claimed that "we must have been in full correspondence by fall of '54"—it was now that the exchange of letters which continued into the early seventies began in earnest. Somehow, in the course of a busy life and many changes of dwelling, a few of the letters Duncan wrote to me have been mislaid, though I am confident that they are not irretrievably lost, for I always treasured them. I have a stack of letters for every year from 1955 to 1972. The written word was not the only dimension of our friendship: from time to time Duncan would come East; in 1963 he and I were both at the Vancouver Poetry Conference; and three times I was in the San Francisco Bay area (in 1969 for six

[6]It is possible Duncan had some half-conscious memory of this moment when years later he spoke of his special feeling for a poem called "Shalom." The "man/going down the dark stairs" in that poem was not he, but it has come to seem to be as much about him as anyone, in the way poems do, with time, come to admit more than their first inhabitants.

months). At these times we would have the opportunity to "talk out loud" rather than on paper and I have happy memories of visits to museums and galleries, to the Bronx Zoo and the Washington Zoo, and of walks in the Berkeley Hills. Over the years we acquired many mutual friends; and during my son's childhood Duncan and Jess befriended him too, sending him wonderful old Oz books they would find in thrift shops. But it was the correspondence, with its accompaniment of poems, newly finished or in progress, that sustained the friendship most constantly and importantly.

Looking through these letters from Robert I am confirmed in my sense of their having been for me, especially in the first ten years, an extremely important factor in the development of my consciousness as a poet. Pondering what I gave Duncan in exchange, besides responding in kind to his admiration and love, I recall his speaking of how writing to me and to Creeley gave him "a field to range in," and in a 1958 letter he writes of me as serving as a "kind of artistic conscience" (not that he needed one). I had, certainly, the great advantage of not being connected to any "literary world" in particular, and being quite free from the factionalism so prevalent in San Francisco.

Both Duncan and I are essentially autodidacts, though he did have a high school and some college education while I had no instruction after the age of twelve, and the education I received before that was unconventional. I had a good background in English literature, a strong sense of the European past, and had read widely but unmethodically. Duncan read deeply in many fields I was ignorant of—the occult, psychoanalysis, certain areas of science. He did not teach me about these matters, which were not what I was really interested in—but he did give me at least some awareness of them as fields of energy. Because of my family background I knew a little about Jewish and Christian mysticism, so that when Duncan mentioned the Shekinah or Vladimir Solovyov I recognized what he was talking about.

207

The Andrew Lang *Fairy Books* and the fairytales of George MacDonald (and some of his grownup stories too) were common ground, along with much, much else—many loves in literature and art. It was in those areas of twentieth-century literature, American poetry in particular, of which at the time of that first "Letter" I had been ignorant, and—more importantly—in the formation of what I think of as "aesthetic ethics," that Duncan became my mentor. Throughout the correspondence there run certain threads of fundamental disagreement; but a mentor is not necessarily an absolute authority, and though Duncan's erudition, his being older than I, his often authoritative manner, and an element of awe in my affection for him combined to make me take, much of the time, a pupil role, he was all the more a mentor when my own convictions were clarified for me by some conflict with his. Perhaps there was but one essential conflict—and it had to do with the role of a cluster of sources and impulses for which I will use "convictions" as a convenient collective term (though no such term can be quite satisfactory). Although, having written poetry since childhood (beginning, in fact, several years before Duncan wrote *his* first poems), I had experienced "lucky accidents" and the coming of poems "out of nowhere," yet I needed, and was glad to get from him, an aesthetic rationale for such occurrences—reassurances to counter the "Protestant ethic" that makes one afraid to admit, even to oneself, the value of anything one accomplishes without labor. Nevertheless, then and now (and I fully expect to so continue) my deepest personal commitment was to what I believed Rilke (whose letters I'd been reading and rereading since 1946) meant in his famous admonition to Herr Kappus, the "Young Poet," when he told him to search his heart for its *need*. The "need to write" does not provide academic poem-blueprints, so there was no conflict on that level; but such "inner need" *is* related to "having something" (at heart) "to say," and so to a high valuation of "honesty"—and our argument would arise over Duncan's sense that what I called honesty, he (as a passionate anarchist or "libertarian") sometimes regarded as a form of self-coercion, resulting in a misuse of the art we served. He saw a cluster, or alignment, that linked *convictions* with *preconceptions* and *honesty* with *"ought,"* while the cluster I saw linked *convictions* with *integrity* and *honesty* with *precision.* Related to this was my distrust of Robert's habit of attributing (deeply influenced as he was by Freud) to every slip of the tongue or unconscious pun not merely the relevation of some hidden attitude but, it appeared to me—and it seemed and still seems perverse of him—*more validity* than what the speaker meant to say, thought he or she said, and indeed (in the case of puns and homonyms noticed only by Duncan) *did* say. To discount the earnest intention because of some hinted, unrecognized, contradictory coexisting factor has never seemed to me just; and to automatically suppose that the unrecognized is necessarily *more* authentic than what has been brought into consciousness strikes me as absurd. Jung (whom I was reading throughout the sixties—Duncan disliked his style and for a long time refused to read him)[7] had made the existence of the "dark side," and the imperative need to respect it, very clear to me; it was Duncan's apparent belief that the dark side was "more equal," as the jest puts it, that I could not stomach.

However, the first time I find this matter touched upon in one of Robert's letters it was not in a way that affronted or antagonized me but one which, on the contrary, belongs with the many ways in which he opened my mind to new realizations. I had been puzzled by some ballads of his,

[7]By the summer of '63 he had somewhat relented, however; "Oh yes, it's true I'm most likely to bridle at the mention of 'Jung.' But, while there is an argumentative cast always in Jung that I find exasperating and dislike finally (the having the answer to things in a schema), there is always much and often so much else that I find revelatory. I look forward with the usual mixture of prejudice and expectation to reading the *Autobiography*." It is amusing to see Duncan claim to dislike argumentativeness, given his own contentiousness!

inspired, in part, by Helen Adam (to whose fascinating work he soon introduced me). I found them, I suppose, a curious retrogression from the exciting pioneering into the "open field" in which we and a few others were engaged. What was the Duncan of *Letters*, the Duncan who in a letter of that same summer (1955) was excited by my poem "The Way Through" (printed in *Origin*) and who shared my love of Williams, what was he doing being so "literary"?—I must have asked. For I myself was engaged in "de-literarifying" myself, in developing a base in common speech, contemporary speech rhythms. "I don't really understand your ballads," I wrote (I quote now from Duncan's transcription of part of my letter in his preface for a projected volume to be called *Homage to Coleridge*), "why you are writing that way. It seems wasteful both to yourself and in general . . . when I remember what else you have written, even long since, as well as of late especially, I can't quite believe they aren't like something you might have written very long ago." My hesitations about questioning anything he did are evident in the circuitous syntax and its qualifiers—"I don't really"—"I can't quite"—"it seems". . . . And in his reply he wrote,

> . . . it is the interest in, not the faith, that I wld take as my clue. Ideally that we might be as readers or spectators of poetry like botanists—who need not tell themselves they will accept no matter what a plant is or becomes; or biologists—who must pursue the evidence of what life is, haunted by the spectre of what it ought to be [though] they might be. As *makaris* we make as we are, o.k., and how else? it all however poor must smack of our very poorness or if fine of our very fineness. Well, let me sweep out the old validities: and readdress them. They are inventions of an order within and out of nonorders. And it's as much our life not to become warriors of these orders as it is our life to realize what belongs to our order in its when and who

210

we are and what does not. I can well remember the day when Chagall and Max Ernst seemed bad to me, I was so the protagonist of the formal (like Arp or Mondrian) against the Illusionary. The paintings have not changed. Nor is it that I have *progressed,* or gone in a direction. But my spiritual appetite has been deranged from old convictions.

This openness was something I was happy in; and indeed, in such passages Duncan often sounded for me a note of "permission" to my native eclecticism that some shyness in me, some lack of self-confidence, longed for. Yet even this liberation was in some degree a source of conflict—not between us, but within me. For years no praise and approval from anyone else, however pleasant, could have reassured me until I had Robert's approval of a poem; and if I had that—as I almost always did—no blame from others could bother me. "The permission liberates," wrote Duncan in 1963 (about a procedure of his own, relating to a habit of "reading too much the way some people eat too much" as he put it elsewhere) "but then how the newly freed possibility can insidiously take over and tyrannize over our alternatives."

Duncan's wit is not a dominant note in the letters but it does flash forth, whether in jest or in epigram. In September 1959 for example, he complains that Solovyóv had been, alas, "a Professor of Philosophy—that hints or sparks of a life of Wonder can show up in such a ground is a miracle in itself. What if Christ's disciples had not been simple fishermen and a whore, and he the son of a carpenter, but the whole lot been the faculty of some college?" Of a highly cultured friend he wrote in 1957, "he has enthusiasms but not passions. . . . He collects experience [but he doesn't] undergo the world." He described San Francisco audiences for poetry readings (preparing me for my first public reading anywhere, in December 1957, which he had gone to considerable trouble to arrange): "The audiences here are

211

avid and toughened—they've survived top poetry read badly; ghastly poetry read ghastly; the mediocre read with theatrical flourish; poets in advanced stages of discomfort, ego-mania, mumbling, grand style, relentless insistence, professorial down-the-nosism, charm, calm, schizophrenic disorder, pious agony, auto-erotic hypnosis, bellowing, hatred, pity, snarl and snub."

Among recurring topics are friendships and feuds among fellow writers: his publishing difficulties (due in part to his very high standards of what a book should look like and in what spirit its printing and publication should be undertaken); and—more importantly—his current reading and its relationship to his work; as well as his work itself. Sometimes poems would have their first beginnings right there on the page, as *Bending the Bow* did; or if not their beginning, the origins of poems enclosed are often recounted. (These, however, I do not feel inclined to quote; they are a part of the intimacy of communion, not to be broadcast—not because they say anything Robert might not say to someone else or to the world in general, but because in their context they are said in an expectation of privacy.)

It is not easy to isolate from the fabric some threads of the essential, the truly dominant theme I have already named— clumsily but not inaccurately—the "ethics of aesthetics"; for the pattern of the whole is complex: negatives and positives entwined and knotted. Everywhere I discover, or rediscover, traces both of the riches Duncan's friendship gave me and of the flaws in mutual confidence which by the 1970s impoverished that friendship.

Perhaps a point at which to begin this drawing-out of one thread is what he says about revision. I had read the notebook excerpts, printed in a S.F. broadside, in which the beautiful phrase occurs, "My revisions are my re-visions." In the beginning I supposed it to mean it was best never to work-over a poem, but instead to move on to the next poem—the renewed vision. But taking it to myself as the years passed, I have come to know its meaning as being the necessity of constant re-visioning *in the very act* of refining: i.e., that changes made from outside the poem, applied as a reader would apply (supply) them, cannot partake of the poem's vitality; the valid, viable *re*working of a poem[8] must be as much from within, as seamlessly internal to the process, as the primary working. Duncan himself in May 1959 explicated:

> I revise (*a*) when there is an inaccuracy, then I must re-see, as e.g. in the Pindar poem—now that I found the reproduction we had someplace of the Goya painting, I find Cupid is not wingd: in the poem I saw wings. I've to summon up my attention and go at it. (*b*) when I see an adjustment—it's not polishing for me, but a "correction" of tone, etc., as in the same poem "hear the anvils of human misery clanging" in the Whitman section bothered me, it was at once the measure of the language and the content—Blake! not Whitman (with them *anvils*) and I wanted a long line pushed to the unwieldly with (Spicer and I had been talking about returning to Marx to find certain correctives—as, the ideas of *work*) Marxist flicker of *commodities*. (*c*) and even upon what I'd call decorative impulse: I changed

> follow
> ~~obey~~ to the letter
> freakish instructions

> to gain the pleasurable transition of l to l-r and f to f-r.
> The idea in back of no revisions as doctrine was that I must force myself to abandon all fillers, to come to correct focus *in the original act;* in part there's the veracity of experience (. . . the poem "comes" as I

[8]I.e., whether or not it takes place on the same day as a first draft or over a span of months or even years.

213

write it; I seem—that is—to follow a dictate), but it's exactly in respect to that veracity that I don't find myself sufficient. . . . I had nothing like "I write as I please" in mind, certainly not carelessness but the extreme of care kept in the moment of a passionate feeling. . . . My "no revisions" was never divorced from a concept of the work. Concentration. . . . I've got to have the roots of words, the way the language works, at my fingertips, learned in the nerves from whatever studies, in addition to the thing drawn from—the sea, a painting, the face of Marianne Moore—before there's even the beginning of discipline. And decide, on the instant, that's the excitement, between the word that's surrounded by possible meanings, and the word that limits direction.

Copying this out in December 1975 I find the dialogue continuing, for I feel I want to respond to that last sentence: ah, yes, and here I see a source of the difference in tendency between your poetry and mine (though there is a large area in which our practices overlap): you *most often* choose the word that is "surrounded by possible meanings," and willingly drift upon the currents of those possibilities (as you had spoken in "The Venice Poem" of wishing to drift) and I *most often* choose the word that "limits direction"—because to me such "zeroing in" is not limiting but revelatory.

In August of the same year (1958) Duncan resumes the theme:

I've found myself sweating over extensive rehaulings of the opening poem of the field and right now am at the 12th poem of the book which I want to keep but have almost to reimagine in order to establish it. . . . It's a job of eliminating what doesn't belong to the course of the book, and in the first poem of reshaping so that the course of the book is anticipated. I mistrust the rationalizing mind that comes to the fore, and must

214

suffer through—like I did when I was just beginning twenty years ago—draft after draft to exhaust the likely and reach the tone in myself where intuition begins to move. It comes sure enuf then, the hand's feel that "this" is what must be done. . . .

He quotes Ezra Pound saying in a 1948 manifesto, "You must understand what is happening"; and makes it clear the significant emphasis is on "what is happening," the present-ness, the process. "Most verse," Duncan comments, "is something being made up to communicate a thing already present in the mind—or a lot of it is. And don't pay the attention it shld to what the poet don't know—and won't [know] until the process speaks." He quotes the passage from T. S. Eliot's *Three Voices of Poetry* in which Eliot, alluding to a line from Beddoes, "bodiless childful of life in the gloom / crying with frog voice, 'What shall I be?'" noted that there is "first . . . an inert embryo or 'creative germ' and, on the other hand, the language . . . [The poet] cannot identify this embryo until it has been transformed into an arrangement of the right words in the right order." And from Eliot he passes directly to a recent poem by Ebbe Borregard—

What Ebbe's got to do is to trust and obey the voice of *The Wapitis.* Where obedience means certainly your "not to pretend to know more than he does." But the poem is not a pretention to knowing; it is not, damn it, to be held back to our knowing, as if we could take credit for the poem as if it were a self-assertion. We have in order to obey the inspired voice to come to understand, to let the directives of the poem govern our life and to give our minds over entirely to know[ing] what is happening.

Most of this rang out for me in confirmation of what I believed and practiced. But I question one phrase—that in

which he *opposes,* to the trusting of a poem's own directives, the communication of "a thing already present in the
mind"; for unless one qualifies the phrase to specify a fully
formed, intellectualized, *conscious* "presence in the mind" I
see no true opposition here. The "veracity of experience"
does not come into being only in the course of the poem, but
provides the ground from which the poem grows, or from
which it leaps (and to which it fails to return at its peril).
"The sea, a painting, the face of Marianne Moore," *are*
indeed the "things drawn from." What the writing of the
poem, the process of poetry, the following-through of the
radiant gists (in W. C. Williams's phrase) of language itself,
does for the writer (and so for the reader, by a process of
transference which is indeed communication, communion)
is to *reveal the potential* of what is "present in the mind" so
that writer and reader *come to know what it is they know,*
explore it and realize, real-ize, it. In the fall of 1965, com-
menting anew on my "Notes on Organic Form" which he
had read in an earlier, "lecture" form, he quotes with enthusiasm: "whether an experience is a linear sequence or a
constellation raying out from and in to a central focus or
axis . . . discoverable only in the work, not before it"—but
in that phrase I meant "discoverable" quite precisely—i.e.,
not "that which *comes into being* only in the work" but that
which, though present in a dim unrecognized or *ungrasped*
way, is only *experienced in any degree of fullness* in art's
concreteness: The Word made Flesh, Concept given body
in Language. One cannot "discover" what is not there. Yet
the poem is not merely a representation of the thing discovered—a depiction of an inscape seen; it is itself a new
inscape, the seen and the seer conjoined. And it is in the
action of synthesizing, of process in language, that the poet
is voyager, sailing far beyond that lesser communication,
the conveyance of information, to explore the unknown.
Duncan seems always on the brink of saying one does not
even *start off* from the known.

At times it seems as if it were his own brilliant intellect he is struggling to keep from domination of his art—beating not a dead horse but a horse that does not exist in me, or in others about whose poetry he wrote. In 1956, writing from a small village in Majorca, wondering if he and Jess can afford to travel to London at Christmas time (their budget was $100 a month) he spoke of,

> . . . craving the society of English speech. My notebooks are becoming deformed by the "ideas" which ordinarily I throw away into talk, invaluable talk for a head like mine that no waste basket could keep clean for a poem. I can more than understand dear old Coleridge who grew up to be a boring machine of talk; I can fear for my own poor soul. And, isolated from the city of idle chatter, here my head fills up, painfully, with insistent IMPORTANT things-to-say. I toss at night, spring out of bed to sit for hours, crouched over a candle, writing out—ideas, ideas, ideas. Solutions for the universe, or metaphysics of poetry, or poetics of living. Nor does my reading matter help—I have deserted Cocteau for a while because his ratiocination was perhaps the contagion; and the Zohar which irritates the cerebral automatism. Calling up, too, conflicts of poetry's—impulses toward extravagant fantasy, my attempt to reawaken the "romantic" allegiances in myself, to Poe, or Coleridge, or Blake, are inhibited by a "modern" consciousness; I grow appalled at the diffusion of the concrete. . . .

And in 1958,

> Sometimes when I am most disconsolate about what I am working at, and most uneasy about the particular "exaltations" that may not be free outflowings of imagination and desire but excited compulsions instead. . . . I feel guilty before the ever-*present* substantial mode of your work.

But of course, it was more than an overactive intellect that he had to contend with; the struggle was often with the sheer complexity of vision. His cross-eyes saw deep and far—and it is part of the artist's honor not to reduce the intricate, the multitudinous, multifarious, to a neat simplicity. In 1961 he wrote,

> It's the most disheartening thing I find myself doing in this H.D. study, trying to win her her just literary place—and what I find (when I reflect on it) is that I lose heart (I mean I get that sinking feeling in my heart and lungs, I guess it is, as if I had played it false). I know I can't just avoid this playing it false—you know, direct sentences like sound bridges from good solid island to good solid island; and contrive thought lines like pipe lines to conduct those few clear streams— because the bog is the bog. [he has previously written of "the bog I get into with prose"] *and I really want to discover it on its own terms,* [my italics] which must be the naturalist's terms. . . . that damned bog would have to be drained and filled in to be worth a thing, but it is a paradise for the happy frog-lover, or swamp-grass enthusiast—and in its most rank and treacherous backwaters a teeming world of life for the biolo-gist. . . .

Instances of particular changes made in poems in prog-ress (and here I return to the interwoven theme of revision) occur in many letters, following poems sent earlier. The mind's bog was fully inhabited by very exact, green, jewel-eyed frogs. Here are two typical examples:

Nov. 29, 1960

Dear Denny, That *Risk!*—how hard it seems for me to come down to cases there. This time it is not the wording (tho I did alter "simple" to "domestic" in "turning the mind from domestic pleasure") but what necessitated my redoing the whole 3 pages was just the annoying fact that I had phrased certain lines wrong— against my ear. I never did read it "not luck but the way it falls choose/for her, lots" etc., which would mean either an odd stress of the phrase on "for" or a stress I didn't mean on "her." I was reading it from the first "choose for her" with the stress of the phrase on "choose"; and that terminal pitch heightening "falls" in the line before. And again: What did I think I was hearing when I divided "I had not the means/to buy the vase" or whatever—was it?—worse! "I had not the means to buy/the vase" etc.? Anyway, here I was going on like any hack academic of the automatic line-breaking school . . . not listening to the cadence of the thing. My cadence, my care, is changing perhaps too—and I was notating this from old habits contrary to the actual music.

Or in March 1963 he gives the following revisions for "Structure of Rime XXI":

"solitude" for "loneliness" . . . "A depresst key" for "a touched string"—a depresst key is what it actually is (when the sympathetic sound rings) and also because both "depresst" and "key" refer to the substrata of the poem.

"steps of wood" = notes of the scale on a xylophone. . .

There are also the occasional suggestions for revision—or for more comprehensive change—of my own work (for until the late sixties we probably exchanged manuscripts of most of what we wrote). Sometimes his criticism was deeply instructive; of this the most telling instance concerns a 1962 poem in which I had *overextended my feelings.* Hearing that a painter we both knew (but who was not a close friend of mine, rather a friendly acquaintance whose work had given me great pleasure) had leukemia or some form of cancer, I plunged, as it were, into an ode that was almost a premature elegy. An image from one of his paintings had already appeared in another poem of mine—"Clouds"— which Duncan particularly liked. In his criticism of this new poem he showed me how the emotional measure of the first (which dealt with matters "proved upon my pulses," among which the remembrance of clouds he had painted ". . . as I see them—/rising/urgently, roseate in the/mounting of somber power"—"surging/in evening haste over hermetic grim walls" entered naturally, although the painter as a person played no part in the poem) was just; whereas in the new poem, focussing with emotional intensity upon an individual who was not in fact anywhere close to the center of my life, however much his paintings had moved me, the measure was false. Although I thought (and looking it over now, still think) the poem has some good parts, I was thoroughly convinced, and shall never publish it. It was a lesson which, like all valuable lessons, had applicability not only to the particular occasion; and one which has intimately to do with the ideogram Ezra Pound has made familiar to us—the concept of integrity embodied in the sign-picture of "a man standing by his word."

There were other occasions, though, when I paid no attention to Robert's criticism because he was misreading. For example, reading my prose "Note on the Imagination" in 1959, he speaks of,

> distrusting its discrimination (that just this is imagination and that—"the feared Hoffmanesque blank—the possible monster or stranger"—was Fancy), but wholly going along with the heart of the matter: the seed pearls of summer fog in Tess's hair, and the network of mist diamonds in your hair. But the actual distinction between the expected and the surprising real thing here (and taking as another term the factor of your "usual face-in-the-mirror") is the contrived (the work of Fancy) the remembered (how you rightly [say] "at

no time is it hard to call up scenes to the mind's eye"—
where I take it these are remembered) and the presented. But you see, if the horrible, the ugly, the very
feard commonplace of Hoffman and Poe had been
the "presented thing" it would have been "of the
imagination" as much as the delightful image. . . .

. . . The evaluation of Fancy and Imagination gets
mixed up with the description. All these terms of seeing: vision, insight, phantasm, epiphany, it "looks-like,"
image, perception, sight, "second-sight," illusion, appearance, it "appears-to-be," mere show, showing
forth . . . where trust and mistrust of our eyes varies.
However we trust or mistrust the truth, necessity, intent etc. of what is seen (and what manifests itself out
of the depths through us): we can't make the choice
between monster as fancy and the crown-of-dew as
imagination.

Here the disagreement is substantial, for the very point I
was trying to make concerned the way in which the active
imagination illuminates common experience, and not by
mere memory but by supplying new detail we recognize as
authentic. By common experience I mean that which con-
forms to or expresses what we share as "laws of Nature."
Hoffman's fantasies, known to me since childhood, had
given me pleasure because they were "romantic" in the
vernacular sense (and my edition had attractive illustra-
tions) but they did not illumine experience, did not "increase the sense of living, of being alive," to use Wallace
Stevens's phrase. In the "Adagia" Stevens says that "To be at
the end of reality is not to be at the beginning of imagination, but to be at the end of both." To me—then and now—
any kind of "sci fi," any presentation of what does not
partake of natural laws we all experience, such as gravity
and mortality, is only a work of imagination if it is dealing
symbolically with psychic truth, with soul-story, as myth,
fairytales, and sometimes allegory, do. Duncan continues,

Jess suggests it's not a matter of either/or (in which Fancy represented a lesser order and Imagination a higher order . . .) but of two operations or faculties. Shakespeare is rich in both imagination and fancy . . . where Ezra Pound totally excludes or lacks fancy. . . . George MacDonald [spoke] of "works of Fancy and Imagination." But I think he means playful and serious. Sometimes we use the word "fancy" to mean the trivial; but that surely does injustice to Shelley's landscapes or Beddoes' Skeleton's Songs or the description of Cleopatra's barge that gives speech to Shakespeare's sensual fancy.

And here I think the difference of views is semantic; for I indeed would attach the words "playful" and sometimes "trivial" and frequently "contrived," "thought-up," to the term fancy, and for the instances cited in Shelley or Beddoes, would employ the term *fantasy*. The description of Cleopatra's barge is neither fancy nor fantasy but the rhetoric of enthusiasm accurately evolving intense sensuous experience: an act of imagination. Fantasy does seem to me one of the functions of the imagination, subordinate to the greater faculty's deeper needs—so that "In a cowslip's bell I lie" and other evocations of faery in the *Midsummer Night's Dream*, for example, are delicate specifics, supplied by the power of fantasizing, for the more precise presentation of an *imagined*, not fancied or fantasied, world that we can apprehend as "serious"—having symbolic reality—even while we are entertained by its delightfulness and fun. The more significant divergence of opinion concerns "the presented thing," as Duncan called it—for there he seems to claim a value for the very fact of presentation, as if every image summoned up into some form of art had thereby its justification; a point of view he certainly did not, does not, adhere to, and yet—perhaps, again, just because he has had always so to contend with his own contentiousness and tendency to be extremely judgmental—which he does seem sometimes to propound, almost reflexively. "What I do," he wrote in January '61,

> —in that letter regarding your essay on Imagination, or yesterday in response to your letter and the reply to _____'s piece . . . is to contend. And it obscures perhaps just the fact that I am contending my own agreements often. . . . Aie! . . . I shall never be without and must work from those "irritable reachings after fact and reason" that must have haunted Keats too—

One of the ways in which what Duncan says here seems, unfortunately, to be true is manifest in this very statement, which assumes without due warrant (I think) that just because Keats saw in Coleridge that restless, irritable reaching, he himself was subject to it. Yet, however contentious, Duncan is often self-critical in these letters—as above, or as when he speaks (Sept. 1964) of "my . . . 'moralizing,' which makes writing critically such a chore, for I must vomit up my strong puritanical attacking drive. . . . this attacking in others what one fears to attack in oneself. . . ." And in the midst of arguments he was often generous enough to combine self-criticism, or at least an objective self-definition, with beautiful examples of his opponent's point of view—for instance, in the Oct. 1959 letter already referred to, discussing Fancy and Imagination, he says,

> Jess said an image he particularly remembers from Tess is stars reflected in puddles of water where cows have left hoof tracks—But, you know, I think I am so eager for "concept" that I lose those details. Or, more exactly—that my "concept" lacks details often. For, where you or Jess bring my attention back to the "little fog" intenser "amid the prevailing one" or the star in the cowtracked puddle: the presence of Tess and Angel leaps up. . . . But for me it's not the perceived verity

(your seed pearls of summer fog from Tess; or Madeline Gleason years ago to demonstrate the genius of imagination chose a perceived verity from Dante where the eyes of the sodomites turn and:

e si ver noi aguzzavan le ciglia,
come vecchio sartor fa nella cruna.

"towards us sharpened their vision, as an aged tailor does at the eye of his needle") I am drawn by the conceptual imagination rather than by the perceptual imagination. . . .

There were other times when Robert objected to some particular word in a poem of mine not in a way that instructed me but rather seemed due to his having *missed* a meaning. He himself was aware of that. In October 1966 he writes:

> And especially with you, I have made free to worry poems when there would arise some feeling of a possible form wanted as I read. Sometimes, as in your questionings of the pendent of Passages 2, such queries are most pertinent to the actual intent of the poem. And I think that even seemingly pointless dissents from the realized poem arise because along the line of reasoning a formal apprehension, vague but demanding, has arisen that differs from the author's form. In a mistaken reading, this will arise because I want to use the matter of the poem to write my own "Denise Levertov" poem. Crucially astray.

He wanted me to change an image of grief denied, dismissed, and ignored, in which I spoke of "Always denial. Grief in the morning, washed away/in coffee, crumbled to a dozen errands between/busy fingers" to "dunked" or "soaked" in coffee, not understanding that I meant it was washed *away*, obliterated; the "errands," the "busy fingers" and whatever other images of the poem all being manifestations of a turning away, a refusal to confront grief.

The attribution to others of his own intentions, concerns, or hauntings, an unfortunate spin-off of his inner contentions, occasioned another type of misreading—a reading-into, a suspicion of nonexistent complex motives that obstructs his full comprehension of what *does* exist.

What is going on," he writes in July 1966, "in your:

> still turns without surprise, with mere regret
> to the scheduled breaking open of breasts whose milk
> runs out over the entrails of still-alive babies,
> transformation of witnessing eyes to pulp-fragments,
> implosion of skinned penises into carcass-gulleys[9]

> —the words in their lines are the clotted mass of some
> operation . . . having what root in you I wonder?
> Striving to find place in a story beyond the immediate.

In this comment of his I find, sadly, that the "irritable reaching" stretches beyond "fact and reason" to search out complications for which there is no evidence. He misses the obvious. Having listed the lovely attributes of humankind, I proceeded, anguished at the thought of the war, to list the destruction of those very attributes—the violence perpetrated by humans upon each other. Because I believed that "we are members one of another" I considered myself morally obliged to attempt to contemplate, however much it hurt to do so, just what that violence can be. I forced myself to envision, in the process of writing, instances of it (drawing in part on material supplied by the Medical Committee for Human Rights or similar accounts; and elaborating from that into harsh language-sounds). There was no need to look for "what was going on" in me, "from what

---

[9]From "Life at War," see *The Sorrow Dance* (New York, New Directions, 1966), p. 80.

root" such images came—one had only to look at the viola-
tion of Viet Nam. And from the misreading of this very
poem stemmed, ultimately, the loss of mutual confidence
that caused our correspondence to end—or to lapse at least—
in the early seventies. But Duncan had conscious justification for such misreadings. In a 1967 interview of which he
sent me a transcript he expounded it in terms of what the
writer himself must do as reader of his own poem-in-
process—but it is clearly what he was doing as a reader of
my (and others') poems also:

> The poet must search and research, wonder about,
> consult the meaning of [the poem's] event. Here, to
> read means to dig, to let the forces of the poem work
> in us. Many poets don't read. For instance, take an
> awfully good poet like Robert Frost; while he writes a
> poem, he takes it as an expression of something he has
> felt and thought. He does not read further. It does not
> seem to be *happening to him*, but coming out of him.
> Readers too who want to be entertained by [or] to
> entertain the ideas of a writer will resent taking such
> writing as evidence of the Real and protest against our
> "reading into" poems, even as many protest the Freud-
> ians reading meanings into life that are not there. The
> writer, following images and meanings which arise
> along lines of a melody or along lines of rhythms and
> impulses, experiences the poem as an immediate
> reality. . . . I am consciously and attentively at work
> in writing—here I am like any reader. But I ask further,
> what is this saying? What does it mean that this is
> happening here like this?

This statement, as always with Duncan, contains, it seems
to me, a valuable reminder of how closely writers must see
what they do, to be responsible for it; and of how readers,
similarly, should not be content with the superficial, the face
value of a poem. But unfortunately, though his "digging for
meanings" results in many felicities and resonances in his

own work, the method often makes him a poor reader of others, a reader so intent upon shadow that he rejects, or fails to see, substance.

Meanwhile, if Duncan did not see what was obvious in that poem of mine, he certainly did see the war. Increasingly, from the mid-sixties on, its dark, dirty, oppressive cloud pervades his letters. In 1965, responding to a form letter I sent out to gather money and signatures for a full page ad in the *New York Times*—"Writers and Artists Protest the War in Viet Nam"—he had written,

> We feel as we know you and Mitch must feel—a helpless outrage at the lies upon which the American policy is run, and at the death and suffering "our" armaments, troops, and bombers have inflicted upon Viet Nam. Count on us for all protests and write if the protest needs more money. We will tell you if we can't make it; but we want to do whatever we can.

And along with his sense of helplessness in face of the outrage—where for all of us the horror itself was compounded by being committed *in our name*, as Americans— he began to worry about my increasing involvement in the antiwar movement.

> Denny, the last poem [it was *Advent 1966*][10] brings with it an agonizing sense of how the monstrosity of this nation's War is taking over your life, and I wish that I could advance some—not consolation, there is none— wisdom of how we are to at once bear constant (faithful and everpresent) testimony to our grief for those suffering in the War and our knowledge that the government of the U.S. is so immediately the agent of death and destruction of human and natural goods, and at the same time as constantly in our work (which must face and contain somehow this appalling and

[10]See *Relearning the Alphabet* (New York, New Directions, 1970), p. 4.

would-be spiritually destroying evidence of what human kind will do—for it has to do with the imagination of what is going on in Man) now, more than ever, to keep alive the immediacy of the ideal and of the eternal. Jess and I have decided that we will wear black armbands (as the Spanish do when some member of their immediate family has died) *always* and keep a period of mourning until certainly the last American soldier or "consultant" is gone from Viet Nam—but may it not be the rest of our lives? until "we" are no longer immediately active in bringing grief to members of the family of man. I started to wear a Peace button for the first time during the Poetry festival in Houston, and I found that it brought me to bear witness at surprising times—a waitress, a San Salvador millionaire, a Texas school teacher asked me what it meant. And I rejoiced in being called to my responsibility. Just at times when I was most forgetting myself and living it up.

Just over a year later, again, February 1967—

I have thought often how, if the outrage and grief of this war preoccupy my mind and heart as it does, the full burden of it must come upon you and Mitch with Nik so immediately involved. [Our son Nikolai was by now of draft age.] And I was fearful in January that you were having a bad time compounded with that other constant claim upon one's life the whole literary structure would make, and where you have a greater exposure in New York. . . . I think also of how much [anti] war groups and other organizations would lay claim. . . . it seems to me too that whatever is not volunteered from the heart, even goodness and demonstrations against the war, when it is conscripted is grievous.

228

There is, I feel, a confusion here. Certainly, as that poem *Advent 1966* and others attest, the ever-present consciousness of the war darkened my life as it darkened the lives of us all. Yet Duncan's affectionate anxiety about me and Mitch was in a sense misplaced. Duncan himself suffered, surely, a greater degree of frustration than we did, because we lightened that burden for ourselves by taking on the other burden of action. Duncan did bear testimony with his peace button and black armband; he attended a number of demonstrations, including the rally of writers, artists, and intellectuals at the Justice Department (which led to the conspiracy trial of Dr. Spock and four others, of whom Mitch Goodman was one) and the huge march on the Pentagon the following day, in fall of 1967; and he participated in group poetry readings given as benefits for the Resistance movement. But he did not join with others on a day-to-day basis in organizing antiwar activities. Meanwhile, even though grief, rage, shame and frustration inevitably continued, and indeed even grew as my political awareness grew and I began to see how this war was only one facet of a complex of oppression, I nevertheless was experiencing unforeseen blessings. Not only was ongoing action a relief, an outlet for frustration, however small a drop in the bucket of resistance to that oppression one knew it to be; but—much more importantly—there was the experience of a new sense of community as one worked, or picketed, or even merely "milled around" with comrades. As a good Anarchist from his youth up, Duncan mistrusted group action; and he was just enough older than I to have a ready suspicion of "Stalinism" every time he confronted some action planned or carried out in a way that did not strike him as entirely "voluntarist." This habit of distrust had shown itself to me as far back as 1959, when he expressed hesitations concerning a magazine he otherwise liked (and which in fact was quite nonpolitical in its concerns) merely because of its "exaggerated estimate of Neruda . . . plus the poem by Celan where I suspected the reference to Madrid as standing for

229

Spain in the Civil War" and added that he had sent "a prodding letter" to the editor, "to see if there was any neo-Stalinism going on there." This fear in him, by being a large factor in keeping him out of more involvement in the Movement during the sixties and early seventies, had two effects: one was that his political awareness, formed in the forties and early fifties, remained static; and the other, that he did not experience the comradeship, the recognition of apparent strangers as brothers and sisters, that so warmed the hearts of those who did feel it, giving us in the difficult present some immediate token of hope for a truly changed future—a comradeship which depended precisely upon a political awareness that was *not* static, but *in process of becoming.* Had he but realized it, the spirit of those days was (except in certain factions not central to the movement) not Stalinist, coercive, and regimented at all, but essentially as voluntarist as he could have desired. But we did gather together, and we did shout slogans—and it was perhaps due not only to ideological difference, but to temperamental distaste, that Duncan did not and could not do so. He was, therefore, isolated in his very real anguish; his blood pressure soared; and he could not see that there was nothing I was engaged in that was not "volunteered from the heart."

But the wedge driven between us by his supposition that I was acting coercively, toward myself and—possibly— towards others (a supposition which had, as I see it, no foundations in truth) had not yet gone very deep. In December 1968, a time of private troubles for me as well as of shared political ones, he wrote,

> . . . to reassure you my thoughts are with you. And a prayer . . . not to something I know, yet "to," but *from* something I know very well—the deep resources I have had in our friendship, the so much we have shared and share in what we hold good and dear for human life, and the service we would dedicate our art to. My own thought has been dark this year and in some part of it I have been apprehensive of how much

more vulnerable and involved you are: I mean here about the crisis of the war and then the coming-to-roost of the American furies. What we begin to see are the ravening furies of Western civilization. And it corresponds with our own creative generation's arriving at the phase when the furies of our own art come-home-to-roost. Denny, just as I have been carried in my own work to a deeper, grander sense of the ground, I have begun to be aware of gaps and emptinesses—in my being? in the ground?—and I have now to turn next to work again on the H.D. book where I had begun to dread having to do with the inner conflicts I sensed at work there. The *World Order* essay, as I wrote, was written in phases of inertia, dread and breakthrus.

Does it help at all to consider that in part your affliction is the artist's? The personal pain is compounded in it.

Well I couldn't speed this off. My sense that I was doing no more than identifying a brooding center in my own feeling with your inner pain halted me in my tracks. Only, this morning, to find that my thought as I woke turning to you still revolved around or turned to the concept of inner trials belonging to the testing of the creative artist, which we as poets and artists come to, as surely as the fairytale hero or heroine comes to some imprisonment or isolation—to dwell in the reality of how the loved thing is to be despaired of. I am thinking of the story of the forgotten bride and groom dwelling close to her or his beloved in despised form.

Only, in this fumbling, to try and say that your dread, pain, and being at a loss—personal as it must be, is also the share of each of us who seeks to deepen feeling. Not an affliction in and of itself but belonging to the psychic metamorphosis—we cannot direct it, or, it is directed by inner orders that our crude and unwilling conscious self dreads. Eros and his Other, Thanatos, work there.

That beautiful letter, in which the feeling-tone of an earlier time in our friendship resounds at a deeper, darker pitch, and which sums up, or rather, is representative of, the rich, the immeasurable gift given me by this association, seems almost valedictory. Yet it was not yet so, in fact, for a month later Mitch and I arrived on the West Coast to spend six months at Berkeley. During this period, though my teaching job and participation in current events (this was 1969, the spring of the Third World strike and of People's Park) prevented me from seeing Robert as often as I had hoped, there were some quiet times of reading current poems to one another (and to Mitch and Jess) and at least one or two walks in the mimosa- and eucalyptus-scented lanes above Berkeley, a terrain he knew intimately and seemed curiously at rest in.

It was not until after that, in the early seventies, that our correspondence faltered and jarred to a halt. I will not deal here with the way every negative element that had ever arisen between us, but especially the false interpretation begun in his questioning of "Life at War," began to take over in our letters, each of us taking fierce, static, antagonist "positions," he of attack, I of defense. It is a conflict still unresolved—if this is in some sense a narrative, the end of the story has perhaps not yet been reached. But I think of my Duncan letters as a constellation rather than as a linear sequence. And in that constellation the major stars are without question the messages of instruction by means of which my intelligence grew keener, my artistic conscience more acute; messages of love, support, and solidarity in the fellowship of poetry. None of my many poet friends has given me more; and when I look back to Florence, 1948, I know I came then upon what was for two decades a primary current of my life.

Herbert Read Remembered

I had begun to read some of Herbert Read's books on art when I was fourteen or fifteen; then his poems, and perhaps *The Green Child*, though that may have been a little later. So that, in 1939, when I turned sixteen, and the ballet school at which I was a full-time student was evacuated to Seer Green, Buckinghamshire, it was tremendously exciting to find that the Reads lived at the next house up the road. My first visit there, with some other ballet students, was, I think, part of an expedition to sell tickets for our first local recital. I said not a word, but used every minute to scan the wonderful paintings—one was a Miro, I recall—and the bookshelves, which, even though I had grown up in a house full of books, were the most enticing I had ever seen. Before long Mrs. Read was kindly filling in as class accompanist when the regular pianist was ill; and I believe she once played for one of our recitals. I seized every opportunity to be the bearer of messages from my teacher to Mrs. Read, in order to return to that magical house, thatched with Norfolk reeds, which represented the whole world of contemporary art and poetry, which I already dreamed of entering (as a painter as well as a writer, in those ambitious days—yes, and a ballerina as well, though I never really believed that part would come true). Sometimes Mr. Read would appear, and I would gaze at him, my hero, so intensely that it must have embarrassed him had he not been too modest to notice it. At least once the senior students—five or six of us—were invited to dinner at the Reads, which gave me the chance to go upstairs to wash, and peer at more paintings and sculptures, more beautifully arranged, brightbacked books. But I never, during that whole year, had courage to say to Herbert Read, "I draw and paint and write poems and I've read your books and I long to talk with you."

Published in *Herbert Read: A Memorial Symposium* (London, Methuen, 1969), which was originally a special issue of *The Malahat Review* (British Columbia, Canada).

I remember one day in the summer of 1940, during the Battle of Britain when sudden explosions of white cloud in the blue skies would reveal the reality of a war that still didn't seem quite real: a day when the ballet school gave a garden party to mark the opening of an art exhibition in our dance studio. The artist was a child prodigy, Plato Chan, who with his mother and sister was a member of the strange assemblage of dancers, evacuees, refugees, Russian exiles, and misfits that formed our household; and Herbert Read had consented to give a short speech on the exhibit. After he'd done so, I escaped from the crowded room filled with local gentry. But the garden was full of them too. Shy and lonely, and imagining Mr. Read to be somewhere among them having a brilliant conversation I wished I were privileged to overhear, I retreated to the garden's furthest edge and slipped behind the tall hedge to be by myself and moon over my poems—and who should I find there but Herbert Read himself, with his little boy, then about two. They were hiding! He too had escaped! I'll never forget the guilty, embarrassed look he gave me. I fled, with a startled "Sorry!"—and said nothing when, back in the crowd, with a tray of glasses thrust into my hand to pass round, I heard people chattering, "Where is Herbert? Where can Mr. Read be?" . . . I was happy in my sense of complicity.

That fall, when the bombing began, I went back to London to be with my parents, and I did not see him again for several years. But when I was eighteen I wrote to him, sending some poems and asking for criticism. He wrote back encouraging me, giving quite detailed comments, and gently reproving me for never having spoken to him when I was his neighbour. Thereafter for three or four years I would send my work to him about every six or eight months, never failing to receive an encouraging but helpfully critical reply. Isolated as I was at that time—in the first two years especially—such letters from a man I so respected and admired were of inestimable value to me. (For years I kept them all safely throughout my many moves and travels; alas, it is now a long time since I have been able to find them—

234

but I don't believe they are really lost: I expect to rediscover them some day.) And meanwhile poems of his—"Cranach" and "The Sorrows of Unicume" for instance—were working in me in deep, still unacknowledged ways. When my first book, *The Double Image*, was published by Cresset Press, in 1946, I dedicated it to Herbert, to John Hayward (who had, as reader for Cresset, accepted the book for publication) and to Charles Wrey Gardiner (who was then editing *Poetry Quarterly*, the first magazine in which my work was printed). At some point in the 1940s I introduced Gardiner to Herbert's romance, *The Green Child*, which was then out of print, and suggested that his Grey Walls Press bring out a new edition of it. (Grey Walls Press being long since defunct, I suppose this edition also has now become rare.) This was the only opportunity I ever had to do something for Herbert in return for all his unfailing kindnesses to me— which included, in 1945, writing a reference for me to get a job in a bookstore (where, being incapable of making correct change, I was an abysmal failure) and, a decade later, recommending me for a Guggenheim Fellowship.

After I came to America in 1948 I saw Herbert occasionally on his visits to read and lecture. He never forgot to have me invited to parties and receptions given for him in New York—and always on these loud, crowded occasions I was reminded of that moment of stumbling upon him hiding behind the hedge at Seer Green, for the guest of honour obviously shrank from being lionized and seemed to long to be invisible. On one such occasion he said to my husband that he believed he had made a crucial mistake at some point in his life, that he never should have let himself become a "public figure," (by then he was *Sir* Herbert), that he would have been a great deal happier raising sheep in Yorkshire or even in Australia, writing more poetry and fiction and less criticism. The very last time I saw him, at Bill Bueno's house in Middletown, Connecticut, during one of his two or more long visits to Wesleyan University, I was deeply saddened by his evident weariness and illness and that sense he had, despite all his achievements, of unfulfill-

235

ment as an artist. Yet his gentleness, and his enthusiasm and concern for the work of others, were untinged with bitterness. Here is the text of his very last letter to me; even though I feel some embarrassment at making public his praise of my poems, I want to show, in tribute to him, that gentleness of his, that integrity and simplicity so characteristic of him:

Stonegrave, York, 16.iv.67

Dear Denise:

Thank you very much for 'The Sorrow Dance'—I've told you again and again how much I like your poetry and this new volume does not disappoint me—indeed, it is better than ever. I like what I would call the objective poems better than the 'didactic' ones—how difficult it is to write about 'events' rather than perceptions. But most of your poems are visual in the sense I mean, the images so clearly seen. The 'Olga Poems' are very moving.

Your letter must have arrived near to the day (April 4) that Sophie had her second baby, here in Stonegrave. She is living in Liverpool now, where her husband Nick is studying architecture. Her first child, Eliza, is now an enchanting girl of eighteen months, very lively and intelligent.

I, alas, have been in and out of hospital and am still not quite better. I went to Portugal in search of sun and warmth, but it was just as cold as Yorkshire. It is lovely here now, thousands of daffodils and all the trees beginning to show their fresh green leaves.

Our second son, Piers, is coming to New York in September on a Harkness Fellowship and will be in the States for 2 years. He has decided to get married first and will bring his bride (18!) with him. He is to take Frank MacShane's course in Creative Writing at Columbia as a beginning. I hope you will see something of him. We all send our love—

Herbert.

Finally, I would like to quote these words of his, copied into my notebook in 1942:

> It is only an unintelligent and superficial realism that demands of the artist a mechanical reflection of the objects which lie in his field of vision. Nor is it much more intelligent to restrict the artist to what is called an interpretation of those objects—the running commentary of the impressionistic journalist. What history demands in its long run, is the object itself—the work of art which is itself a created reality, an addition to the sum of real objects in the world.

That definition—the work of art as an addition to the sum of real objects in the world—gave me, at eighteen, floundering in the beginnings of my life as an artist, a ground to stand on, a measure to try and fill. I think there was much experience that came to me later that I would not have been ready for if I had not then taken those words into my life.

Herbert Read was a wonderful friend to me for nearly thirty years. I shall miss him always.

Beatrice Levertoff

My mother was born on June 29th 1885 and christened Beatrice Adelaide. Her father, Walter Spooner-Jones, M.D., was a grandson of Angell Jones of Mold, the tailor, teacher, and preacher, to whom Daniel Owen, "the Welsh Dickens" was apprenticed, and with whose son John Angell Jones, (my great-uncle, if I am counting generations correctly) whose shop doubled as a kind of literary and intellectual salon in the 1870s, he subsequently worked until setting up in business for himself. Angell Jones the elder, my great-great grandfather, is depicted by Daniel Owens in *Rhys Lewis,* a novel I long to read but of which the only English translation is long since out of print and unobtainable. My cousin Myfanwy (Mrs Illtyd Howell of Newport, Gwent) shares this descent. She grew up in Llangefni (Anglesey) and was one of the prime movers in Welsh language broadcasting, and later in TV also.

My mother's parents were from Caernarvon and Llanberis. Her father, who inherited the deft hands of several generations of master tailors, studied medicine and surgery in Scotland, married even before he graduated, and brought his young Llanberis bride, Miss Margaret Griffiths, to the mining village of Abercanaid, near Merthyr (next along the Taff valley to Aberfan), where he was employed as a junior doctor by the mining company. Often he used to have to go down the pit to operate at the site of an accident, when a man was pinned by a fall and had to have a limb amputated there and then. He was known and trusted as an excellent surgeon, though he did not really like the practice of medicine. When my mother was two and a half her mother died in childbirth, the baby dying likewise. Dr. Spooner-Jones

---

This brief account of my mother's life was written in 1977 before her death, at the request of the editors of *Poetry Wales* after they had heard me read some poems by her. Its publication in the magazine did not take place until after her death, so she did not see it.

remarried, but was not very happy; and my mother was increasingly neglected by her step-mother. However, this very neglect gave her childhood the partial solitude which enriched it—so that all my life her memories have been to me a fascinating oral storybook. Had she grown up in the bosom of a large, happy, well-ordered household perhaps the habits of observation and reflection would not have been so well developed in her. Like New England's Sarah Orne Jewett (but at a much earlier age) she sometimes accompanied her father on his house calls (made on foot) and to this day—at ninety-two—can tell anecdotes about many of the people they went to see, describing their appearance down to details of dress. One family that has always stuck in my mind from her childhood reminiscences, kept a pub somewhere on the Nightingale Street edge of the village, and were especially musical, all singing and playing the harp, even a little girl not much older than my mother (who would have been between six and eight at this time), all having curly golden hair and beautiful milky complexions (and all, alas, riddled with T.B.). Sometimes at night, after supper, she would go with her father to visit a miner friend of his who had built himself a telescope. All along the street the men would be singing, sitting on their heels in the dusk after a long day down the pit. The music and the stars must have been mysteriously connected for the little girl, out and about when the other children of the village had been put to bed; as they were connected for me at the same age, listening to her tell about it.

When she was ten or so, there was a move into Merthyr, and not long afterwards the step-mother died. By the time she was twelve her father died too—still in his early thirties— and she was taken to live in the very different atmosphere of Holywell, Flintshire, where her maternal aunt Elisabeth— Auntie Bess—was the wife of a well-known Congregational minister, the Rev. David Oliver. Neglect and freedom were replaced by strict care and many duties, in a household from which most of the older children had gone, into marriage or career, but in which her two youngest cousins were close to her own age. The next ten years of her life gave rise to a still larger and more detailed crop of stories. Whether Holywell had more than its share of eccentrics, or whether—as I think more likely—a quiet, observant, humorous girl simply saw what others often missed or took for granted, these tales fascinated me no matter how often I heard them, and have always seemed to me distinctively Welsh in some way I can't define: I don't believe an English town of the same size at the turn of the century would have yielded anything quite comparable. It is perhaps a question of the emotional intensity involved—pent up in a besieged culture, a fervent but restrictive religious mode, a mountainous land. My memory being relatively poor and vague, I prevailed on my mother to write down some of her "Tales of Holywell" some years ago, and I treasure the many exercise books that contain them, though they present only a few of the many memories, and of course it is not quite the same thing to read them, especially the amusing ones, as to have heard them acted out, complete with imitations of people's comical speech and manners. One that comes to mind is about a man known as Man the Lifeboat; he was a devoted member of the church and had a cousin who was a famous professional singer, and so got appointed *dychraewr canu*,[1] but he really couldn't sing and when, at "socials," he would be invited to give a solo, invariably sang "Man the Lifffffeboat" with a tremendous splutter on the f, from which the audience used to discreetly duck. Or the famous visiting preacher whose new false teeth were hurting him; so he slipped them quietly into his handkerchief pocket; but as his sermon developed, so did his *hwyl*, so much so that he made *himself* weep, not only the congregation—and sweeping his handkerchief out to dab his eyes, out flew the teeth, straight into a portly lady's Sunday-best lap.

In those years Beatrice went through high school and teacher training, developed her beautiful singing voice (of professional quality if she had had the opportunity to go

[1]Choir leader.

further), played hockey, drew and painted, did a lot of
housework, was deeply affected by the Revival,[2] read all
the books she could get her hands on (not a wide choice)
and loved the mountain with its sheep-cropped grass and
tiny flowers and the sound of the distant sea you could hear
in a clump of pines if you closed your eyes. And because,
despite basic kindness and affection, she always felt like a
"poor relation" in some ways, and hankered secretly after
some of the freedom of her childhood, she always dreamed
of travel. The way to travel was to teach. Her Uncle David
would not let her be a governess in Paris, because Paris was
a sinful and dangerous city; but he did let her take a job in
Constantinople, because it was at a girls' school run by the
Scotch Mission. So off she went—never having been further
than Liverpool and Cardiff before—on the Orient Express.
She had signed a five-year contract, but it was not long
before she met my father, a young Russian Jew who had
converted to Christianity and had begun his lifelong task of
attempting to reconcile Jews and Christians. My mother and
he were soon engaged; she broke her contract, returned to
Wales to introduce him to her relations, was married in
London from the house of another aunt, (also the wife of a
minister), and went to live in Warsaw (then part of the
Russian Empire). From Warsaw they went to Germany—
were prisoners of war in Leipzig (not in a camp, but under
house arrest) during WWI; "displaced persons" in Denmark
after the Armistice, before being able to cross the mined
North Sea to England (another cause of delay was the fact
that my father was a Russian citizen still); and eventually
settled for many years in the London area, in the Essex
suburb of Ilford. My father was ordained in the Anglican
Church in 1922. I will only summarize the next two decades
of my mother's life: work as my father's amanuensis; bringing up her two children (my sister was nine years older than
I though, so that in some ways my experience was that of an
only child) which involved giving me daily lessons (I did not

[2]The religious revival which swept Wales in the first decade of the
twentieth century.

go to school); writing a novella and an (unpublished) novel for children; hard and selfless work rescuing refugees from Hitler and finding homes and work for them in Britain; reading aloud virtually all of nineteenth century fiction, and much else, to her family (and especially to me, for I was a voracious listener); reading as much history as she could manage (she should have gone to university and studied it—but then it would have been another life . . .);[3] surviving the drudgery of keeping house through the years of bombing and rationing; nursing my father through his painful last illness. Then, ill herself at the time, she came to live with me and my son and (now ex-) husband in New York City, a whole new adventure gamely undertaken—and soon, even more of a step into the unknown, accompanied us to Guadalajara, Mexico, where we proposed living for two years. While we were there she went at one point to Oaxaca, in the south of Mexico, to be a paying guest for a few weeks with a Mexican family. They asked her to stay longer—she did; longer still—she did; and eventually became the adopted grandmother—"Abuelita"—and in many respects the mainstay of the household, bringing up the youngest daughter (who was born after she went to live there) on Beatrix Potter and *The Wind in the Willows*, etc. She has now been in Mexico almost twenty years. And during that time she has not stood still in her life, but—reading, painting watercolors, thinking, beginning to write poems—has been constantly growing. (While, as she would add, shrinking in physical size, as people do in their eighties!)

After she left Wales in 1910 to go to Constantinople she never really lived there again, though of course she visited from time to time, the last occasion being just after my father's death in 1955. But she has never lost a great love for and pride in Wales. The Welsh hymns, and secular songs like *Davydd y Garreg Wen*, sung or remembered or heard on records, never fail to bring tears to her eyes. One of her

[3]She also researched and painted a foldout panorama of first-century Jerusalem, together with a text and line-drawings, published by S.P.C.K. Press (London).

great joys in Oaxaca in the days when she was still strong and agile enough (i.e. into her eighties) was to go "for a good tramp" on the bare grassy hills just above the town, reminiscent of Welsh moorland. As I, her only surviving child, began to become well-known in America as a poet, she rejoiced, and not merely in my worldly success but more deeply in my work itself which has often moved her; but it was a special pleasure to her when I read to a Welsh audience, as I did a few years ago, and particularly on my 1976 visit when, at Barry, I really felt I had made some contact with the vital literary life of Wales, meeting a number of poets and writers. What she does not realize is that if I was given a measure of acceptance as a person less alien than a visiting American with a Russian name might be supposed to be, it was in large part because I had read to that audience a poem of *hers* about her childhood in Abercanaid.

The other thing she doesn't know—though I have told her—is that though I may have inherited from my father some of his verbal gifts (he was a prolific writer and an admired preacher) it was she who, as I have written,

taught me to look,
to name the flowers when I was still close to the ground,
my face level with theirs;
or to watch the sublime metamorphoses
unfold and unfold
over the walled back gardens of our street.

I could not ever have been a poet without that vision she imparted.

(Beatrice Spooner-Jones Levertoff died on June 8th, 1977, a few months after this memoir was written. D.L.)

One summer evening, led by her. . . .
—Wordsworth

One spring morning, led by a surge of common sense and
the hand of the Muse—who must by then have been exasperated by my precocious infidelity—I quit my ballet class
never to return. Actually I did return, the very next day; but
with a change of spirit. I was sixteen at the time, and had
suffered unrequited love for my ballet teacher for almost
four years. I would never have enrolled in the ballet class in
the first place if my much-older sister had not placed me
there to give herself a little vicarious satisfaction. It was she
who had really wanted—too late—to be a ballerina. To
make sure I stuck (first preparing my desires by taking me
to see the de Basil Russian Ballet Company two or three
times a week during their London season) she told me, as a
big secret, that Madame thought I was so talented she was
giving me a huge, possibly a whole, scholarship; but I was
never to thank her, never to say a word about it to anyone.
Madame wished it to be an entirely private matter. My
thanks might be in the form of my eventual success. When I
made my grand debut, my first prima ballerina role, then
and only then might I say to her, "I owe everything to you."
I was already under a spell by the time my sister imparted
this breathtaking information to me. She conned my parents, too, of course. By the time it was discovered that my
sister had been paying for my classes all that year, with
money taken from them—(cash from a desk drawer? I
forget. But anyway, eventually found missing—it took a
while as Father was no businessman) I was hooked, on
Madame and the dream of dancing Odette/Odile. And my
sister was gone. *Incommunicado. Disparu.* It was about a
year before they traced her, and by that time my father had

Written *c.*, 1964, revised 1980.

adjusted to paying my ballet school bills. Madame made him a slight reduction because he spoke Russian—not because she thought I was gifted. I suppose my outcries of despair at the idea of having to stop my lessons and give up the dream that had been painfully grafted into me were more than he could take—on top of his older daughter's disappearance, anyway.

So, though I preferred to paint and read, and above all to write poems; yes, though I had known ever since I was nine or ten, or even before, that I was a poet; even though my very bones told me daily that I would never be more than mediocre as a dancer—I had, by the summer I was sixteen, spent four years in a perverse slavery. *Elevation good; arms graceful. Denise, come to the front of the class and demonstrate that step.* My moments of ecstasy. *Turn-out poor, pointe work bad, Fouettés terrible. Denise, what are you doing? Idiote! Shto takoi?* Despair, and I stumble about in the back row, or retire immobile to a corner and weep, ignored. My moments of misery so outnumber the moments of ecstasy that indeed they are not moments but the dark fabric out of which little joys jump, rarely and briefly. And among the joys are those occasions when Madame lets me walk to the Underground station with her, carrying her hold-all, and talks to me about Paris, about Gurdjieff, about—what? I'm damned if I can remember, or care to. Oh yes, the mimosa at Juan les Pins. So I spent my pocket money buying hothouse mimosa—but she sniffed it with a grimace and said it had no smell. She was an unworthy object of love, violent, insensitive, a capricious authoritarian, with a poor taste in music—and indeed in the arts generally—and a fanatical belief in her own importance.

The virtues of this tiny, aging woman were her energy and her bitter loyalty to her family—(old mother, ne'er-do-well brother, sister and various nephews) most of whom I think she supported. She worked very hard; worked her students and her accompanist very hard; and shouted abuse at them eighty percent of the time. It's a wonder most of them didn't leave. But her reputation—based on her late

245

husband's extreme eminence as a dance teacher—did a great deal for her; and it's true that for professional dancers a class with her meant an intense, fiery workout, charged with action to the limits of endurance. They already knew what to do, and she made them do it. She was a dynamic drill sergeant rather than a teacher, in fact. The remaining twenty percent of the time she gave, with a sort of primitive cunning, to flattery, cajolery, and—oh twist of the knife!—to pathos. To me she was a swan—Odette/Odile herself—a tragic figure who would have been the most famous of all dancers if she had not broken a knee long ago—a dark angel whose ill-temper was righteous (an Olympian fire) and whose kinder moments were glimpses into depths of tender wisdom. She was about five feet two, wore black bell-bottomed pants (in a decade when no one else did) and must have been about fifty at that time, I suppose; maybe more.

When the second World War was declared, the school, like much else in London, fell apart. I'm not talking about the bombing; that didn't begin till a whole year later. I mean that the theaters closed, travelling ballet companies cancelled their London seasons, mothers of younger students removed their children to the country, and not enough pupils attended to make it profitable to pay the rent on the huge studio. Anyway, Madame too moved to the country, together with her dependents, and gathered around her a few devoted students and a larger number of people with no place else to go. It was to be not only a ballet school, but an academy. The personnel was random but suggested a certain adequacy. There was dear Babushka, her mother— very old, very mumbly, very moustached and bearded, with her two ancient and smelly pekinese; she was to teach Russian. (And she really did teach *me* some, though regular classes never got under way. We read *The Little Hump-backed Horse* together, and she gave me tea in a glass with a few white hairs floating in it. Happy hours. Dear old woman.) There was the brother, Vanya, a pianist in the blood-and-thunder arpeggio style (with missed notes) and composer (improvised variations on themes by Rachmani-noff) who might perhaps be persuaded to give music les-sons to a talented few. (This did not occur.) There was Vanya's wife, who only played patience, but didn't eat much; and Auntie Sonya who did not even play patience, but gave tone to the establishment, being a Princess (by marriage) and very gracious (and indeed, like Babushka, very kind) and had the bluest eyes I ever saw, and dyed black hair. Later I realized Madame dyed her hair too; I even knew it then, though I would not admit it. Auntie Sonya's husband the Prince visited only rarely. It was said he worked in a bank. But there was Alexey, also a prince, who had loved her when she was young, and asked for her hand, and been refused, and had gone away to war, and she had married, and then came the Revolution and he and she and her husband all met in Paris, where she and her husband started a restaurant; and Alexey had been shell-shocked and could not speak or think, but they gave him a job washing dishes. So here he was, and could wash the academy's dishes. He was pale, thin, and silent; only at night he would sometimes bring out his balalaika and sing to it.

Then there was Mrs. Hong, a Chinese lady whose hus-band was in the Secret Service and had disappeared when war was declared. She was kind but noisy and not easy to understand. Late at night, when Alexey brought out his balalaika, she would be seized by a desire to cook, and would create stacks of delicious pancakes stuffed with greens, called Dai-bangs, and, using a pan and its lid as a gong, would rouse the sleepers young and old, who came trooping into the kitchen to eat, rubbing their eyes and yawning. Mrs. Hong was nervous, not knowing where her husband was, and suffered from a mild case of klepto-mania. She would occasionally take the sheets off one's bed and hide them in her room. But we knew where to look; she never took anything out of the house. Her ten year old daughter, Angelina, was a ballet-student, and her eight year old son, Socrates, was an artist.

Who else? Oh, Elizaveta's mother. Elizaveta was one of

the senior students from London days, a really good dancer, and her mother, a German refugee, was the widow of a Russian exile. Mrs. Patrinsky had a heart condition and was always enquiring plaintively for a *physician* (she never said a *doctor*). Her morale was poor, or at least pessimistic, if one can so describe morale; her culture was high. She would teach German and French. She was in fact an excellent teacher; but factors too numerous to mention prevented the exercise of her talents during the year I lived in that house.

With Mrs. Patrinsky and Elizaveta, (who was eighteen, a good dancer and a good girl, but spiritless) came, as in a package, *die kleine* Trudi, seventeen, a refugee and orphan whom Mrs. Patrinsky had taken under her wing. The character of Mrs. Patrinsky had about it something that suggested a benevolent vampire or boa constrictor. She fed upon sorrows; she crushed anyone she could crush—but tenderly. Elizaveta and Trudi were encouraged to stay in bed when they had their periods. Suffer! Suffer! How Mrs. Patrinsky loved it when I would start to cry and not be able to stop. A sadist she was not, but a sense of humor she did not have. Her one pleasure was the giving of doleful sympathy, and this necessitated a doleful person to give it to. A Mrs. Gummage from the Court of Weimar . . .

Trudi was neither spiritless like Elizaveta nor given to torrential weeping like me; but she was very young and unformed and frightened, and glad to get under a warm hen's wing even if the hen was a boa constrictor.

Add Rita, surely the original Lolita, a nubile and ravishing child of eleven, and Minette, her roly poly little sister; Sara, fourteen, and Laura, ten, also sisters, one tall and thin and the other short and plump, and probably the two most sensitive and intelligent of all the inmates. Their American parents, long resident in Europe and loyal to it now the war was on, had moved them from place to place and school to school all their lives; they were not very happy but nothing surprised them. There was also Ernestine, ten, who was frankly homesick: her parents raised coffee in Kenya. She spent her holidays down in the West Country at a manor house with her grandmother, who at seventy still rode to hounds.

Our male dancer was Peter—Peter the Partner, indispensible for practising "double work": he was, oh, twenty-three? twenty-five?—a con-man if there ever was one, from Berlin; now also a refugee, and playing the son to Mrs. Patrinsky. No doubt Madame was well aware he constituted no danger to us girls—but I was not, and since he was, without exception, the only young man I knew at the time, I felt a certain interest in him: of which, having sworn undying and exclusive loyalty to my grumpy little idol, I was ashamed. Oh, I almost forgot—there was another young man around, a boy of seventeen, Arthur, the Madame's oafish nephew (the composer's son) who spent his school vacations with us—but he was a nondancing Caliban who spat and picked his nose. He was waiting impatiently for Rita-Lolita to turn twelve and notice him. (She did.)

Finally—(not really finally, for many others came and went, including a series of genteel governesses for the children and an even longer series of piano accompanists, few of whom could stay the pace for more than a few weeks) there was Madame's tough, gallant daughter, Mab, who did all the cooking, and her husband, Abe, a jazz musician from Whitechapel, who dried the dishes and fixed things and watched the proceedings of these assorted misfits with patience and irony. I used to think him the wittiest and also the sanest man I ever met—but in retrospect I see he was as crazy as the rest of us, just to *be* there. People used to say he was lazy, which angered me; but maybe it was true. Why else would he have stayed?

The academy of liberal arts, as I have adumbrated, failed to materialize. Personalities were in too much conflict for schedules to be agreed upon. Even the little ones' schooling lapsed between governesses (and Britain's usually firm school inspectors no doubt had their hands much too full, that year of mass evacuations from the cities, to bother with us). But meals and ballet classes were supplied with regularity. Every morning and every afternoon we danced for two-hour stretches—sometimes longer. In the evenings we rehearsed for recitals we were to give in the neighborhood. What other students did the rest of the time, I can't remember; but as for me, when I was not dancing I read (I had a Boots Lending Library subscription and could order what I wanted) or darned my dancing shoes, or hung around Mab and Abe in the kitchen, washing the dishes in the frequent unexplained absence of silent Prince Alexey.

That early summer morning in 1940 when I walked out of class I'd been living in this ménage about seven months. Madame had just yelled at me that, my right arm upraised, my head turned to the right as directed, I looked as if I were smelling my armpit. I had heard this before, not only directed at myself—any student might hear it at least once a week, though not usually if their mother had come to visit the class (but then mine never did, and I was glad she didn't, for I preferred to keep my worlds separate—and home *was* another world). But on this particular morning something in me said "enough." It was like the opening pages of *The Wind in the Willows*, when the Mole also has had enough, and stops spring cleaning his house, and pushes his way up and out, into the sunshine, and finds the River, and the Rat, and begins all his adventures. I just stopped dancing, turned around, and quietly walked out of the room. No one paid any attention.

I went up to the room I shared with the little girls, changed out of my tunic and tights and pointe shoes, and walked out of the house. No one saw me. I walked very fast for about a mile, not looking at anything. Something was pulling me. I say it was the Muse because it wasn't just a wave of disgust and impatience at that whole sick, phony, second-rate, imitation-Chekhov household and at my silly, hopeless crush on a bitchy little ballet mistress that was pulling me: it was the knowledge, the remembrance, that I was a poet, a writer, a person whose life had from the first centered in language, not in learning to use my muscles; however beautiful an *arabesque* did seem to me, it was in truth as something to watch, not to do.

250

When I slowed down and looked about me I saw it was spring. A chaffinch—I remember that it was a chaffinch because next day I looked it up in a bird book—was singing on a branch that overhung the lane in which I found myself. It had rained the night before, and now in mid morning the earth still smelled damp and fresh. Leaves and grass were that new light green I associated with the Middle Ages and with some of the earliest English poems. Rivulets rippled in the ditches, and there were small wildflowers in the hedgerows. Only a month or two before, I had written sadly to my closest friend saying I felt I'd lost the intensity of sight, the passion for looking at the world, I'd had as a child. Now I realized I was taking in with restored vision all that I had thought was lost to me. I was released from a dull enchantment into a quiet spring day in Buckinghamshire that was not only different from, but indisputably more important than whatever was going on indoors, at that very moment, in the ballet school.

I spent the whole day walking. My pockets were empty; but hunger was itself a pleasure. I didn't try to walk like a dancer: I strode and stumped along, and swung my arms, and sang out loud, and kicked stones along the road. Whenever I came to a fieldpath I'd climb the stile and leave the road, not caring where the path led to, as long as it was away.

Here and there I'd sit down for awhile, but not for long; I was too restless, too eager to see more and smell more and hear the birds in the next spinney. I came to Burnham Beeches, and though I knew they were not the ones in Macbeth, I liked to pretend they were, and shouted to them, "And Birnam Wood shall come to Dunsinane!" There was no one to hear me; all day I was blessedly alone. The beech trunks were massive, smooth and gray as rocks. There were primroses underneath them. I knelt to touch the pale sweetness cool against my cheeks.

But I did go back. When I got in it was getting dark and supper was over. Mab had saved me a portion. Madame was furious with me and said that if I had been five minutes later she would have called my parents, and then the Police, to say I was missing. That frightened me. But it was a relief to know she hadn't actually done it. "Where were you?" "Oh, I just took a walk to Burnham Beeches."—I was defiantly casual. Up in the dormitory the little girls were in bed but awake. They giggled at me, half in admiration, half askance; all but Sarah, the fourteen year old American. (She and her little sister became my lifelong friends as it turned out.)

So next day I was back in class; and I stayed on at the school through the summer, hearing the big guns from all the way across the Channel as the "phony war" started to become "real," and seeing in the midsummer sky the puffs of white that were the Battle of Britain—and once even a parachute slowly descending like a dandelion fluff—until the autumn, when the bombing began and I wanted to be in London with my parents. And even after that I didn't quite give up on being a dancer; it took me several months of agonizing (and unsuccessful) auditions at such theaters as were open, attempting to get into "Panto" or any "classical" chorus line—to complete the severance.

Patient Muse! How you watched me that last summer of my ballet studies—even giving me a whole valley-full of nightingales! Sara and I would sit on top of the dormitory chest-of-drawers with our feet dangling outside the wide-open window, moonlit nights, to listen to them and watch the silver mist filling the cleft between the ridge where the house stood and the opposite ridge. Up there, against the moon, the night train ran, and added its owlish hoot to the delirium of the nightingales.

As for Madame, I did not suddenly repudiate all of my devotion to her; but from that day I began slowly to see her with a certain detachment. My poetry had been at a standstill, blocked by the idea that I ought to create tributes to her, but that summer I wrote out of what I *really* felt, really saw, instead of out of what I had been *trying* to feel and see. Among the poems I wrote before I left the school was the first one I ever published; it was called "Listening to Distant

252

Guns." My pointe work and my fouettés showed little improvement; but my ears were alert. From the day of my walk to Burnham Beeches there began to work in me—to ferment—a sense of what I couldn't do and what I could do: of who I was.

> . . . after I had seen
> That spectacle, for many days, my brain
> Worked with a dim and undetermined sense
> Of unknown modes of being; o'er my thoughts
> There hung—

not a darkness, as Wordsworth has it, but a little light.

I have been a nurse for three years, and have worked in four different hospitals; soon I shall be at a fifth. I saw my first corpse on the second day of the two weeks "intensive training," which was to make me a member of the Civil Nursing Reserve. I looked long at the dead face, thinking I would always remember it, not realizing how many faces of the dead I was to forget that year, and the next, until all that remained was a composite mask, waxen and sexless.

But the impact of death was less shocking to me than that of old age and poverty. I began for the first time to understand, to "prove upon my pulses," things which I thought I had known before. I had read pamphlets about slum clearance schemes and the means test; now, going out on Ambulance Days to bring in cases from shack towns in the Essex Marshes, I saw, smelt, and touched poverty.

There were all the lousy-headed children, and the rickety ones, and the snuffly ones; there was the old washerwoman, doubled up with arthritis, who lay rubbing her swollen knuckles together all day, muttering, "Done all the woolens now. Only got the whites to do. Done all the woolens." That was poverty suddenly real to me.

But the combination of poverty with old age was the worst. Money can at least buy a certain measure of respect for the senile; the senile poor are herded into big wards, their bottoms are slapped jocosely by healthy young women, they are scolded in public for making messes they cannot prevent—all this in a spirit of obtuse good-nature and lack of imagination. Such indignities are of little account to the feeble-minded; but when I saw them visited upon the mentally alert I was sickened. In my first weeks in hospital I could think of nothing else—death, pain, humiliation. It amazed me that others seemed to accept it calmly: how

---

Written in 1944 for *Gangrel*, a magazine edited by John Pick. I was then twenty-one.

could they bear it? I would look from some laughing nurse as young as myself to the faces of patients, and think, "Golden lads and lasses must as chimney sweepers come to dust." Most of the patients on these chronic wards where I was working had been poor all their lives, but sometimes some "decayed gentlewoman" would come in, still possessed of a few faded relics of better days—nice handkerchiefs, a bottle of scent. She would try at first, with desperate gallantry, to "keep up appearances," and the nurses would make rather a favourite of someone clean and well-spoken. But as she grew worse—a cancer case, perhaps, or paralyzed, she gradually succumbed to the crude atmosphere, her small niceties forgotten.

I became very depressed, was haunted by the idea of decay, and took a morbid interest in the details of gangrenous bedsores, the ravings of delirium, the wasting away of the carcinomatous, and the curious mobility of the flesh of the dead—I would spend considerable care in moulding their lips to the desired expression: neither a grotesque grimace of pain nor an unreasonable smile.

At nineteen I was very "green" and priggish; at first it seemed to me that almost all the other nurses were rough and hard-hearted. When some old hospital bird caught at my apron and croaked "Ah, there's *my* little nurse! You're the only one as does wot you're asked, ducky," I believed it and was flattered, until I overheard her say the very same thing to another nurse!

I discovered that there was broad comedy to be found as well as sorrow: my struggles with armfuls of bedpans on the unaccustomed slipperiness of ward floors; the ninety-seven-year-old great-grandmother, long bedridden, who got up and danced a jig after drinking her Christmas beer; Fat Annie stuck in the bath, and she and I laughing almost to hysteria as I tried to pull her out; the deaf cockney bellowing very intimate complaints from behind the screens while a shy young visiting curate blushed at the next bed.

I began to develop a defensive humour against the blows of unpleasant reality, and to find that many of those I had thought so abominable were likeable people. The staff of this hospital were divided into two main groups—the Good, who all lived in the Nurses' Hostel, and the Gay (in 1944 "gay" did not connote homosexual), who lived out if they got the chance. The Good were stodgy girls who spent their evenings writing home and making khaki socks. They became animated over knitting patterns and were popular with the maids because of their neat dressing tables. The Gay were tough. They drank hard, danced hard, swore hard, and were far more efficient and more genuinely kind, I found, than the Good. They might make rude jokes about Granny this or Daddy that, but attended to their needs thoroughly, while among the softly-spoken were some who would hold a patient's hand for half an hour and leave him in a wet bed.

Once I was accepted by the Gay as "not a bad kid," I started to feel happier. I learned to look away from misery, and to seek what was amusing. Cleaning out sputum mugs in hot lysol while Nurse A. was testing urines on the draining-board was not so bad if we were both singing "O, the pity of it all," with mournful gusto, and I ceased to be snobbish about popular songs. I learned also how and when to make myself scarce. When the Assistant Matron did her morning inspection I was always to be found scrubbing the bath out: she could hardly find much wrong there.

I used to like "doing the flowers." Coming from the sluice where I had been rinsing filth from icy sheets under the open window, the bathroom, where the flowers were kept till the ward was tidy, seemed comparatively warm; I would shut the window and run the hot tap until the air was steamy, and luxuriate in sweet scents, almost dissipating the remembered stench.

I was pleased and excited when, after three months, I was put on night duty. It was much less hard to saunter down the village street to work in the evening than to run down it half asleep on winter mornings, tripping over cottage doorsteps in the blackout. The work was no less hard—thirty beds to make in the morning, breakfast to cook and clear, dirty linen to sluice, bedpans to give etc., etc. and all to be finished by 7:30 by two—or sometimes only one—inexperienced nurses. And the difficulty of keeping awake at zero hour was sometimes agonizing, especially when an empty bed confronted one invitingly. But there were distinct advantages; there was no dusting or polishing to be done and the days were your own to sleep or not as you liked, so long as Home Sister didn't catch you out. Moreover at night there was less contact with the authorities. I had already been in several scrapes—caught smoking in the grounds, singing in the corridors, talking to a military patient from another ward (about politics as it happened), and reported for answering back—this last was when a short-sighted Sister sent me back three times to "clean that cupboard properly" and I protested that what she thought were dirt spots were really places where the white paint had flaked off. On night duty it was easier to get on with the job without such clashes—the only one I clearly recall was when a recently promoted Sister, determined to be a proverbial new broom, reprimanded me for not standing stiffly to attention while addressing her, and I lost my temper, saying I wasn't in the Army and didn't intend to behave as if I were,—and a good deal more. For a day or two afterwards, I lived in fear of being sent to Matron's Office, but nothing more happened that time.

The fear of the Office Door is something which has often puzzled me. Why did I go white when Sister said "Matron wants to see you immediately Nurse. What have you been up to now?" Why did I tremble as I knocked at the august door? I had none of the usual reasons—ambition, fear of losing my job and getting a bad reference, or even a guilty conscience, for although I might know quite well what the trouble was I didn't feel wicked: what the hell did it matter if I *had* come in at 12:00 P.M. instead of 11:00 the night before? If I had failed to attend fire drill on my morning off? If I showed too much hair beneath my cap? These were not mortal sins; yet I shook and stammered before the Matron. This kind of fear is an infection—a sort of mass hysteria. There is such a strong tradition of awe for the sacred precincts that even the most rebellious are physically affected by it. The telephone suddenly ringing in the duty room, the peremptory summons, the curious or pitying glances of colleagues as you straighten your cap at the mirror and suck off excess lipstick before scuttling down the endless shining corridor (at Hospital IV it was a quarter of a mile long) trying to hurry without running—all this has a pernicious psychological effect.

No wonder the nurses' representative council which was formed at Hospital II had little support, despite constant grumbling about the grievances which it was designed to settle. No girl of little character and intelligence, coming straight from school, perhaps, to that atmosphere, has a chance to develop the necessary courage and initiative to bring about reforms, and the few who are endowed with these qualities can do nothing without the support of the many.

The authorities themselves often maintain ridiculous rules from stupidity, rather than from malice or love of power. I once had an argument with a Home Sister: "Nurse, I see you have not once come to breakfast this month. If you are absent again I shall have to report you." "But Sister, I'm not hungry so early in the morning." "That is not the point. Anyway, you surely like a cup of tea before you go on duty?" "No, Sister, I prefer to wait till nine o'clock break. Surely I needn't come to table if I neither eat nor drink." "What you eat is entirely your own affair, Nurse, but the rule is that you are to attend breakfast. Besides, *we've* done it all our lives, why can't you?" She was a kind old soul, and though she couldn't see my point I continued to miss breakfast and she never reported me.

I spent eleven months in Hospital I, and became a probationer at Hospital II, a small Fever training school and T.B. Sanatorium, rather because it was in a convenient locality than from any great desire to rise in the profession. However, I had a real interest in physiology and medicine (I hated anatomy) and in spite of the increased discipline, the caterpillars in the greens, and a more sober atmosphere than at Hospital I, I was not sorry for the change. Lectures were a welcome break in the day's work, unless they fell in an off-duty period, and the work itself, mainly with child patients, was much easier.

I am in the habit of saying I dislike nursing, but I must in justice admit that there were weeks and even months of my year at Hospital II that I really enjoyed; times when I was working under reasonable and pleasant Sisters, who believed in developing initiative, and would sit talking by the kitchen fire in the evening when the work was done—a quiet time that never comes in the rush and tumble of a big general hospital. I enjoyed some of the work—bathing the children and letting them splash; giving injections and seeing the effect; the odd feeling of benevolent power that is given by making someone comfortable.

There was more unity of feeling among the nurses here, and it was pleasant to know that, if I had stolen through the hedge after the gates were locked, the fire-escape door was sure to have been left open by some staunch friend. I enjoyed drinking tea out of tooth-glasses in a minute bedroom filled with girls and tobacco smoke. I enjoyed strictly forbidden visits to wards where friends were on night duty, and running silently back over the moonlit grass afterwards. I enjoyed asking posers in the lecture room.

But these pleasures were of a very juvenile kind, and although I preferred them to loneliness I used to think how wrong was a life which kept young adults at a stage of mental development that was satisfied with so little, when life was rich, exciting and only waiting to be grasped. Some of us had plenty of outside and intellectual interests, but the majority had not: their life was that small world, and any desire for another was too weak to become active. An examination which I was pleased to pass from sheer vanity was to them an event of major importance. By the time the results were out I was feeling restless and cramped, and instead of doing the second year of training I left and went to Hospital III, as an assistant nurse.

Hospital III, an old-fashioned dust-trap proud of its "voluntary tradition" was a gloomy episode in my career, from which I quickly escaped to Hospital IV, by far the best of the lot in every way, where I lived out and was on permanent night duty.

Almost all the time I was there—six or seven months—I was on the same male ward. I have found more to admire in men as patients than in women. Men usually are neighbourly to each other, and help the overworked nurse as much as they can, so long as she doesn't try to bully them. To see the convalescents hopping out of bed in the morning to make the tea and push the trolley round, or to hear them disputing among themselves about the proper way to tuck in a sheet was quite charming. Sitting at the desk trying to do some writing while the charge nurse was at midnight dinner I would look down the dim-lit ward at the twenty-four beds—all occupied—and listen to the different kinds of breathing, like an old hen counting her chickens. Some of the patients were there for almost the whole of that six months and I grew really fond of many of them, taking a personal pleasure in their recovery.

After a year of fever-nursing, which is cheerful because the greater number of cases get better and go home within a definite period, to return to a general hospital was to return to tragedy; but now I could see sides to it that I had missed before. I remember gentle Mr. F., an elderly Jew, dying of a diseased liver, who spoke of the beauty of life; I remember S. dying of a cerebral tumour, who in his last lucid moment told me about his dead wife, whom he fancied I resembled a little, and who kissed my hand because, he said, I "had the patience to listen." I remember H., the ex-violinist, who roused himself out of semicoma, by sheer effort of will, to join fiercely in a conversation about Mozart that the other nurse and I were holding as we made his bed. I remember Lily Bloom. . . .

Although I am still nursing I am beginning to be able to estimate the good and bad effects of these experiences on myself and on my efforts to write good poetry. The danger of hospital life to an intending artist is less the ugliness and endless drudgery themselves than the easy happiness on a

260

low level. It is too easy to sink into a sort of bog of comfortable chatter. After twelve hours of hard work, often among terrible sights, your back aches, your feet ache, your brain is numb; it is not surprising that the conversation in the staff sitting room deals only with shop, gossip, clothes and boyfriends—the latter mainly imaginary. The Fifth Form at St. Monica's mind is as much a form of defensive reaction against difficult truths as the "tough girl" attitude.

The continual conflict with petty authority is degrading; it makes one either deceitful or aggressive.

But the contact with tragic realities I consider very valuable. To *feel* death and poverty and disease and dirt, not merely to know them intellectually, made me appreciate the humour and gallantry and human virtues which sometimes spring from them like flowers from a wilderness, and I value them more than I could have done had I continued to lead a "sheltered life," or if I had become a ballerina as I once desired. I would have avoided the horror, and living arrogantly among dreams, never have seen the beauty.

VI OTHER WRITERS

Hilda Morley

*This was written in the late 1960s as an introduction to a book of
Hilda Morley's which, however, remained unpublished. A different
small book of her poems,* A Blessing Outside Us *did appear in
1976. For publication as a statement here, I have altered only those
few sentences which referred specifically to the ill-fated volume,*
The Bird with the Long Neck.

After reading Hilda Morley's mainly unpublished poems,
each so perfect, each a separate pleasure, I find myself
shaking my head at the strangeness of what used to be
called fate, a word currently out of fashion. For here's a
woman just about my own age; who grew up, like me, in
England; her education mostly informal, like mine; her life
spent, like mine, writing and thinking about poetry from an
early age; and who has experienced many of the same
influences: yet I've begun to lose count of the books I've
published, while she, whose poems seem to me so finely
wrought, surely *at least* as well wrought as my own, is only
now publishing this first book.

Partly it is because Hilda Morley has made, all these
years, almost no effort to have her poems go out into the
world. But then, despite appearances, neither have I, as
people who know the strangely lucky, "coincidental," history of my relationships with publishers could attest. No,
this has to do with "fate" or the even more old-fashioned
concept of Dame Fortune. That these poems have, for the
most part, not been printed even in magazines is not necessarily to be interpreted, however, as due to Dame Fortune
having been scowling upon them up to now: rather it seems
to me that she has been *keeping them up her sleeve.* When
they see the light, it is in full ripeness. We fall silent before
them.

It is evident that Hilda Morley's poetics is based on that of
Pound and Williams; that she learned much from Olson;
and, like Duncan and Creeley and myself, has looked to

H.D. also for help and wisdom. In this tradition she has evolved an unequalled exactitude. The lucid, the *illuminated* quality of poem after poem is given them by the precision of their structure. By the sureness with which she breaks her lines, indents to indicate nuances of pace and emphasis, articulates with spaces within the line (as fingers are articulated by their joints), and employs other devices to sonic and expressive ends, she gives the poem its head: it can race straight into the field of the reader's head (if his gate be open). The reader will not know how it happened— unless he too happens to be a technician, and examines the process: but such a reader too will *first* experience their affect, for there is nothing gimmicky here to distract the attention to *how* it is done *before* the magic force of *what* is being done is felt. But afterwards, yes: there is indeed much to learn in such poems.

Yet although the student can observe in them all one intends to signify when one talks about *accuracy of diction, concrete images, close attention to the visual, transmutation of the visual and other sensuous perceptions into the sonic structure,* and so on, the sum of the parts is, as in all the "open secrets" of nature and of art, beyond accounting: the *duende* is dark within transparence.

This is a time when perhaps more women are writing poetry than ever before, and certainly more poetry by women is being published and read. Since much of it is excellent, this is a matter for rejoicing; yet there are certain factors I deplore in the situation.

Some recent poetry by women is feminist first and poetry afterwards; some consists of statements in verse by people who are not really poets at all. Some of it is not feminist but is a poetry that—following what the writers take to be the example of Sylvia Plath and Anne Sexton—is neurotically, excessively, self-indulgently preoccupied with death, or rather with suicide in one form or another. (This genre is of course by no means exclusively written by women.) And floating over the whole field of poetry by women is the misconceived banner upon which is inscribed, "Women's Poetry." I have formed a habit, of late, of asking, when I hear this term, what the speaker thinks of Women's Mathematics or Women's Geology.

Women poets who are also Black are perhaps the only ones who escape being asked about their art in gender-dominated terms, and that is only because they are assumed to be (sometimes of their own volition) *Black* poets. What is ignored is that, while women poets may be dealing with the role of women in our society and with their struggle, and while Black poets, male or female, may be dealing with Black consciousness and struggle, any poet—male, female, black, white, or green—only is a poet insofar as his or her poems manifest a peculiar relationship of the imagination to language itself. The failure to recognize this adequately results in some inferior work being acclaimed, while some of the best is given less than its due.

For example, one of the most moving and accomplished of living American poets, Hilda Morley (widow of the com-

---

Published in *National Observer,* 1974.

poser Stefan Wolpe) remains almost unknown and entirely without book publication. She is fifty years old, has masses of manuscripts, works constantly. Subtle sensibility and rock-firm craft are united in her poems; but she is not self-destructive nor self-exploitative, and her poems would not excite the sadistic, voyeuristic impulse that derives a thrill from the very real anguish of a Plath or a Sexton.

Hilda Morley, alive and unpublished at fifty. And now I have before me the first book[1] of poetry by Michele Murray, book-review editor of *The National Observer* until her death last March, whose lack of national recognition among poetry readers while she lived is regrettable, and whose loss at forty is a tragedy for American literature.

Michele Murray's death of cancer, a death she did not court but struggled against, and which she and her family met with exceptional courage, dignity, and grace, is to me so much more representative of what an artist's, a poet's death should be like than are the pitiful dramas (for which one must feel sorrow and pain, not scorn—but not admiration either!) that are frequently taken to be typical of creative sensibilities.

But I would not have undertaken to write about her if strength, grace, suffering, and the spirit that asks, explores, demands, wonders, and accepts were not present in the structure of her poems, in her images and her language, as well as in her life. All those qualities *are* in her poems; and with them a rich sense of further possibility, of ongoing development, that makes heartrending the knowledge that this book is posthumous.

"Morning opens in the household of my body" begins the first poem in the collection, fittingly. The line, the image, the immediacy of it *as* an opening line (yes, opening indeed . . .) sets the tone of the book as a whole. But when I speak of acceptance and courage, whether in the encounter with illness and death or in the struggle of the artist to know and obey his/her means or medium (for the struggle is to

[1]*The Great Mother and Other Poems* (New York, Sheed and Ward, 1974).

learn to surrender, not to conquer!), I don't mean to suggest anything like resignation or a wilful upbeat in these poems.

No, it is the very fact that she did not want to die, that she knew passionately that she was alive and had beloved people to live for and with, that makes her death truly tragic, and not merely pitiful. Here there is nothing narcissistic, no love affair with death. Her love was for life, and she was willing to put hard work into it as into a marriage. Likewise, her full engagement with the power of precision in language, the stern obligation to honesty (the only road to true originality), gives to her poems a tension and at times a harshness that does not let the reader off any hooks, and stamps them indubitably as works of art, not works of self-expressive therapy.

One can see that she explored a variety of formal means. "A Box of German Blocks: 1939–1969" is five and a half pages long: not so very long, yet so full of time—time past, time present—that it has the weight of a "long poem." "The Dreams of Beautiful Women" contrasts, with a subtlety akin to the subtle color sense of some fine weaver working in muted colors, the dreams of those who "feel in the bone unearned mastery that transforms," with the poet's own dreams:

> . . . of windfalled apples
> still crispy and juicy,
> of the sky before snow
> grey and stretched
> longing for release.

Some poems (for instance, "Summer Country in the Kitchen" or "Staying Home,") have a steady margin and lines of fairly even length. The last of a group of four called "Under the City" adopts the stepped indentation of late Williams; "Making Love" is in "articulated" lines (lines in which there are spaces, pauses, indicated by typographical spaces) and is wholly composed of gerund phrases.

269

The content of Michele Murray's poems, because it relates closely to her life rather than being distanced from it by the adoption of personae or by dramatic or epic modes, is, unquestionably, the content of a woman's personal experience; but this is incidental. One feels, that is, that if she had lived, and had chosen at some point to write in those modes, she was fully capable of doing so: she was not a poet impelled by one theme alone, the theme of *being aware of being a woman* (though this awareness is a strong force in her work).

It is the complexity of being a *human being*, rather, that is implicit in these poems even when—naturally, simply, plainly—they are about women as another woman sees them, about being a mother, about "five thousand dinners," about what it feels like to inhabit the skin of femaleness, to have breasts and a womb.

I long since abjured the publication of negative criticism, deciding that it was only rarely usefully didactic. Therefore I seldom write reviews at all, and when I do it is from the desire to pay tribute to what I admire. The best way to fulfill this tribute, then, to a poet I deeply regret not having known during her lifetime is to quote in its entirety her "Death Poem," a kind of epitaph for herself that affirms her life.

Death Poem

What will you have when you finally have me?
Nothing.
Nothing I have not already given
freely each day I spent
not waiting for you
but living
as if the shifting shadows of grapes
and fine-pointed leaves in the shelter
of the arbor would continue to tremble
when my eyes were absent
in memory of my seeing,

or the books fall open where I marked them
when my astonishment overflowed
at a gift come unsummoned, this love
for the open hands of poems,
earth fruit, sun soured grass, the steady
outward lapping stillness of midnight
snowfalls, an arrow of light waking me
on certain mornings with sharp wound
so secret that not even you
will have it when you have me.
You will have my fingers
but not what they touched. Some gestures
outflowing from a rooted being, the memory
of morning light cast on a bed
where two lay together—
the shining curve of flesh!—
they will forever be out of your reach
whose care is with the husks.

The poem is astringent but not bitter; if it is defiant, there
is nothing brash in its tone, which is calm, sober, restrained.
It does not lapse into self-pity, nor sentimentality, nor yet
into pious resignation. "Stoic" does not describe it, for it is
passionate, but the passion is reserved for what is living;
towards death it is cool—no, devastatingly, contemptuously,
cold. It sings, it celebrates—and it despises. Rilke wrote,
"He was a poet, and so, of course, abhorred the approximate." This death, "whose care is with the husks," knows
only the approximate. Michele Murray was a poet.

We mourn the death of the woman—but her poetry now
makes its entrance into our lives, generous, profound, and
precise.

Bert Meyers

Bert Meyers' death has deprived us of one of the best poets of our time. I feel strongly the irony of my making that statement, since I "discovered" his work only months before his death; and that discovery need not have been so tardy, for I had seen his name, seen (but not really read) poems of his in *Kayak* and perhaps elsewhere, and even—some six months before I did at last recognize the value of his work— had met him. Fortunately I did enter the world of Bert's poems before finding out that he had cancer; so that I have had no need to wonder whether knowing that he was seriously ill influenced my response. It was only after I wrote to tell him I had fallen in love with poem after poem in *The Wild Olive Tree*,[1] the manuscript of which he had sent me, that he wrote back telling me he had been found to have lung cancer. (And reading that letter I shuddered to recall having noticed that he was a heavy smoker.)

Bert Meyers' work seems all to have been lyrical; he was not drawn to the epic, narrative, or dramatic modes and eschewed the hortatory or didactic. For clarity of discourse, I would reserve the term "major" for poets whose range of genres and also quantity of work seem equal in breadth to the depth of their poems. But the term "great" should be applicable to those who produce deep and exquisite work in fewer modes, or in a single one; though here too some sense of abundance seems to form part of what "great" implies. I feel Meyers can be called *great* because of the extraordinary intensity and perfection of his poems and the consistency with which he illumined what he experienced, bodying it forth in images that enable readers to share his vision and thereby extend the boundaries of their own lives.

Published in *Follies*, August 1979, a tabloid in Los Angeles that no longer exists.

[1] Published in 1979 by West Coast Poetry Review Press, Reno, Nevada.

The image is unequivocally at the center of his work; indeed, a sequence of short poems, now posthumously published in the volume *Windowsills*,[2] is named simply "Images." Often there are single lines, or brief syntactic units, within longer poems of his, that seem fully poems in themselves—random examples would be:

> Night lifts the moon like a coffee cup
> from the skyline's cluttered shelf,

or

> Fog—
> sailing for hours
> in the same spot;
>
> and the joyful sound
> of the invisible sea.

Or this:

> All around me, butterflies,
> ecstatic hinges,
> hunt for the ideal door.

It is apparent that Meyers himself recognized, and cultivated, this ability to find images that can function autonomously; the "Images" section of *Windowsills* begins with a two-line poem, a discrete image:

> Bales of hay—cartons
> of sunlight fading in a field.

And the poem "Train" begins and ends with single lines that are entities separated from the middle stanzas: "Sunlight

[2]Published in 1979 by Common Table, New Haven, Connecticut.

plays its flute in the treetops," says the first one, and "Green keeps changing itself from green to green," says the last. But he also knew that the image was a building block out of which he could construct longer poems: one of his strengths is the way in which every longer poem of his is built up of an accumulation of such image blocks, each of which has such integrity that the whole edifice is dense and strong. In this way his poems, like the best haiku, are capable of imparting a sense of his life and values, his emotions and deepest loyalties, with a minimum of stated opinion. Though an intense feeling for the beauty and strangeness of the sense-apprehensible world informs most of his work, he does not ignore the hideous nor shrink from the ugly terms necessary to depict it:

> And here are also filthy streets,
> leprous walls that sunlight
> never touched, smeared with crud,
> battered like garbage cans . . .
> the cracks in a stone
> are the landscape of nerves;
> the air's a perpetual fart
> and even the shadows wear rags
>
> (from "Paris")

Though he did not like "engaged" poetry, feeling that it violated what he believed was the essentially evocative and nondidactic nature of the art, he at times encompassed historical comment, e.g., "Arc de Triomphe":

> Nothing but grey seen through the arch
> as if triumph were an abyss
> into which a nation marches

And in a poem such as "Saigon" (though I believe he decided to pull it out of The Wild Olive Tree which was in process of publication at the time of his death) he did make a very direct criticism of the corrupting influence of the

United States—the poem's epigraph is, "In our own image we created them," and it describes teenage thugs in pre-liberation Saigon:

> Their smiles are gunbelts,
> their brains, nuclear clouds;
> and they speak a dialect
> that sounds like money . . .
>
> Around them, the landscape's
> a flag that fell from the sky:
> red roads, bloody stripes;
> whitened by bones
> and stars that explode;
> blue, like genocide's queer smoke.

Again, though a love of the earth and its creatures and things, and of his friends and family, is the predominating spirit in his poetry, anger recurs in a poem like "To My Enemies," and once more is seen to be, despite his anti-polemical bias, a social criticism:

> . . . Maddened by you
> for whom the cash register,
> with its clerical bells,
> is the national church . . .
>
> . . . Your president
> is a tsetse fly . . .

In this poem his humor (like James Stephens' in "A Glass of Beer") finds expression in a curse:

> May your wife go to paradise
> with the garbage man,
> your prick hang like a shoelace,
> your balls become raisins,
> hair grow on the whites of your eyes.

These are the wild arabesques in which a gentle man draws
his rage; a hard man would curse without fantasy.

His eye is keen as an animal's; in "Paris" he sees that

> A child carries a long,
> thin loaf of bread.

O.K., any of us would have seen that. But he sees more:

> Its sides are chipped
> like the molding of a gilded frame.

That's a detailed observation both of the loaf and of its
analogue (he had been for years a frame maker) demon-
strating how the *habit* of observation can provide metaphors the occasion of need for which could never have been
foreseen. And from the security of image that this combination of quick gaze and verbal accuracy established, there
arose, in turn, a further kind of image, a taking off into an
analogy that could not have been predicted but which, "far-
fetched" though its reference may be—who could believe,
in advance, that one could leap meaningfully from bread to
picture frames?—is "earned." It therefore satisfies one's
sense of aesthetic propriety and enables one to see and feel
that *baguette*, almost to smell it; and at the same time to feel
one's imagination pulled into an exotic revelation:

> The crust looks warm, dented,
> as if the baker were a blacksmith
> who hammered and sold the sun's rays.

That's the reward of fidelity to the object, of a humble,
intense, disinterested and unflinching attention.

In a Machado-esque portion of the same "Paris" poem
something similar happens:

> In a little square, a man
> fills a bottle at a fountain.

> The sound of water stops, continues.
> A woman leans from a window
> to see how the sky feels.
> Clouds rub their silver polish over the sun.

Here we have four lines of plain description, "poetic" only in their simplicity and the clustered associations of "little square," "fountain," "the sound of water," "leans from a window." Then in line five a subjective estimation of what the woman is doing makes poet and reader look up and *see* the sky she sees—and like her we experience the visual in empathic tactile terms, becoming, as we do so, the diaphanous clouds paradoxically engaged in the homely action of rubbing, and at the same time the sun itself, *being* rubbed, its fire a white glare behind the gauze.

Because most of his images are such direct fusions, montages that synthesize into a new image, he was able to use the word "like" on occasion with the authority of genuine simile rather than in imperfectly realized metaphor:

> On the horizon, late at night,
> a ship glows like the last café
> still open
> at the end of a boulevard
> after the rain.

The difference between such simile and the immediacy of a montage-image can be clearly seen in these lines:

> Passengers board the ship at twilight.
> The people who wave from the pier
> light matches—they become
> a crowd of candles on the shore.
> The boat, a huge altar, dissolves in the fog.

The syntactic difference is called for not merely because altars don't typically dissolve in fog, don't even *seem* to dissolve in fog, but because the degree to which the boat is felt by the poet to *be* an altar—not only visually but because it bears what is sacred to the people who are watching it, and who themselves have been for the nonce transformed into votive candles—is intense: this boat isn't "like" an altar the way the other boat is "like" a café; it *is* one, and at the same time it is still a boat. The simile, on the other hand, is a device that itself conveys something of the wistful sense of distance one experiences in looking down that long boulevard towards the café, its lights (and the street lights, too) reflected in the wet pavement, an Impressionist painting. . . . It is a mark of the most profound poetic instinct to comprehend, in the act of making poems, the degrees of analogy: and so to avoid muffling the perception of *coalescence,* which demands metaphor, with the word "like"; or, on the other hand, failing to note *resemblance* with the appropriate figure of speech, simile. It seems obvious enough so stated, but thousands of poems bear witness to the unacknowledged confusion of all but the most gifted poets regarding this essential matter. Bert Meyers' intuition in this, as in other things, seems to have been faultless.

Jim McConkey's invitation to participate in the Chekhov
Festival at Cornell in the spring of 1977 released memories
of the period in my life when I first read Chekhov. It so
happened that when his letter arrived I had been working
on a group of discursive, semi-narrative poems, written
mainly in rather long lines; and the way in which Jim described the kind of festival he had in mind, (which reflected
his own love for Chekhov and his sense of him, akin to my
own, as a positive force in readers' lives) combined with the
expansive or elastic mode in which I was already writing,
made possible for me the poem[1] which I ended up presenting at Cornell months later, instead of a formal lecture or
informal talk. I am grateful for having been given the opportunity—and the stimulus—to recollect and reflect upon
an important phase in my own growth; but I hope that the
autobiographical material will be recognized as not being in
the poem merely for its own sake, but to provide the context
in which Chekhov began to affect my life, as he has continued to do and as, no doubt, he always will.

His influence was not on my work as a writer, directly (it
would be interesting to know if any poet ever considers any
writer in other literary forms a direct influence, or if such
influence is possible, indeed, on a craft or technical level).
For me, as for any other reader, including the lifelong friend
with whom I shared the experience of his work, it was
Chekhov's vision of life that I received and cherished, and
which, however imperceptibly, affected my own vision and
consequently the course of my life.

It is a feature of Chekhov's artistry that his vision, his
attitude, enter the reader without the *apparent* mediation of

---

Written in 1977.

[1]"Chekhov on the West Heath," in *Life in the Forest* (New York, New
Directions, 1978). First published early in 1978 by Woolmer & Brotherston
(Andes, New York) in a limited edition for Friends of the Cornell Library.

style; that is to say, his style and structure have the transparency Pasternak speaks of as Zhivago's goal: "It had been the dream of his life to write with an originality so discreet, so well concealed, as to be unnoticeable in its disguise of current and customary forms; all his life he had struggled for a style so restrained, so unpretentious that the reader or the hearer would fully understand the meaning without realizing how he assimilated it. . . ."

The word "hearer" in that quotation reminds me of the fact that my friend Betty and I, in our teens, used to read Chekhov *aloud*. As she was ill at the time it was usually I who did the reading. Reading aloud was something her family and mine did as a matter of course, and in fact my introduction not, strangely enough, to poetry, but to fiction, came as a listener rather than a reader, for my mother read most of the English nineteenth century classic novels and much else, (including *War and Peace*) aloud to me during my childhood. So as part of my "nonlecture" at Cornell I decided to read a Chekhov story; my choice was *Gooseberries*, which, besides being a beautiful work, represents the particular balance of negative and positive—of despair at *what is* countered by a vision of, and aspiration towards, *what might be*—that is to me the most profound and essentially Chekhovian characteristic of his fiction.

Before the time of my association of Chekhov with Hampstead Heath, the site of our readings, Betty and I had seen several of his plays performed in London with admirable casts that included Edith Evans, Peggy Ashcroft, John Gielgud, Lawrence Olivier, and many other first rate performers. (I wish I had kept the programs!) Also I had seen, as a child, some rehearsals and eventually a performance of *The Seagull* by a company of amateur actors my sister had assembled, and which she had previously directed in *Paul Among the Jews,* by Franz Werfel, translated by my father, and Turgenev's *A Month in the Country*, revised by him from the standard translation. She did not direct or perform in *The Seagull*, so its rehearsals did not take place in our house and garden as had those for the other productions; but I saw enough of it to have dimly gleaned a sense of how the lives of the young actors were in some way mimicking or parallelling those of some of the personae of the play—it had caught them up in itself. (They were young clerks and typists from a London suburb; I know nothing of what became of them afterwards.) However, it was perhaps the intimacy of the stories, and the narrative, reflective element in them—Chekhov's own commentary on scene, situation, and character—that elicited from me a deeper response than the plays.

The typical negative-positive balance I find in, for instance, *Gooseberries*, *The Bride*,[2] *My Life*, and *The Black Monk*, and which I believe is dominated by a sense of the positive (yes, even in the controversial *Black Monk* which many people interpret in the opposite sense) became, one might say, the essential subject of my poem, "Chekhov on the West Heath." Chekhov saw, objectively and yet with passionate disgust, the injustices, the sloth, the philistinism and the barbarities of the life around him, and he had great compassion for the variously warped lives of individuals caught in the societal spiderweb. But time and again he expresses, through his characters as in his letters, the sense of aspiration, of belief in life, of the hope of change for the better even though that change will come too late for him and for them to see it. To be human, his stories seem to say, is to be a creature in a state of modulation, of evolution, not a forever fixed category; to be human, as we experience it, is to belong to a species of *forerunners*, to some of whom is given from time to time a glimpse of a distant future for which we carry the potential. He never asserts that we shall fulfill that potential, but he does assert its existence; and that qualified, cautious assertion, made with delicacy and wistfulness, is more inspiring by far than any bombastic claims, any unironic "Democratic vistas," could ever be to a child of

[2] Also known as *The Betrothed*, *A Marriageable Girl*, and perhaps other titles.

281

our time. This is what I tried to celebrate in this poem, as I looked back to Hampstead in 1941 and into the lives of the two girls who sat reading in Judge's Walk.

An earlier poem of mine (from a series called *Modulations For a Solo Voice*) called "Like Loving Chekhov," speaks of Chekhov's voluntary journey to Sakhalin and of the ugly inkstand I had seen in his Moscow flat and office, which he had cherished because it had been given him in gratitude as a great treasure, the utmost she had to give, by some poor seamstress he had treated without charge (and to whom it had probably been given carelessly by some rich lady who wanted to get rid of it). It is Chekhov's way of backing up his vision, as expressed in the stories, with actions modestly undertaken in his daily life (among which should be remembered the long periods of dangerous and frustrating work he put in as an organizer of rural public health care during cholera epidemics and in other extremely difficult situations) that gives context to the vision itself, and reinforces it as a dynamic resource in a reader's life.

I have only a smattering of German, and consequently know
Rilke's prose far better than his less satisfactorily translat-
able poetry, yet he has been for me an important influence.
There is a depth and generosity in his perceptions that made
them go on being relevant to me through the decades. I had
already been writing for many years, and had been reading
Rilke for seven or eight, when I first came to America and
began to read Williams, Pound, and Stevens. Before long I
met Robert Creeley and through him I encountered Olson's
ideas. I remember Creeley's grimace of distaste for Rilke, or
for what he imagined him to represent; but though I was
excited by the new ideas, and open to their influence, I
didn't give up on what Rilke meant to me, for I knew it was
not the mere web of sentimentality Creeley accused it of
being. It is true that Rilke could be pompous and sancti-
monious at times—but those episodes are minimal in pro-
portion to his strengths. Thus all the useful and marvelously
stimulating technical and aesthetic tendencies that I came
upon in the 1950s were absorbed into a ground prepared not
only by my English and European cultural background in
general but more particularly by Rilke's concept of the
artist's task—a serious, indeed a lofty, concept, but not a
sentimental or a smug one.

Although I went on to read other volumes, it was through
my original encounters with him that his influence continued to hold. The first of Rilke that I read was the *50 Selected
Poems* (from *Das Buch der Bilder* and from *Neue Gedichte*)
translated with notes and introduction by C. F. MacIntyre
(University of California Press, 1941), which my father gave
me at Easter 1942—a bilingual edition. MacIntyre was a

Adapted and revised, 1981, from a lecture given at a conference on
religion in Chicago *c.* 1975.

translator who exasperates most readers (he did versions of *Faust*, Verlaine and Mallarmé as well as of Rilke) but he did have the virtue, for which I honor his memory, of a passionate involvement with his subject and a willingness to take verbal risks to advance his peculiar, crotchety, but loving relationship to the chosen poet. This is particularly true in regard to Rilke's work: he loved it but he was not given to swooning over it; his notes have an acerbity of tone quite free of the *schwärmerei* that often surrounded Rilke both as man and writer (not without his collusion, no doubt) and which has continued to cause the kind of distrust Creeley expressed in 1950. MacIntyre helped me to place the poems in a cultural context, and also (quoting it in his introduction) first acquainted me with that famous passage from *The Notebooks of Malte Laurids Brigge* that tells, with only a slight degree of hyperbole, what a poet must have experienced in life in order to write a poem, or even a single line, of value. That was my first lesson from Rilke—*experience* what you live: to the artist, whatever is *felt through* is not without value, for it becomes part of the ground from which one grows. (Or as Goethe said—but I only read that years later—"In order to do something one must *be* someone.") Rilke's words reinforced my assumption that I did not have to undertake special (academic) studies to develop my poetry, but need only continue to read and write, and to be open to whatever might befall me; the rest must depend upon my native abilities and the degree of intensity and persistence that I was prepared to devote to the service of the art.

The next Rilke that I read was the *Letters to a Young Poet* in the Reginald Snell edition (London, Sidgewick and Jackson, 1945). Here, of course, it is in Letter I that he speaks at more length, and more specifically, about the needs of the poet than in any of the other ten, (perhaps because it soon became clear to him that Herr Kappus was not destined for the life of art, and would be a receiver rather than a maker). That first letter in the series was my second lesson: again it was a reinforcement, a seal of approval for the instinct which had always told me not to run hither and thither seeking advice. Like everyone else I needed occasional reassurance, a word of approval, a warning against some weakness; but I knew, somehow, what Rilke's words now stated for me, that the underlying necessity was to ask not others but *oneself* for confirmation. And he specified the primary question not as "Is what I have written any good?" but rather, *"Must* I write?" I came at some point to recognize that when he says Herr Kappus ought to continue only if he could honestly answer "Yes," he meant the question (for every poet) to be a perennial one, not something asked and settled once and for all. Likewise, when, in the same letter, he states that "a work of art is good only if it has grown out of necessity," he is not merely repeating that injunction; the first imperative had to do with an initial sense of being inexorably drawn to the making of poems, while this second one demands that the poet apply the same standard to each separate work.

Rilke does not emphasize to Kappus the aesthetic, structural, needs of each poem; but his own *oeuvre* amply manifests that concern. Thus one is provided with a threefold basis for artistic integrity: scrupulous attention to three necessities—need as a person to write in order to fulfill one's being; the need of each separate poem to be written; and the aesthetic needs of each poem—each line. This implication of a standard of aesthetic ethics does not exclude the playful, the role of the artist as illusionist—it encompasses it. And it is important to remember, too, that Rilke did not scorn irony, but goes out of his way to tell Kappus that it can be "one more means of seizing life," but that it is a dangerous resort in unproductive moments (leading then, he implies, to mere cheap cynicism) and that it does not function at the profoundest depths of experience.

Another lesson from Rilke which reinforced something I knew already concerned the value of solitude. (Isn't all that we really learn the affirmation of what our experience already hints or what our intuition can assent to?) I had learned as a child to enjoy being alone; now I saw how Rilke pointed to solitude as necessary for the poet's inner development, for that selfhood that must *be* in order to experience all the multifold otherness of life. Later on, the phrase he used in relation to marriage or a comparable relationship, "the mutual bordering and guarding of two solitudes," dimly understood at first, became a cardinal point in my map of love; and still later in my life I came to see solitude, and the individual development for which it is a condition, as the only valid ground on which communion of the many, the plural Other of brother-and-sisterhood, can take place. (Rilke himself, of course, shunned the many in practice, and can scarcely be claimed as democratic in theory either; yet there are letters of his written in the revolutionary Munich of 1918 which show him to have been too open-hearted, apolitical and aristocratic though he was, to have been altogether irresponsive to that stir of new possibility, even if he soon became disillusioned with it.)

When I think of the *Selected Letters* (translated by R. F. C. Hull; London, Secker and Warburg, 1946) which was the third, and in many ways the most important, book of Rilke's that I obtained, it is as if of a palimpsest. So many passages, read at different times in my life, have yielded up so many layers of significance to me. Some I know almost by heart; yet there are others that I come upon as if for the first time. Early in 1947 I began making my own index for this volume, to supplement the ordinary one; and—like the wonderful poem-titles of Wallace Stevens—this list alone gives quite a strong, peculiar sense of the contents: *autumn the creator—standing at windows—as ready for joy as for pain—how can we exist?—the tower of fear—the savour of creation—each step an arrival—vowels of affliction—alone in cities—our conflicts a part of our riches—strings of lamentation—the mouse in the wainscot—further than work—open secret—* and so on. From each passage I received, of course, something specific; but they all combined—and not only those I indexed but, importantly and enduringly, others in which he described and evoked the working life of Rodin and Cézanne—to increase my understanding of the vocation of art, the obstinate devotion to it which, though it may not lead to any ordinary happiness, is nevertheless at the opposite pole to the morbid self-absorption often mistakenly supposed to be typical of artists. The models Rilke presents as truly great—even though he sadly reports on what he perceived as Rodin's decline from integrity in old age, and even though he did not underestimate Cézanne's mistrustful and surly personality—were heroically and exhilaratingly impassioned about art itself, and unflagging in its alluring, demanding service. "Work and have patience. . . . Draw your whole life into this circle," he quotes Rodin as saying. Rilke's emphasis on "experience," on living one's life with attention, is always balanced by an equal emphasis on the *doing* of one's art work, a zeal for the doing of it, not for the amateur's wish to *have done* it; an appetite for process.

Rilke's intense joy in the visual (whether in art or nature) recapitulated for me a direction towards which my mother had faced my attention very early in my life. "I love *inseeing*," he wrote in what I've always found a delightfully comic passage about *really looking*, (for which "insight" has become too abstract a term): "Can you imagine with me how glorious it is to insee, for example, a dog as one passes by—*insee* (I don't mean in-spect, which is only a kind of human gymnastic, by means of which one immediately comes out again on the other side of the dog, regarding it merely, so to speak, as a window upon the humanity lying behind it—not that)—but to let oneself precisely into the dog's very center, the point where it begins to be dog, the place in it where God, as it were, would have sat down for a moment when the dog was finished, in order to watch it under the influence of its first embarrassments and inspirations, and to know that it was good, that nothing was lacking, that it could not have been better made. . . . Laugh though you will, dear confidant, if I am to tell you where my all-greatest feeling, my world-feeling, my earthly bliss was to be found, I must confess to you: it was to be found time

287

and again . . . in such inseeing, in the indescribably swift, deep, timeless moments of this divine inseeing."

There is joy in so much of Rilke's letters, despite the early bouts of soulfulness and the later times of torment when (quickly recovering from his brief fall into collective pro-war hysteria in 1914) he perceived the frightfulness of WWI and intuited that it presaged the further horrors that we are witnessing (and the worse horrors we fear). It was not that he had any ordinary political astuteness; but his sensitivity to subsurface tremors, to ominous shadows, (and also to the delicate counter-rhythm, the stir of seeds struggling into light), was acute. As a nonparticipant he did not undergo the daily bestiality of the war; but this peculiar sensitivity gives his overview a special kind of validity. And considering that that faculty made him highly vulnerable, it is remarkable that his sense of wonder and delight survive, so that, regaining Paris after "those terrible years," he is able to feel again "the continuity of (his) life": on October 20, 1920, he wrote, "here, here—la même plénitude de vie, la même intensité, la même justesse dans le mal: apart from political muddle and pother, everything has remained great, everything strives, surges, glows, shimmers—October days—you know them. . . . *One* hour here, the first, would have been enough. And yet I have had hundreds, days, nights,—and each step was an arrival." The joy he found in his last years, in the Valais, in the little Chateau de Muzot where his wanderings came to rest, is not simple confrontation of an appreciative sensibility with the world's beauty, but the profounder joy of a struggle won, the lifelong struggle to transform "the visible into the invisible," that is, to *internalize* experience—and to use "the strings of lamentation" to play "the whole paean of praise which wells up behind all heaviness, anguish and suffering," ("*später auch den ganzen Jubel zu spielen.*") "Our conflicts," he says, "have always been a part of our riches"—and one feels he had earned the right to say that, for out of much inner conflict he had made works that give off energy and joy to others. In this way he provides an example for poets who follow him, just as a Cézanne or a

288

Rodin, through their dedication and the work that resulted, provided examples for him. An example of persistence and of realism. He faced up to anguish and kept on creating: he could see both "Cézanne, the old man, [who] when one told him of what was going on, . . . could break out in the quiet streets of Aix and shriek at his companion: 'Le monde, c'est terrible . . .'" and the Cézanne who "during almost forty years . . . remained uninterruptedly within his work, in the innermost center of it . . . the incredible freshness and purity of his pictures is due to this obstinacy. . . ."

This kind of influence, first on a young beginner, and then throughout the life of a working artist, represents one of the most deeply useful kinds of mutual aid. It is an influence not on style, not on technique, but on the attitude towards one's work that must underlie style and craft: it is out of that basic stance, a sense of aesthetic ethics, that they must develop (in whatever measure accords with the individual's innate and indispensible gifts). If the underlying attitude is shaky, the movements of style will be shaky too—desperate gestures made to maintain balance or hide the fear of falling. Rilke presents to any young poet an example of basic attitude that can remain relevant throughout a lifetime because it is reverent, passionate, and comprehensive. His reverence for "the savor of creation," as he calls it in a diary excerpt, leads him to concrete and sensuous images. His passion for "insee-ing" leads him to delight, terror, transformation, and the internalization (or absorption) of experience. And his com-prehensiveness, which makes no distinction between meet-ing art and meeting life, shows the poet a way to bridge the gap between the conduct of living and the conduct of art. Because he articulated a view of the poet's role that has not lost its significance as I have read and reread Rilke's prose for almost four decades, he remains a mentor for me now as he was when I was a young girl. No reiteration can wear thin such words as these:

> . . . to those who have not, perhaps, worked their way fully into their tasks . . . I wish that they may

keep joyfully to the road of long learning until that deep, hidden self-awareness comes, assuring them (without their having to seek confirmation of others) of that pure necessity, by which I mean a sense of inevitability and finality in their work. To keep our inward conscience clear and to know whether we can take responsibility for our creative experiences just as they stand in all their truthfulness and absoluteness: that is the basis of every work of art. . . .

Some New Directions Paperbooks

For complete listing request complete catalog from
New Directions, 80 Eighth Avenue, New York 10011   † Bilingual